The Philosophical Practitioner

by

Larry Abrams

TELEMACHUS
PRESS

The Philosophical Practitioner

The publisher does not have any control over and does not assume any responsibility for author or third–party websites or their content.

Edited by Fred Dinas

Originally published by LuLu Enterprises, inc. 2010

Published by Telemachus Press, LLC
http://www.telemachuspress.com

ISBN # 978–1–935670–53–7 (eBook)
ISBN # 978-1-935670-94-0 (paperback)

Version: 2011.07.28

Printed in the United States of America
10 9 8 7 6 5 4 3 2 1

Acknowledgements

Thanks to Thomas Adcock, Carolyn Hardin, Bill Kelley, Casey Kelley, Jim Lank, and Dianne Lawson for their helpful comments and to Murray Franck for his detailed suggestions. Thanks also to Fred Dinas, my editor, for his.

The Philosophical
Practitioner

1

I had my feet up on my desk and my hands clasped behind my neck, trying once again to puzzle out why science progressed so much faster than everything else, when she walked into my office unannounced. Nothing wrong with that since I didn't have a secretary. But she didn't even bother to knock.

She paused on the threshold for the space of a heartbeat while her dusky eyes ticked off the contents of the room – me, my desk, my computer, a desk clock, a coffee machine, and my client chair. I could see her adding these up to a sum that must have meant something to her. She sat in the chair and said, "I saw your sign."

I hadn't yet seen her blink. A tall, big–boned woman, she had on the barest suggestion of lipstick and could have been anywhere from nineteen to maybe twenty–five.

I nodded.

"On my way home I looked up at the building and saw your sign in the window. So I took the elevator. Just for the hell of it."

"Just for the hell of it?"

She crossed her legs and did a little trick with my hormones. She wore a moss–green sweater, plain black pumps with maybe two–inch heels and flesh colored hose under a pleated gray skirt. Sexy but comfortable.

She shrugged. "I told you. I saw your sign."

"Lots of people see my sign. Lots of people ignore it."

She draped an arm around the back of her chair. "Let's say I'm curious. I never heard of a philosophical practitioner. I thought I'd see what kind of things you say. What kind of answers you give. How you're different from a psychologist."

"Depends on the questions. Psychologists tend to emphasize feelings over theory. We generally reverse that. But not always." I paused. "Something's on your mind or you wouldn't have stopped."

"Tell me what kind of practice you have here. What exactly you do."

I shook my head. "Every client is different. It would help if you told me why you're here."

She gave me a long look and brushed back a few strands of straight black hair that had fallen into her eyes.

"It's not that simple."

"It never is."

"I have no idea if you're any good. I might be wasting my time."

"You might."

Her lips pursed as she studied me. When she finished she stood up.

"Why don't we call it a day. What do I owe you?"

"I charge a hundred and twenty–five for a forty–five minute session. Less if the session is shorter. You have more than half an hour left if you want it. You've gotten nothing for your money so far."

She fished some bills from her handbag, placed them on my desk and moved to the door.

"Maybe you'll give me extra good advice if I come back."

"Call ahead next time."

"If I decide to come. If I think you can help me."

"You haven't told me with what."

"You noticed." She opened the door. "I'm about to kill a man. You may get a chance to talk me out of it."

She started to leave, then spoke over her shoulder.

"Or not."

And she slipped out.

2

Three weeks went by before I saw her again. I went through my routine, shuttling from my two–room apartment on West Eighty–Fourth to the office in the morning and back again at night. I had a lot of time for reading since the demand for philosophical practitioners seemed to be somewhat less than for exorcists. Well, a lot less. The dawn of the twenty–first century did not usher in any mass passion for the philosophical endeavor. People still tended to think of philosophy as too abstract to have any meaning for their lives. It would take a while for that to change. The trick was to be around when it did. Well, at thirty–six I could wait. And although my life savings came to a total that would impress no one, I'd long ago committed to looking at the bright side. If I sometimes had a little trouble finding it, that had to be temporary.

The way it happened, I'd skipped breakfast that day and ordered out for a pizza at the office. When I heard footsteps outside the door, I thought the kid with my extra cheese and anchovies had arrived, so with my anticipation levels peaking near maximum I watched as the nameless lady sauntered in the second time without an appointment and plunked herself down in the chair. This time she had on a clingy blue dress. Silver hoop earrings. Redder lipstick. Light brown pumps that looked like deerskin. Sometimes the way a client dressed meant something. Sometimes not. I let her settle in.

"Nice to see you again."

"Is that a crack?"

She quirked one black eyebrow and held it there.

"Does it sound like one?"

"Hey. You're not supposed to be a shrink. Talk straight."

"Why did you come back."

She took out a cigarette and lit it.

"Mind?"

"Most of the time, yes. Right now, no."

"That some kind of special dispensation?"

I smiled. "We can begin whenever you're ready."

"You think you're a pretty cool guy."

I waited.

"Self image like that, it's like a taste for cigars. You gotta cultivate it."

I waited some more.

She watched me, dark eyes challenging. She blew out a long, thin stream of smoke. At least she didn't blow rings. I let the silence build.

"If you're done, maybe this time we can get to why you're here."

She took another deep drag, let it out audibly.

"I'm not sure."

"As I recall, when we left off you were going to kill someone. How did that go?"

"Okay, you proved you're cool. Except you're also a real wise guy."

Someone knocked on the door. Had to be the pizza.

"It's open," I called out.

I paid the kid and put the box on my desk. After the first bite I knew the pizza was a winner. The anchovies tasted salty but not fishy, and the cheese was firm enough that it didn't run but soft enough that if you tried hard you might be able to inhale some of it. I held out a piece.

"Want some?"

She just looked at me. I shrugged and took another bite. I held out another piece.

"You sure? Excellent stuff."

She didn't reply. She studied me. I ate some pizza and let her.

"What's your name, by the way?"

"You don't need to know that."

She rummaged in her handbag, one of those cream–colored, large–grained Coach jobs, fished out another cigarette, went through the business of lighting it, took the first drag.

I tried raising one eyebrow. I couldn't do it the way she did, but I made up for it by not caring.

"Right. Killers don't give out their names. Makes it too easy to catch them."

I looked at the pizza. Two lone pieces waited their turn at immolation. I considered whether I could stuff down one more. My hunger had vanished but the pizza tasted so good I took another piece on principle.

"You're not going to kill anyone."

She glared at me. "You don't believe me?"

"Killers don't walk into a stranger's office and tell him they're going to do a kill. Never happens."

"I'm just telling you a fact."

"Right."

"Fine." She stood, picked up her handbag.

"What do you intend to use?"

"What?"

"Knife, poison, gun? Anything like that in that bag?"

She gave me a black glare. Her blackest, in my judgement.

"You know, for a soft philosopher, or whatever you are, you take an awful lot of chances."

I watched the flex of her calf muscles as she marched out.

Soft? Me?

***

"I had a visit from a woman today."

I sat in a corner booth of an Italian restaurant on the south side of restaurant row on Forty–Sixth. Sheila, wearing outsize sunglasses, sat with me. She had a break between films so she flew in from Hollywood to spend some time with her roots. I'm one of her roots.

"I know that's lucky for the woman. Is it lucky for you too?"

"Not so far."

"Going to pursue it further?"

"She's a client."

"Is she hot?"

"In more ways than one. She says she's going to kill someone."

"Going to? What is she, confessing before the crime?"

"Unless she's got an agenda."

"For sure she's got an agenda. But why you? Why would she go to a philosophical practitioner with a story like that?"

"She wants me to stop her."

"She said that?"

"No."

"But you've philosophically detected it."

The waitress came with my veal picatta and Sheila's garden salad.

"If you always order just salad, why did you want to eat Italian?"

"Atmosphere." Sheila dug into her lettuce, a small woman whose hazel–flecked green eyes and generous mouth were known the world over. We both tried to ignore the people who had seen past the sunglasses and tried not to stare. She was better at it than I.

I took a bite of the picatta. Savored it a while.

"You should taste this."

"No thanks."

"You could offer me a bite of your salad."

She gave me her gamin grin. Audiences all over the world had to pay good money to see that grin, but I got it for free.

"Let's see. I think the last time I saw you eat a garden salad was... hmmm. Gee. I guess never."

"But I eat my asparagus."

"Why would I be in New York if you didn't have some redeeming features?"

She'd come to New York because both of us hoped we might get some sort of resolution to our relationship one day. We dated in college years ago, before she hit the big time. We liked the same plays, the same jokes, the same music, and many of the same books. I'd wanted to get serious but she hadn't, and after graduation we drifted apart. After she was famous she looked me up and said she was ready. But by then I wasn't. I'd seen how different our goals were. And the lives we led and wanted to lead. She liked the high life. Fame, adulation, lots of money to spend. According to the media she owned four cars, closets full of clothes, and a twelve–thousand square foot house in Beverly Hills. I liked quiet and privacy. I made enough money for my needs but not much more, had no cars, rented my small apartment, and owned the same number of sport coats as she had cars. I loved Manhattan and dealt with people's problems. She lived in make–believe land and dealt with fantasy.

She pushed her plate aside and leaned in toward me.

"So why did she come to you? Why not a psychiatrist or psychologist?"

"She said she was passing by and saw my sign."

"Right."

"Do I detect sarcasm?"

"Not at all. Woman wants to kill someone, she sees a sign advertising a philosophical practitioner, which nobody knows what it is anyway, so naturally she stops in and confesses to a crime she didn't yet commit."

"Which nobody knows what it is anyway?"

"You want style or substance?"

"Good point."

"So what's your answer? Why you?"

The waitress came over. We ordered coffee. Cream and sugar for her, espresso for me.

"I don't know why me. Maybe it's like she said. She saw my sign and walked in."

She let it go. "So what are you going to do?"

"What do you do when you're shooting a scene but the script changes aren't ready?"

"We wait for the pages."

"I'll wait till she comes in again."

"And if she doesn't?"

I shrugged and took a sip of my espresso. It tasted refreshingly bitter.

"That's plan A. There's no plan B."

3

"Hello, doctor." He arrived twenty minutes late. I had long since given up trying to make sure they knew the difference between an MD and a Ph.D or between medical and non–medical. Maybe it made no difference to them. Doctor was technically correct, so I let it lie.

"Hello, Jeremy."

He had a spindly body with a long pale face and quick slate–colored eyes and the title of chief financial officer of a Fortune 500 company. When he got excited, which had happened only when the subject of the stock market came up, the color in his face deepened to match his eyes. Sometimes his nostrils twitched. Then I knew we were onto something earth–shattering. According to him he had a seven–figure income, a big house, a gorgeous wife, a girl aged eleven and a boy aged sixteen. He wore a navy blue Brioni suit, which I recognized from their ads, with a white jacquard shirt and a power red tie. He held himself straight in my client chair looking up at the ceiling above my left shoulder. Behind the gold wire frame glasses his eyes did a lot of speed blinking.

"So I thought about what you said last time. About definite answers to definite questions." He cleared his throat. "I'm not quite sure where to begin."

"At the end of the last session you were talking about your wife."

"Yes. Well." He shifted in his seat and cleared his throat again. "This is not a very comfortable chair."

I waited.

"See, the thing of it is, I can't really give you a definite take on that, I mean what we talked about, whether I love her, because I don't really know what love is. I'm not sure anyone knows. I mean, what's the difference between loving someone and liking them? And how much difference does it make anyway?"

He delivered this in an affectless voice somewhere between a contralto and a tenor. It struck me that the language lacked a word for a voice like that. His voice inhabited a descriptive limbo. Life was not always fair.

"What do you think the difference is?"

"I think there's not much difference. They're on the same scale. Love is just higher up."

"You think so?"

He stared out the window.

"That's the thing, isn't it. That's the thing."

He said nothing more for a while, eyes fixed on the sky as if hypnotized.

"Qualitative differences," I said.

"What?" His eyes snapped back to me.

"On that scale."

"Yes. Yes, of course." He frowned. "But that would mean – wouldn't that mean they weren't on the same scale?"

I leaned back in my chair. This guy dealt in abstractions. He was at home with numbers, which most people thought of as very concrete but are really abstractions. For Jeremy, any abstraction was better than the messy real world. Especially his personal life.

"Jeremy. Do you love your wife?"

"I don't know."

"Sure you do."

"I'm telling you I don't know."

"Did you love her when you married her?"

"I was just a kid. What did I know."

I didn't reply. Finally he said, "Okay, yes. I suppose. I mean, hell, I was twenty–three years old, my hormones were shooting out of my skull. I wanted to be with her all the time."

He sounded calm and uninvolved, as if describing a routine sunset.

"And now?"

"Now it's different. Look, she's a nice woman. But she hasn't done anything with herself, she hasn't grown. Mentally I mean."

"The way you have."

"Right. I have a career, I do important work, I come in contact with, I have to say it, important people. She takes care of the kids. She doesn't keep up with the world. She's not as interesting as she used to be. Maybe it's not her fault because the kids take up so much time, but there it is."

"You're clear on that."

"Yeah."

"Look, Jeremy. Two things. First, you have to decide what you want. Then we can talk about whether it's a good idea. Second. You don't really need me to help you explore your feelings. If that's all you want, you probably want a psychiatrist or a psychologist. You're not getting your money's worth here."

"Isn't that what you do too? Help your patients find out who they are?"

"Yes, but feelings are not necessarily my focus. It's a matter of emphasis. Mainly I try to help them find out who they could be. And maybe sometimes who they should be."

I rose. "And you're not a patient. You're a client."

***

Thinking deep thoughts and sipping a diet coke at my desk, I barely had time to look up when my mystery woman reappeared. She strode in again without knocking and sat down in my client chair. Today she wore a red peasant blouse with a straight black skirt and black hose. I didn't know how she knew I wasn't in session. Maybe she didn't care. She took out a cigarette, this time without asking. She seemed to think her special dispensation had permanent status. I let it go.

"If you wanted an appointment, why didn't you call my secretary?"

"You don't have a secretary," she said in the slow throaty voice I remembered.

"Just wanted to see if you were paying attention."

I waited. She waited.

"You forgot to pay last time."

She looked at me for a beat. Then a corner of her mouth arched up in what might have been a sneer. She dug into her bag of the day, one of those open duffle type things with a drawstring around the top, leaned toward my desk, flung down a handful of bills, and leaned back again. I looked at the money. It was ten dollars too much. I picked out a ten and slid it over to her side of the desk. I let the other bills sit there.

"When we left off last time, you were going to kill someone but hadn't gotten around to it yet."

She took a deep drag on the cigarette. Her pupils looked preternaturally large, as if she were hyped on amphetamines. Maybe she always looked that way when intent on something.

"You think this is a joke?"

I reached behind me to my new mini fridge for another diet coke.

"Want one?"

She didn't answer.

I took a sip of the coke.

"You're not really going to kill anyone. If you were you wouldn't need or want to talk about it. But you want me to give you reasons not to anyway so you can stop thinking about it. Are we agreed so far?"

She shifted in her seat so that she faced me at an angle.

"No."

"No?"

"No. I don't know how you are as, what do you call yourself? A philosophical practitioner. But you're pretty lousy as a psychologist."

"Uh huh." Patience was a virtue in my profession, but my stock of it might not be deep enough.

She shifted back toward me and crossed her legs. Her skirt rode up almost enough for me to tell whether she wore pantyhose or stockings. Most women didn't bother with stockings these days, but this was not most women. She thumb-flicked her cigarette, spilling a half-inch of ash on the floor.

"You spilled ash on the floor."

She ignored me.

"All wrong. I'm going to do it soon. And you can't talk me out of it, never mind what I said that first time. Not you or anyone else."

I drank some more coke. I held up the glass. "Sure you don't want some?"

She glowered at me. "Do you know how easy it is to kill someone? All you have to do is study their habits and wait for the right time. All it takes is planning. Anyone can be gotten to if you don't have a time deadline. Anyone. If someone wants to kill you bad enough, that's it. You're dead."

"Look, let's stop fooling around. If you really want to kill someone tell me who and why. Otherwise we're finished here."

She smiled a surprisingly wide, generous smile, which she shut off so fast I wondered if I'd imagined it.

"See," she said, "it's not me who wants to talk. It's you."

My patience had just about given out. Maybe I had too little after all.

"Last chance. Who do you want to kill?"

Her eyes locked onto mine for several seconds.

"Why, you, of course. I'm going to kill you."

She reached into her handbag and came out with a gun. Not your usual ladies' nickel-plated .22. This was a blued steel snub-nosed .38, which anyone who ever saw a cop show on TV would recognize. Nothing much in the accuracy department beyond fifteen feet or so unless you had a very steady hand and a lot of practice, but her chair was maybe three feet from my desk.

Nothing much I could do. Diving under my desk seemed undignified and pointless.

"If it matters, I'd rather you didn't."

She said nothing. She held the gun rock steady, pointed at the center of my chest.

"Whatever your reasons, you're making a big mistake."

She showed me a grim smile. "I don't think so."

"As far as I know, I haven't done anything to you. I never even met you until you waltzed into my office that first time."

"I could do it right now." She sounded relaxed and calm, as if having a dinner conversation with a friend. "Just a little pressure on the trigger and everything ends for you." She let it hang. "But I won't. Not now. I want you to have plenty of time to think about it."

I couldn't think of anything to say.

"Think about what you've done that would make someone want to kill you. I want you to know why you're going to die."

I thought of pointing out to her that she could simply tell me, but given what she intended to do once I knew, that seemed counterproductive.

"I don't know what you're talking about."

"Probably not. But now you're going to think about it. You'll think about it when you get up in the morning and when you brush your teeth and when you eat breakfast. You'll think about it when you're in your office trying to listen to your patients. You'll think about it when you leave your office to go home because you'll be out on the street and vulnerable. You'll think about it when you're trying to go to sleep. You'll be trying to figure out who I am. You'll be looking for a way out."

She got up and slung her bag over her shoulder, still brandishing the gun. "But there is no way out. You can't go to the police because you don't know who I am or where I live, and they'd never believe your story anyway. What are you going to tell them, some woman I never saw before threatened to kill me, please stop her?"

She backed toward the door.

"You'll be seeing me again."

She reached behind her for the knob.

"Oh, one more thing. If you try to follow me I'll shoot you."
She closed the door behind her quietly.
Almost fastidiously.

4

She might be crazy. But not definitely. You didn't have to be out of touch with reality to have the urge to kill. Hell, sometimes you're out of touch with reality if you don't have the urge. But the urge is not the deed. We all have urges. We control them. It's called civilization.

Maybe she just wanted to scare me. For what reason, I had no clue. Or she might be dead serious. Either way, she got one thing right. Anyone could kill anyone if they tried hard enough. I had to assume she meant what she said.

To have the best chance at stopping her I needed to know what she thought I'd done. I had no idea where to begin.

I didn't feel like working any more today. I cancelled my remaining appointment. At a little after five I walked up Fifth Avenue with throngs of people who had just completed eight hours of whatever they did for one third of their lives in order to have full control over how they spent the other two thirds. The sun angled in low from New Jersey, bouncing flat bursts of muddy light off the tinted glass of the Trump building.

At the entrance to Central Park some people browsed at a couple of red kiosks filled with second hand books. I turned onto Central Park South and continued on my way to my place on the upper west side.

Apparently the gun lady wanted me to review my life and figure out why she hated me, an impossibility given that I had no clue about her identity or the source of her hatred. Sure, some people didn't like me. If you took any actions or had any opinions at all you couldn't get through life without that being a given. But none of them made it a project to kill me. Until now.

At my second floor walkup Circe set up a series of escalating meows even before I put the key in the lock. Whenever I left for more than a couple of hours she'd be waiting at the door to reproach me. I picked her up, cradled her on her back and rubbed her belly fur, which kick–started the purring machine.

"You're so easy," I said.

She arched her neck to give my fingers easier access to the underside of her throat, which I obediently massaged. This had the effect of downshifting the purring machine. When it redlined a few seconds later I figured she forgave me. I opened a can of tuna for her and went into the living room to look through the mail. I tossed out catalogs for window coverings, auto accessories, kitchenware, cigars, foot care, hunting gear, gadgets of the future, stationery, and stock trading systems, keeping a couple on men's fashions so I could remain well informed about what I rebelled against. Then I leafed though the envelopes looking for checks, but as usual wishful thinking had no effect. Bills, however, were never in short supply. I had just settled down with the pile when a ball of gray fur smelling of tuna rocketed onto my lap, squirmed around a little and settled in.

Trapped. I picked up the phone and called Sheila.

"Hey," she said.

"Hey. How's it going?"

"Oh, a little thisa, a little thatta, with an emphasis on the latter."

I laughed, remembering that we'd shared a love of old musicals in our dating days. The plots weren't much, but the singing and dancing gave us the kind of lift others got from cocaine or speed.

"How about you?" she said in her smoky voice. In another era that voice would have launched a thousand ships.

"Remember that lady I told you about? The one who wants to kill someone? Guess who she wants to kill."

"Not me, I hope."

"No, but you're warm."

"What? What do you — ? She wants to kill you?"

"That's what she says."

"That's crazy! Why? And why would she tell you that?"

"Those are the right questions. I don't really have the answers. She seems to think I wronged her in some way and she wants me to squirm."

"Wronged her? How?"

"She wouldn't say."

"What are you going to do?"

"I need more information. I have to figure out how to get it."

"You'll think of something."

"I hope so."

"You always do."

"I wish that were true."

"You don't give yourself enough credit."

"You give me too much."

"No."

"I'll let you know if I come up with anything. Any suggestions, give me a call?"

"Of course."

*✱✱

Getting a gun permit would take too long. I'd have to fill out several pages of forms and then wait for the city officials to check me out. At the end of the process they'd reject me anyway, because by their definition I wasn't in a hazardous profession. In fact by their definition I probably wasn't in a profession at all. If they looked up practitioner, philosophical in whatever manual the city issued them, I knew what they'd find. Nothing. Same if they switched the words around.

So the next day, a Saturday, I took a train to Philadelphia because I'd heard the gun laws in Pennsylvania were more lenient than in New York or New Jersey. I'd looked up the address of a gun shop on Market Street. The owner had shoehorned it into a space the size of an average New York dining room on the second floor of a small office building that for some unfathomable reason had a stainless steel statue of an armadillo in front of it.

The guy behind the counter looked bored, which didn't surprise me given that he had no customers. He looked to be a fit forty–five or fifty with broad shoulders and the kind of flat army crew cut I hadn't seen in a long time. Which might have been the fault of the places I frequented. Or didn't.

"Help you?" he asked as I came up to the counter. Three glass cases displayed three rows of handguns, old ones and new ones. The rifles stood upright in a larger case behind him.

"I'm looking for something small and light. Easy to carry, easy to conceal."

"I can help you better if I know what you want to use it for."

"Self defense."

"You know anything about guns?"

"Assume I don't."

"The smaller and lighter you go, the less stopping power. You don't want to go less than a .38." He unlocked a sliding glass panel and handed me a snub–nosed Smith & Wesson revolver. It felt amazingly light.

"Aluminum. That's your baby."

"What's that one?" My eye had caught the blued steel of a second hand gun. The blueing had worn off around the business end of the barrel, but it was a beauty.

"That's a Walther. World War Two gun. German."

He took it out and handed it to me. "But it's a .32. Not as much stopping power as the S&W." He flicked a catch on the bottom of the grip. He handed me a spring clip.

"This is where you load the ammo. Holds twice the number of bullets as the S&W. But like I said, not as good stopping power. And it's heavier."

I hefted it, aimed it at a corner of the room. "This gun probably killed a lot of people." All of a sudden it wasn't so beautiful.

He shook his head. "No."

I held it out to him. "Look at it. Well used. World War Two. German."

"That gun never killed anyone. No gun ever does. People kill. Not guns."

I stared at him. I looked at the gun. I thought about it. He watched me like a patient parent. I hefted it again, raised it, and sighted along the barrel at one of the rifles. It felt light. Not as light as the S&W, but it balanced perfectly in my hand.

I took out my wallet.

5

I decided to install a camera outside my office door near the ceiling. Now it showed a tall, heavyset guy with his finger on the bell. No way he could be a five foot eight woman in disguise. I let him in and led him to my client chair. Some day if my practice catches on and I start doing couples I'll buy another one. Or maybe I'll be feeling optimistic sometime and just buy one on spec.

"I saw your sign," he said. "I don't know what the hell it means, but I thought I'd give you a try."

"Fine. My rates — "

He waved a manicured hand. "Tell me something – why should I trust anything you say?"

"I'm sorry?"

"How do I know you know anything? Anything worthwhile. I mean, Socrates said the wise man is the man who knows he knows nothing, right? But you have that sign out there, philosophical practitioner. So what do you know that Socrates didn't?"

I tried to maintain my calm. After a few seconds I succeeded.

"I work on specific problems. Tell me what's bothering you and let's see how I can help you."

He laughed. It came out more as a giggle which sounded odd coming from such a beefy guy. He had blue eyes and blonde hair cut long, set off by a soft textured gray suit and a light blue shirt. He wore brown slip–ons which I recognized as Cole Haans. A thin gold watch with a face the color of his eyes decorated his wrist.

"I'll tell you what's bothering me."

He waved his hand above his head in a broad arc. "All this? The things people do every day? The jobs, the kids, the sex, the cars, the houses – none of it matters. None of it!"

I steepled my fingers and looked at him.

"And you say that because?"

"It's all bullshit! If you don't know that you don't know anything. What's the point? We're all gonna die anyway, so what's it all for, all the scratching and clawing? For nothing. For nothing! It's all just a con game."

"Games have arbitrary rules."

"Yeah. So?"

"Life is not a game."

"You know what I mean."

"Let's start from the beginning. Well, maybe the middle. What work do you do?"

He shifted around, glanced out my window and crossed his Cole Haans at the ankles.

"Banking. I'm a banker."

"Is that investment banking or people walking in off the street banking?

"Regular banking. I'm a loan officer."

"So I take it you don't enjoy your work."

"People want a loan, they open up their financial life to me, I say yes or no. That sound exciting to you?"

"So why do you do it?"

He shrugged. "It pays fine. I got a degree from Wharton with a major in banking. It's what I know."

"There are plenty of other jobs for someone with financial savvy."

"You don't get it. There's no point. It doesn't matter. Whatever I do, it's all bullshit in the end."

I decided to shift tactics. "What would make it not bullshit?"

"What?"

"Can you think of any way to change things for the better."

He cocked his head at me. "Sure. Absolutely. If I didn't have to die, that would be better. If I could live forever."

"So then you'd enjoy your job. Your work would be enjoyable."

"I suppose. Sure. Yeah. Why not?"

"Why?"

"Why what?"

"Why would it be fun if you did it for, say, five hundred years, but not if you did it for forty?"

He just looked at me.

"It's the same work," I continued. "If anything, I'd think it might get a bit boring along about maybe year two hundred or so."

He stared some more. I waited.

"So what are you saying. That it's not good to live forever? That it's good to die? I should be glad?"

"I'm suggesting that you're preventing yourself from enjoying work which you indicated you could find enjoyable under other circumstances. I'm suggesting if you think it over you might not need the other circumstances."

He pursed his lips and looked up at the ceiling. Then he looked out the window. Then he got up and took out a wallet stuffed with cash. He took out a folded check.

"How much do I owe you?"

I told him. He paid me.

"I'll call you."

I felt like a school girl on her first date.

"Be nice to know your name."

"Bernie. Bernie Feld."

He held out his hand. I took it.

***

On the way home I stopped at the police station on West Fifty Fourth. In a small anteroom to the left of the entrance two women and a man sat on stools at a counter, filling out forms. All were dressed in what one might charitably call second hand eclectic. The woman held a big shopping bag between her legs. One man had a ponytail gone gray, tied with a red rubber band. The other had a week of black stubble on his face. He squinted at the forms as if they were an IQ test with a bunch of tricky questions. He held one end of a pen in his mouth. I hoped it wasn't the pointy end.

The desk sergeant, a heavy guy in his late thirties with unfortunate red blotches on his face, sat in a hard–backed chair on a small built up area about three feet off the floor. He looked down at me and waited. I looked up at him and spoke.

"I wonder if I could talk a little with your sketch artist."

"What's the problem?" He sounded bored.

"It's a little complicated."

"So uncomplicate it."

"Someone threatened to kill me. I'd like to work up a sketch of her from my description, then see if it matches anyone in your files."

"Her?"

"Yeah."

A precisely placed yellow pencil bisected a memo pad on his desk. His index finger stroked the eraser on the end of the pencil.

"We don't work like that."

"Like what?"

"There's gotta be a crime. We can't do anything unless there's a crime."

"Until she carries out the threat? If she does I'll be dead."

"We don't call in an artist or anyone else unless there's a crime."

Three cops, all under five ten, walked in and nodded to the guy behind the desk. Crime fighting standards had changed since my childhood.

"You have any suggestions?"

"You want, you can fill out a report form."

"Any other suggestions?"

"A woman?"

"That's right."

He tried to suppress a smile but a twitch at the corners of his mouth gave him away.

"Get some pepper spray."

I started to go but stopped myself. His attitude was his problem, not mine. I turned back to him.

"She had a gun. A thirty–eight."

His attitude changed instantly. The smirk vanished.

"A gun? She pointed it at you when she made the threat?"

"Yes."

"That's a crime." He picked up his desk phone, punched in a two–digit number.

"Detective? Got a guy here needs to talk to you. Armed threat. Right. Sending him up." He replaced the receiver.

"Second door on the left when you come out of the elevator."

Detective Stone, who I would have taken for an accountant, was middle–aged, bald, and bored. He read me questions from a form and typed in my answers. When he finished he directed me to a sketch artist who the department had just hired.

"You're lucky," he said as I was leaving his office. "We used to use freelancers. You'd of had to hang around until we located some-one. Maybe an hour. Maybe more."

The new hire, an attractive Hispanic woman, asked me a lot of questions about age, hair, face shape, nose shape, eye spacing, com-plexion, eyebrows, mouth, and ears. When she drew something I thought was not quite right she erased it. In less than an hour she had a reasonable likeness.

"Wait here. Our files are computerized. I'll scan it in."

When she returned she shook her head. "No match. Sorry."

I thanked her and left.

6

"I've been thinking," Jeremy said. He came in late again, which was mildly annoying, but he had a saving grace. He always paid for a full session.

We had nearly reached the end of his time when he started to bring up a new subject.

"I've been reading this book, *The Myth Of Self*. It says the self is an illusion. There's no one home, no man in the machine. Just the machine."

"Jeremy. What about your wife? Have you decided what you want? Do you want to stay with her?"

"Wait a minute. I'll get to that. First I want to talk about this other problem."

"What problem?"

"What I just said. If it's all an illusion, if there's no self, then it doesn't matter."

"What doesn't?"

"Anything. Everything. Me. Wife. Everything." His voice took on an intensity I never heard before. He thought his way out, his ticket to tranquility, lay in denying the self. If "Jeremy" was an illusion, he wouldn't have to think about any of his problems any more. Even better, he wouldn't have problems any more, since there would be no him. How this bizarre thought could possibly give him comfort eluded me, but then so many things did.

"There's no self?" I tried to keep my tone neutral. Hard under the circumstances, but not impossible.

"It's not just this book. A lot of informed neurologists are saying the same thing. And computer scientists."

"Tell me something. When I talk to you, to whom am I talking?"

He didn't speak for a few moments. "You think these guys are wrong?"

"I think it's absurd on the face of it. And I think you know it."

"I'd like to hear your reasoning."

"Okay. Let's start with when I talk to you, to whom am I talking?"

He played around with it in his head.

"If I answer that, if I say, "me", it cuts off the discussion."

"Sort of."

"And that's your point."

I shrugged.

"What if I say you're not talking to anyone?"

"You can say it if you believe it."

He looked deflated. There wasn't going to be an easy way out of his troubles after all. Happiness still eluded him. He still had to decide what to do about his wife.

He sat back. "I want to think about this."

I rose. "I'd like you to think about something else too. We can discuss it next time."

He got up and I walked him to the door.

"Like what?"

"Like where your life is going."

Fascinated, I watched him furrow his brow, hollow his cheeks, and purse his lips in what looked like one fluid motion. Maybe he had some unique muscle connections no one else had. Or maybe he could do slight of face, the way some people could do slight of hand. Either way, without uttering a word he managed to convey a notable lack of pleasure at my homework suggestion.

Well, it was his life.

When my doorbell rang my camera reassured me that the lady waiting expectantly outside was my next appointment and not the gun lady. I let her in.

"Tell me why I should get out of bed in the morning," Sally Carter said when she settled herself.

She appeared to be in her early fifties with bleached blonde hair worn in a becoming pageboy. She had on a blue blouse of some synthetic material and sensible low–heeled shoes. She didn't look like a person who would ask that kind of question, but then, I didn't know what a person who would ask that kind of question would look like, since no one had ever asked it of me. From what I could see of her bone structure, she had probably been quite beautiful once.

I knew nothing about her except that she'd told me on the phone that I'd been recommended by an old client of mine, a woman about her age named Myrna Shaeffer who taught art history at a community college and worried about the relevance of her subject to today's world. Given her opening line, I also knew that Sally was prone to drama.

"You understand I'm not a psychologist."

"I don't need one. There's nothing wrong with me. Besides, that's not a question for a psychologist or a psychiatrist anyway. It's a question for a guy like you."

"Tell me something about yourself."

"What do you want to know?"

"Why don't we start with what you think I should know."

She got to her feet. "Mind if I pace a little?"

"Go ahead."

She chose a route between her chair and the window. When she reached the window she didn't pause to look out, turning sharply and pacing back to her chair. After about half a minute she stopped, facing me, her hands on the back of the chair.

"I'm divorced. Both kids are grown and gone. I live alone. Well, with Leslie, my dog."

"Nice name for her."

"Him."

"Leslie's a him?"

"I named him after an old–time actor. Leslie Howard."

I had seen some of Howard's movies. He had a slight build and mainly played sensitive types. Ashley in *Gone with the Wind*. The deceptively foppish Scarlet Pimpernel. Others in the same vein. Definitely not a muscle man or an action hero.

"You're a fan?"

"He was my favorite." She started pacing again.

"Unusual choice."

"Why? Because he had a brain?" She stopped at the window. She peered out but I had the feeling the view didn't register. She came back toward me.

"Lots of women like a man with a mind. I'm one of them." She sat down opposite me. "What else do you want to know?"

"Tell me what a typical day is like for you."

"Boring. That's what it's like for me."

"Do you work?"

"Depends on what you mean by work."

"Tell me what you mean by it."

"I read a lot. Mainly novels."

"You're calling that work?"

"It gives me an outlet. It lets me feel. That's a kind of work. Arranging your life so you can feel something."

She hesitated, seeming to search for words.

"Normally I don't feel anything. My life is not exciting. In the books I read, life is exciting. And I learn things."

"What about when you're not reading. I gather that financially speaking you don't need a job. What do you do with your time?"

"My husband was a successful entrepreneur. Computer games." She shifted suddenly in her seat. I thought she would start pacing again, but she settled into the new position, legs crossed in a ladylike way, facing me at a slight angle.

"When I'm not reading I putter around the house. Go to the supermarket and the dry cleaner. Walk the dog. Go to the movies." She looked at me. "Exciting, right? Really gets your motor going."

"You keep using that word. Exciting. If that's what you think your life is missing, what do you think would bring it back?"

"Bring it back? You're assuming I had it once."

"Did you?"

She looked away from me. "Yeah."

"When was that?"

"When the boys were young. When they were in school. I made a couple of documentaries. Won a prize for one of them. It was about kids who did drugs and what it did to their brains. I interviewed kids, parents, teachers, doctors in hospitals, and doctors in private practice. I showed what drugs do to a life. A lot of schools bought copies. One of the networks too. They gave it repeat showings for a whole year."

"Why did you stop?"

She shrugged. "It was a lot of effort."

"Sure. Was that the whole reason?"

"I didn't see the point. The world was turning before I came and it'll keep turning fine after I'm gone. What did I change? I thought I could make a difference. I was so excited. But the drug problem now is worse than before I made the film. Much worse. I accomplished exactly nothing."

"That might not be right."

"What?"

"Maybe you did have an effect. You don't know how much worse the problem might be now if you hadn't made the film."

She leaned her head on the back of the chair and closed her eyes for several seconds. "I'd like to go now. I need to think about this."

"We haven't gotten very far on your question."

She got up and took a check from her bag, a canvas tote decorated with representations of book spines in red, green, blue, and black. "I'm looking forward to next time."

Given the idiosyncrasies of my clients, knowing there would be a next time was something of a luxury for me. I decided to bask in it for a while, but I quickly realized I didn't know how.

7

Sheila, in a black skirt that matched her hair and a pale yellow T–shirt, waved at me from her seat on my couch when I returned. I'd given her a key and she hadn't used it until now. Circe, the traitor, abandoned her usual place in front of the door for the warmth and security of Sheila's lap. I acknowledged the wave. "Hi. Come here often?"

"Not as often as I'd like, big fella."

"Big fella?"

"Wishful thinking."

"Ouch."

"Not to worry. I like smarts better than muscles." She stood up and handed me the cat, whose purring circuits were engaged to the max. "I made coffee."

At the kitchen table she extracted some dark brown slabs from a paper bag.

"I also made you some chocolate. I found a new recipe in a book by some woman in Houston. You mix cocoa powder with peanut butter and almond extract and substitute stevia for sugar."

"I didn't know you could cook."

"It relaxes me."

"Well, thanks." I broke off a piece of the chocolate and bit into it. It tasted rich and thick with texture.

"I love it. But what have I done to deserve it?"

She took a piece for herself and sipped her coffee. She stirred her coffee with a spoon and took another sip.

"I'm working on an answer."

From her perch Circe, who had staked out my lap, craned her neck over the edge of the table to investigate the chocolate. She wasn't allowed on the table, but she pushed my limits whenever she could.

I broke off another piece and held it out to her. "You wouldn't like it." She took a long sniff, snatched her head back and looked up at me, as if to say, "Why are you wasting my time?"

"I see the woman who wants to kill you hasn't succeeded so far," Sheila said between sips.

I ate some more chocolate.

"You don't seem worried. You need to take a threat like that seriously."

"I do."

"Have you taken any measures?"

"My office door is locked, there's a surveillance camera outside, and I bought a gun."

"A gun?"

"World War Two souvenir." I flicked my coat open and showed her the holstered gun up near my armpit.

"A gun? You're an intellectual, for God's sake. Do you even know how to use a gun?"

"I did some research. You point it and pull the trigger."

She reached across the table and covered my hand with hers.

"Don't joke. You don't know what this woman is capable of. She could be very dangerous."

"I know."

We sat like that for a while, just looking at each other across the table. My endorphins began shoving a bunch of other neurotransmitters out of the way. We didn't speak. I reached down with my left hand and put the cat on the floor. She padded off without protest.

Sheila withdrew her hand and cradled her cup of coffee. She made no move to drink it. We sat there like a couple of adolescents, wanting the same thing, knowing it probably wasn't a good idea with our relationship this unsettled but wanting it anyway, neither of us knowing what to do about it. Finally she gave her head a little shake, as if she had won a debate with herself. Or maybe lost.

"What makes you think," she said, and stopped, because her voice came out a little funny. She cleared her throat and started again.

"What makes you think this crazy woman won't find out where you live? She found your office. She could find you here."

"The home phone is unlisted."

My own voice could have used a little shoring up too. If she noticed, she didn't let on.

"That wouldn't stop anyone with a little determination. She could follow you home. She could hire someone else to follow you home."

"I know."

"She may be crazy but that doesn't mean she's stupid."

"I know."

I decided on a change of subject.

"How's the fame business going?"

She smiled. "Threats on your life not an interesting enough topic?"

"All talked out on that. Why don't we sit on the couch."

She put the remaining chocolate back in the paper bag and put the bag in the fridge. We went into the living room. Circe watched us from the rug in front of the couch. Her head rested on her paws. I could see her thinking about whether or not to jump onto my lap. Her eyes shifted to Sheila's lap, then back to mine. The conflict must have been unbearable. Her tail began to twitch.

"The fame business, as you delicately put it, is alive and well. They pay me money, I make movies for them. People sometimes recognize me when I walk down the street. I have no complaints." She paused. "We've had this conversation before."

Could she be remembering the first time it had come up in our junior year at college? We'd just emerged from a local eatery where we'd had what in our student days passed for a pre–theater dinner. Spaghetti and pizza, extra cheese, heavy on the anchovies. A few doors away a movie marqee put the world on notice that an actress whose name I never heard of starred in a movie I had no interest in seeing. As we passed beneath it Sheila turned to me, eyes intense.

"I want people to know my name."

It took me by surprise. "People?"

"Everyone. The whole world."

While I considered this, she said, "Don't you?"

A cool Spring evening. The stars slowly winking into place. If you swivelled your head a little the sky turned into a celestial kaleidoscope. Students in jeans, khakis, shorts and T–shirts mingled on the sidewalks with townspeople in tailored slacks and shirts and blouses. To each his own.

I took a deep breath and inhaled May. "Maybe not everyone in Transylvania."

She didn't smile. "I'm serious."

"I see that."

"So?"

"Why would I want people who don't know me to know my name?"

"Because then they'd know you."

"In what sense?"

She shook her head. We'd arrived at the theater for a student production of *Hamlet*. Once inside the question of the evening was no longer fame. It was To Be Or Not To Be.

Well, I thought now, in the four hundred years since Shakespeare not all that much had changed regarding his question. The meaning of Not To Be never seemed obscure, and everyone always knew that To Be meant more than just breathing in and out. But the specifics? There's the rub.

Circe got up, arched her back and stretched. I knew that stretch. She'd made a decision.

"Nothing missing?"

"I didn't say that. And it's not a fair question."

I let it pass.

"Fame is not so bad, Eric. It's a time–honored goal. People have worked for it for thousands of years. In every society, right up to today. Nobody wants to be a nobody."

"Ah."

"I didn't mean you. Come on. I'm here, aren't I?"

The approach–approach conflict was too much for Circe. She sprang onto the couch and settled in on the middle cushion, exactly halfway between us.

"Anyway, I don't think there's anything wrong with it. I'm surprised you do," Sheila said.

"No you're not."

She nodded. "I'm not. But you know what I mean. I still don't understand."

"There's nothing wrong with it if it comes because you've done a really good job at something you love. Done it really well. There's a lot wrong with it if it's your main goal."

"Why?"

"Too much dependence on other people's opinions."

"What other people think is important."

"Sure."

"But?"

"Not all that important."

"Meaning?" She was beginning to sound impatient.

"Not enough to make it a life goal."

"Other things are more important." She made it a statement.

"Yes."

"Like?"

"Your own opinions."

She thought about it. "Well, okay. Sure. But people do things to impress other people. They don't do things to impress themselves."

"Yeah, they do."

She regarded me with a steady gaze. We'd touched on these things before, in bits and pieces, but they always made her uncomfortable and she shied away from pursuing them. I wondered if she would do the same now. She crossed her legs, which given the fashionably short skirt she had on and the shapeliness of her legs, had the interesting effect of both calming me down and perking me up.

"How is that even possible? You already know yourself. How can you impress yourself? You can't fool yourself."

"People do it all the time. You know that." I paused. "But in one sense you're right. When you do something you know you shouldn't do, on some level you do judge yourself the same way you'd judge anyone else who did the same thing. In the end, deep down, you aren't fooling yourself at all."

I got up to get some more chocolate from the fridge. Circe followed me, but when I took out the chocolate and she saw it she lost interest. I went back and offered a piece to Sheila. No interest there either.

I took a bite. "It's really great." I took another. "Your own opinion of yourself is the one that counts."

"My opinion of myself is alive and well."

"And living in California."

She shrugged. "Like I said. No complaints."

"Except when I ask you if there's anything missing, you'd rather not say."

"Nobody's life is perfect, Eric. There's always something missing. So like I said, it's not a fair question."

"Would it be fairer if you could ask me the same question?"

She smiled. "Now you're cooking." She ran her fingers through Circe's neck fur. "Maybe if you went first."

I took a deep breath, gathering my thoughts. She held up a hand. "I said maybe. I'm not really ready for this yet."

8

Sheila had to go back to Los Angeles. She'd been chosen for the lead in a film that started shooting in a week. The good news was that all her scenes could be shot back to back in a single two–week block. She played a sexy divorcee who stumbled on the door to a time warp which enabled her to see alternative lives she could have lived with three of the men she once dated. Not too original, but still an interesting premise. They hadn't worked out the ending yet. Three writers on the payroll were working 24/7 on three different endings. I wished them luck. When we said goodbye at the airport I stood and waited until she reached security. I always took pleasure in watching her walk, but watching her walk away made it a mixed bag.

***

The gun lady sat behind my desk pointing her gun at me when I came into my office at a quarter to nine the next day. I guessed she'd probably used the old credit–card–in–the–doorjamb trick against my spring–bolt lock, then relocked it from the inside and settled down to wait for me. I stood with my back against the closed door. I'd not seen her until I'd closed it behind me.

"Sit." She waved the gun toward my client chair.

I sat.

"What have you got to tell me?"

"Put away the gun and we can talk."

She wrinkled her nose as if smelling something distasteful.

"Oh, please. Don't waste my time."

"Your time? It's my time that's ticking here. I've got a client in ten minutes."

She opened my desk drawer, pulled out my appointment book and flicked it onto the desk without comment. She knew I had no client until eleven.

"Look. I told you before. I have nothing to say. I have no idea what you want from me."

She regarded me with speculative interest. I had no way of knowing whether she was capable of pulling the trigger right then and there, and no time to reach under my jacket to get my gun out of its holster with her gun pointing straight at my chest.

"Pity," she said in a whispery voice. The gun never wavered. At last she came to a decision.

"Tell me, a man like you, an honest to God philosophical practitioner. All those dry philosophy texts you have to remember. Those endless, boring, unreadable outpourings of diseased minds, men who couldn't live in the real world so they made up fantasy worlds in their heads and tried to pass them off as real. You have to remember all that crap, don't you."

I didn't answer. She wasn't looking for one.

"You must have a terrific memory. Do you have a terrific memory?"

"What's your point?"

"Let's see how good a memory you have. Do you remember Clara Thompson?"

"I never knew a Clara Thompson."

She gave me a long, wide-eyed stare.

"Here's what I want you to do. This is a very specific assignment, real easy for a Ph.D like you." She leaned in toward me.

"I want you to think about Clara Thompson. Think real hard, because next time I see you will be the last time, and we're going to talk about her before I kill you."

I stared at her. Only Kafka could have felt at home in a situation like this. Maybe he could think of a reply.

She stood up and went past my chair, giving it a wide berth and keeping the gun trained on me. She left without another word.

9

I Googled Clara Thompson and got nothing that related to any memory I had. I slipped the gun from its holster and aimed it at the doorknob and immediately felt a little better. After a few seconds the good feeling went away and I felt silly, so I put it back. At eleven o'clock Bernie Feld walked in. I didn't know how he managed to get an hour off before lunch hour. Maybe his title of loan officer carried privileges.

"Hello, Bernie."

"I thought about what you said last time. It made some sense."

Not a man to waste time on pleasantries.

"Good."

"But I'm still not happy."

"You're not happy in general, or you're not happy with what I said?"

"Both. Right now it's the same thing."

It's always nice when someone tells you that an argument made them unhappy because it implies that an argument could make them happy.

"Was there something you wanted me to clarify?"

Bernie frowned, resplendent in a well–tailored blue suit with a white jacquard shirt and red silk tie. Standard power outfit, and a sharp contrast to my khakis, no–iron rust shirt and brown tweed jacket. Well, they weren't coming to me for tips on haberdashery.

He put his hands on his knees, risking a flattening of the knife crease in his pants, and leaned forward.

"Let's say you're right with the job argument. Why I should be able to like it, enjoy it, without thinking so much about my mortality. That sounds okay."

"Good," I said again, in my most encouraging tone.

"So let's say I can get past that. I accept your point. But I still don't get what it all means."

"It?"

"Let's say I find a way I can be happy. Say banking. Say I'm a happy banker, okay? But I'm still not happy, if you get me. I feel like I should be part of something else. Something bigger than just me. Something that really matters."

"Such as?"

"I don't know. You tell me."

"I can't."

His eyebrows shot up and stayed up.

"I can't because I don't think you need to look outside yourself to find something that matters."

Now his face took on a pained expression, as if he had just bitten into something sour.

"You matter. You, your happiness, your life. You don't need outside justification for your life."

Bernie sat back in his chair and crossed an ankle over his knee. His expression changed slightly. His face screwed up and his heavy lips worked as if trying to get rid of the sour taste.

"That makes no sense."

I said nothing.

"Sure, I matter. Whatever that means. But I mean, so what? I'm talking about something else. I'm talking about being part of something really, I don't know, significant."

I reached over to the coffee pot and poured myself a styrofoam cupful. I offered one to Bernie. He nodded.

"Cream and sugar."

"Black is all I've got."

He shrugged and reached for the cup. I took a sip of mine. It had been standing a while and become bitter, but they didn't come to me for gustatory delights either.

"Okay, you're looking for something that matters, by which you mean something really significant. Right?"

"Yeah. This coffee is awful."

"True. Bernie, what would you say is the one thing that matters most?"

"To who?" he said ungrammatically. "To me?"

"Let's say to you."

"I just told you. I don't know. Maybe being part of something, like I said before. I don't know." He spread his hands in the universal gesture of helplessness.

I laced my fingers around my cup. A little heat managed to work its way through the styrofoam.

"If you asked me the same question, I'd say happiness."

"Happiness," he repeated without inflection.

"My own happiness is the most important thing to me, and I suggest yours is the most important thing to you."

Bernie placed his cup on the floor next to his chair. Apparently he needed both hands to gesture his impatience, which he now did.

"My own happiness. Sure, okay. Of course. But what about beyond that. It's a big world out there. That can't be all there is."

"Ultimately it's all there is, Bernie. For each of us."

He looked at me. "I don't believe it. It's too...shallow."

"Depends on what you think will make you happy." I waited for Bernie to say something. He remained silent. I went on.

"Most people are not happy. Real happiness is a significant achievement."

Bernie grunted and levered himself out of his chair. He started to say something, then stopped. He shook his head a few times. Then he cut the session short by simply leaving. Not all my clients reacted to me with equanimity.

I got my Aristotle from the desk drawer and spent the extra time with one of the best minds that ever lived. A mind that had studied the components of a happy life in great detail.

***

I called Sheila around ten o'clock that night. Seven her time. I didn't want to call her too late because she had to be on the set at six in the morning.

"Hello?"

"Checking in on my favorite actress."

"You sound a little funny. You okay?"

"I'm lying on my bed. Circe is lying on my chest. She weighs fourteen pounds."

She laughed, producing a sound I never tired of hearing. It started deep in her throat and modulated up to a girlish giggle. I never heard anything quite like it.

"In bed with the other woman," she said.

"A guy has needs."

Probably the wrong thing to say, as it put a little too much focus on the strained artificial nature of our current relationship. A topic we usually managed to stay away from. She stayed away from it now.

"Find out anything more about the lady with the gun?"

"No." I didn't see any point in telling her how misplaced my confidence in door locks had been. Besides, I hadn't really found out anything more about the gun lady. The sum of my knowledge remained that she said she wanted to kill me.

"How's the shooting going?"

"On schedule so far, which is a minor miracle."

"Conrad not known for sticking to the budget?" Conrad was the director.

"I don't think he really tries. But his pictures gross big, so they give him a free hand as long as he doesn't go wild."

"You okay? The schedule isn't too much?"

"I'm fine. Why don't you come down for a visit. I can introduce you to anyone you want. Well, almost anyone. In the film business."

"You think they'd want to hook up with a philosophical practitioner?"

"Want to, or need to? They all need to."

"But wouldn't want to."

"They wouldn't know what a philosophical practitioner is. Nobody does."

"We're trying to change that."

"We?"

"We have a society now. With a website and everything."

"Wow."

"Yeah. Today obscurity, tomorrow the world."

"I thought you thought obscurity suited you."

I didn't want to talk about this.

"Anyway, if I came out there you'd be enough."

"No urge to meet movie stars?"

"Anyone you think is interesting would probably be fun."

"No one as interesting as you. So when are you coming?"

"Not when you've got to be on the set at six every morning."

"There's always dinner."

"And we'll always have Paris," I said. She laughed, which I thought was generous.

"What would I do for the rest of the day while you're shooting?"

"I could get you onto the set. You could watch the filming."

"Didn't you tell me being on a movie set was boring?"

"I hoped you forgot. Besides, it isn't always boring."

"I'll take a pass for now. Maybe when your shoot is over. And no one is threatening to kill me. And my client load lightens up a little."

"Whatever. You know, we really need to talk."

"I know."

"About us."

"Yeah."

"About where we're going. Assuming we're going anywhere."

"I know."

"Things have changed for both of us. We're not who we used to be. At least I'm not. And I'm not talking about the movie star stuff."

I cleared my throat. "We could start where we left off last time. You asked me what was missing in my life."

"Actually you asked me and I threw it back at you."

"True."

"Eric? I really don't want to go on this way. I need some kind of closure. One way or the other."

"I'll call you soon." We hung up, which got Circe's attention. She stretched her neck and licked my face once, then sat back and eyed me. After a while she decided one lick was all I'd get. I went to the kitchen and found a piece of Bonbel cheese and a coke. I thought some more about Sheila's lifestyle and mine. About what each of us wanted out of life. About whether it could work. Obvious questions, but elusive answers. When I climbed into bed for the night I had resolved pretty much nothing.

***

When Jeremy came into my new office the next day, late as usual, he didn't even glance around. Not that all that much was different. I'd only had to move a desk, a chair, a computer and the mini fridge out of the old place, but in a fit of blind optimism I splurged and bought two more chairs. Three clients at once would be two more than I ever had and would be my form of group philotherapy.

Philotherapy. I liked the sound of it. Maybe some day they'd come up with a Nobel prize for philology.

I'd found a locksmith who claimed he could install a secure lock on my door. I decided to see if I could outfox the gun lady for a change by opening a new office and fortifying it with the new lock and a new camera. The phone was unlisted, so I'd called all my clients and given them the new address and phone number.

Jeremy sat in one of the chairs. "I'm not sure I agree with what you said last time."

"Which part?"

"About the self."

"Jeremy. You're the client. Do you want to stick to abstractions, which we can do if you like, or do you want to talk about your life?"

Jeremy cocked his head on one side.

"As long as I pay your fee, why do you care?"

"As long as you get your money's worth, I don't. But I want you to get your money's worth. As it is, your sessions are shortened when you come in late."

He nodded. "Okay. I appreciate that. Fair enough." He glanced at his watch. From where I sat it looked like a stainless steel model. I looked again. Nope. Not Jeremy. White gold.

"If there's no self," he said, jumping right in again, "it doesn't matter if I live or die."

"I'd say that was true."

"But that doesn't mean there's a self. It feels like there is, but that could be an illusion."

"If it's an illusion, who's being deceived?"

"You keep saying that." He wore the same generic outfit as the last two times, standard blue suit, white shirt, polished black shoes. He took off his glasses, holding them carefully by the wire frame, and polished them with a yellow pocket handkerchief. Then he carefully refolded it, replaced it, and looked up at me. For several seconds he said nothing.

"That can't be the whole answer. There are books written on this. Saying that it's all an illusion."

I shrugged. He was repeating himself.

"We can talk some more about that. Or we can pick up where we left off last time. Your problems with your wife and where your life is going. Your choice."

Jeremy remained silent. I remembered his lack of enthusiasm when I made this suggestion at our last session.

"Or you could tell me your last name. That might be helpful."

He shook his head.

"No names."

I smiled and spread my hands.

"Well, we'll always have Jeremy."

"Not my real name."

It stopped me.

"Any particular reason for keeping your identity a secret?"

Jeremy, or non–Jeremy, just pressed his lips together, shook his head and said nothing. I made one of the lightning quick calculations for which I was yet to become famous. If he had lied about his name, maybe he'd lied about everything else too. Which could mean he didn't have a big house and wasn't CFO of a Fortune 500 company. Maybe he wasn't CFO of any company. Or maybe he told the truth about all that and just wanted to keep his name secret.

"I'm not going to be much help to you if you're feeding me wrong information."

He let out a small sigh.

His deception disappointed me. Someone wanted to kill me, a threat that never stopped pushing at the back of my mind like a pin at a balloon. On top of that my clients lied to me. One of them, anyway. These things did nothing for my mood or my desire to continue this session.

"I think that's enough for now."

He gave a short nod, got up and paid me in cash, as usual. No checks meant no name on the checks for me to see. The cash made a little more sense now.

***

Twenty minutes after Jeremy left, two tentative knocks on my office door interrupted my fantasies about the entire world population adopting rationality as the ordering principle of their lives. I didn't think I needed to check the camera because I had an appointment with a new client starting now. Besides, the gun lady never knocked, and in any event, one thing she wasn't was tentative.

Of course she might be crafty enough to know I'd think that way. With an inward sigh, I checked the camera. Diana Rogers stood in front of my door. I let her in.

A small mixed–race woman of about forty, she had straight black hair that reached her shoulders. She looked more Eurasian than anything else. Whoever made the mixture got it right. She had a pouty mouth, a valentine face and large dark eyes that fixed on me in an intense stare.

"I'm not sure I'm in the right place."

I looked at her.

"I thought maybe I should go to a psychologist. Or a psychiatrist. Oh, I just don't know."

She crossed her legs, which were fine, in a quick nervous gesture. She wore a light green skirt of some soft material that came to her knees and a sweater the same color. Her brown shoes had medium heels that looked comfortable for walking. On her left wrist was a stainless steel Seiko watch with matching band. All together, tasteful, yet casual and understated.

"Maybe if you told me a little more about what's on your mind."

She twisted her hands in her lap, not answering right away. When she finally spoke her words came in a rush.

"I'm in love."

"Sounds good so far."

"You don't understand. I don't know what to do."

I waited. Waiting is a very underrated activity.

"I'm scared."

I waited some more. I like to think I waited inquiringly.

"He's so...so..."

We were not making rapid progress.

"Yes?"

"He's so...everything. He's very smart. And he's funny. He makes me laugh. And everyone likes him."

"You left out handsome."

"Oh, who cares about that." She waved an arm as if brushing my comment away. Which is what it deserved.

"So, what's wrong? He sounds great."

"He is. Oh, he is. That's the problem."

"I'm missing something."

"I'm scared," she said again. "What if he tells me he loves me? What do I do then? I don't think I could handle it."

"He hasn't said anything to you?"

"Not about that. No."

"Does he know how you feel?"

"No, of course not."

"Why of course not?"

"I can't just blurt out a thing like that. He has to go first."

"Diana, this is the twenty–first century."

She shook her head, swirling her black hair around her face.

"Some things don't change. The man has to go first. The man is the risk taker."

"Not if men and women are equal."

She kept shaking her head.

"Let's go back to the hypothetical. Let's say he tells you he loves you. So now it's mutual. You said that would be a problem? You couldn't handle it?"

"Look at me." She got up and stood in front of my desk, then turned in a slow circle. She remained standing for several more seconds. Then, her point apparently made, she sat down again.

"I'm pretty. Men like me. But that won't last. Everyone gets old. What then? In the end it all comes down to who you are. Not what you look like. And who am I? Who am I, really? I'm a cute computer programmer. Soon the cute will go away and there'll be just me. I know a lot about computers, but not a lot else. I'm not interesting. I'm not funny. I don't have what people call a winning personality."

She paused and blinked several times, trying to hold back tears.

"I couldn't hold him," she whispered. "Never in a million years."

And the tears came, soundlessly. She sat, shoulders shaking, blinking away the fullness in her eyes, looking straight at me, hands clasped in her lap, letting the wetness run down her face, leaving crooked trails in her makeup. I took a couple of tissues from my drawer and handed them to her. She dabbed at her cheeks but the tears kept coming. She made no apology for them. I gave her all the time she needed and placed the tissue box on the corner of my desk nearest her. When the tears ended she blew her nose, which seemed to settle her.

"Thanks."

She threw the crumpled tissues into my wastebasket and sniffled twice.

"I don't usually do that."

I nodded.

"I can't remember when I cried like that."

"No shame in crying."

"I know. Except you feel so out of control. It's like you can't handle your life. Like you've given up."

"It makes you feel helpless."

"Yes."

"That's okay, as long as you remember that you're not."

She held her lower lip with her teeth. "In this case I am."

"You're not helpless. You haven't given up."

She looked at me.

"You came here."

She considered this. It had the virtue of being hard to deny.

"Diana, you've told me how you see yourself. Why don't you tell me how your friend sees you."

"I told you, he hasn't said anything. I don't know how he feels."

"Then why not wait and see."

"You don't understand. He'll find me out. Then he'll leave. I'll lose him."

She looked as if she wanted to cry again. I hoped she didn't. I'm sure she hoped so too. Our time had about run out, and we hadn't gotten anywhere.

"I hope we can talk some more about this next time," I said.

She left, looking sad. I hoped I could make some progress with her next time but I had no time to think about it right now because my next appointment, Bernie Feld, arrived at the door.

10

Bernie went straight to the middle chair of my three client chairs, bypassing the one on the left closest to the window and the one on the right nearest the coffee. The middle one centered directly in front of my desk. So far every client had chosen the middle chair. I thought about the significance of that and decided it had no significance whatever.

"What did you mean when you said last time that real happiness is a significant achievement? In the first place why did you say real happiness? There can't be an unreal happiness. Either you're happy or you're not. But if you are, you are. Period."

Bernie had plunked himself down with his customary lack of greeting. I thought about whether to treat him in kind. I decided against it.

"Hello Bernie. Nice tie."

"Thanks."

I leaned over and poured myself some coffee. No question about it, I'd become an addict. I found this thought singularly undisturbing.

"Want some?"

"No thanks."

Who could blame him. He knew how bad my coffee tasted. I cast about for a place to begin.

"Look. You've been happy plenty of times in your life, right?"

"So has everyone."

"So, would you call yourself a happy man?"

"If I was I wouldn't be here."

"So feeling happy plenty of times doesn't necessarily mean a person is happy? Doesn't that sound strange?"

"I suppose it's a question of how often. That's not exactly rocket science."

"Why do you think more people aren't happy?"

"People get it wrong," he said.

"In what way?'

"Every way. They don't know what they want."

"You think that might apply to you?"

Bernie stood up, took off his jacket, hung it on the back of the chair nearest the window, and sat down again.

"No. I always knew what I wanted. But so what? Nobody feels good all the time."

I nodded. "Because, of course, bad things happen to everyone. But some people can put those things behind them. They still feel good about themselves and about the world. They feel good about being in the world."

"Why don't you just say they feel good about being alive," Bernie snapped.

This was a hostile guy. The hostility probably wasn't directed at me, since he'd only recently met me. At the world? If so, one day his anger would almost certainly be directed at me.

I smiled. "Anyway, people who feel that way most of the time are pretty rare."

"You know why it's rare? Because sensible people have their eyes open and have the courage not to block out all the shit that goes down in the world every day. I don't think ignoring those things is an achievement."

I took another sip of my drug of choice, then put the cup back on the desk. When I became rich and could afford a fancy desk of polished wood with lots of burls I'd buy a set of coasters to protect it. Until then one more water ring on my desk made no difference. Besides, all my cups were styrofoam.

"It's not denial, Bernie. Happy people are very much aware of what goes on around them. They're just as devastated as anyone else when a 9/11 happens. Where they're different is how they feel about life day in and day out, when life is normal."

Bernie shot his cuff and glanced at his watch.

"I gotta go. I'll pay for the whole hour."

He stood up, retrieved his jacket, and instead of leaving stood for a moment looking out at the distant outlines of New Jersey, his square jaw working as if chewing gum. Then he turned back to me.

"Assuming you're right, how do they get like that?"

I stood and walked him to the door.

"New topic. Next time," I said.

***

At home I retrieved a short message from Sheila asking me to call back. I didn't carry a cell phone because I didn't like to be randomly interrupted. Of course I could shut the phone off and have it take a message, but my home phone could take messages just as well and I had no need to call anyone while walking in the street. Technology is great, but I liked my time to be my own.

Sheila, though, as a card carrying important Hollywood personage, said she couldn't do without hers and carried it all the time. She'd told me I could call any time because she always turned it off on the set.

I called her now but she didn't pick up. When her voicemail came on I said, "Hey, babe. We got your message. Circe sends her regards."

Not entirely true, as Circe was busy scarfing down the cat food I'd poured into her bowl, chomping away with her usual single–minded concentration. When she ate, I and the rest of the universe ceased to exist. Still, I didn't think a little exaggeration would constitute misrepresentation in this case.

For dinner I opened a can of sardines and a can of beans. Then I read a while before turning on the news. People on the other side of the world were killing other people who disagreed with them on any of a variety of issues. One day men and women and children went about their business, living their lives as best they could, making plans for their future. The next day they ceased to exist, along with their hopes and dreams. All because large numbers of human beings did not choose to live as human beings. They chose to live as animals, settling their differences or their imagined grievances by force instead of reason.

After I'd had my fill of the day's mayhem and gone to bed the cat padded into the bedroom, looked up at me with a loud questioning purr, jumped onto the bed and curled around my feet without waiting for an answer. She had long ago figured out I was a sucker for confident women.

Unless they were trying to kill me, of course. The gun lady was still loose in the city with mayhem on her mind and me as her monomania. If I wanted to get some sleep I had to try cementing her behind a mental wall for a while. However my only experience with mental walls involved trying to break them down in some of my clients.

My subconscious arranged a compromise. It kept me awake for about an hour before retreating back into its cave and letting the darkness take me.

***

In the morning I had a new client. She made the appointment over the phone. I checked the camera to make sure it wasn't the gun lady under a false name and made out enough detail to satisfy myself.

"I'm a prostitute," Valerie Marsh said without preamble. She had a full figure with long chestnut hair and open features that made you want to trust her.

She waited for me to reply, and when I didn't she went on.

"Well, do you want me to leave?"

I shook my head. Valerie arranged her skirt around her knees. She wore a fitted business suit in forest green, a tan silk blouse and brown alligator pumps. She had used a minimum of makeup. Most people would take her for an executive from a tall steel and glass tower, which she no doubt intended.

"I got your name from a friend. A long time ago. Well, a few years ago, anyway."

I nodded.

"So you're willing to take me on as your patient?"

"Client."

"Whatever."

"Sure."

She took a deep breath and smoothed her skirt.

"There's a couple of things I want to get out of the way."

I waited.

"I want to make sure...you're not going to ask me what a nice girl like me is doing in a profession like this, are you?"

"Not if you don't want me to."

She reached down to her plain black leather handbag on the floor. It didn't match her suit or her shoes, which I'm sure meant something, but I didn't know enough about women's fashions to know what.

She extracted a pack of cigarettes.

"Mind if I smoke?"

"I'd rather you didn't."

She hesitated, trying to decide if that meant she could if she really wanted to. Then she nodded and replaced the cigarettes.

"I need to know what you think of prostitutes."

"Why?"

"What do you mean, why? Because I don't want to be here if you think I'm the scum of the earth."

"I don't think that."

She stared at me, waiting for more. I held her glance. Outside a car horn sounded and another answered in two sharp staccato bursts. She took another deep breath did a slow exhale.

"Do you want to know how much money I make?"

I shook my head.

"Not curious at all?"

"You're a beautiful woman. I'm sure you do very well."

I saw her eyes narrow.

"Just to be clear here, you're not coming on to me, are you? Just because I do what I do – "

"If we're going to get anywhere, you've got to be a little more trusting." I reached over to the coffee machine, poured a cup and held it out to her.

A quick head shake. "I'm a nicotine girl."

"You're not missing much. It's pretty bad coffee."

She shifted around in her seat so she faced me at a slight angle.

"I'm perfectly happy doing what I do."

"Uh huh."

"I've been doing this for four years. I'm twenty–five now. A little long in the tooth for this job I know, but in two or three years I'll retire. Then I can do what I want for the rest of my life. How many people can say that before they reach thirty? How many can say it ever?"

"I thought you were already doing what you want to do."

She regarded me coolly.

"You know what I mean. I meant there's nothing wrong with it. With being with a lot of men. Taking money from them. But it's for a purpose. I get to live my own life later."

"I don't hear a question in there."

Her hand dropped to her bag and jerked up again.

"You sure I can't smoke?"

"I'd rather you didn't," I said again.

She nodded twice. The smoking question was settled in her mind.

"I do want to ask you something. Two things, really. First, why do men always want to talk first? It's like they can't just do their business and leave. They have to talk before they start. Then they want to talk some more after."

"That bothers you?"

"It's so boring. Where do you come from, have you been doing this long, what's a nice girl like you, and on and on. Why do they do it?"

I drank some coffee.

"Maybe to establish some kind of human connection."

"Why? Why not just do what they came for and be done with it?"

"I'm not an expert on this. I don't know if there are any experts on this, come to think of it. But I'd guess men don't just want to have sex. They want to have sex with a person. Asking you all those questions might be a way for them to feel that the sex is not just a matter of mechanical friction."

"But that's what it is."

I waited. Valerie looked thoughtful. "The other thing I want to ask you..." She stopped, searching for words. "I want to know what you think of me."

"That's not why you came here."

"How would you know why I came here?"

"I don't. I'm hoping you'll tell me."

She leaned forward, started to say something, stopped, opened her mouth again and closed it. She leaned back.

"Okay. The truth? I just wanted to talk and have someone listen. I'm not sure why."

"If this were the beginning of the session, I could ask you some questions and maybe we'd find out."

She rose.

"I don't think I got my money's worth."

"You didn't."

"I'm not sure I'll come back."

"If you do, I recommend we get into some of the things that matter to you."

She looked at me sharply. "Like what?"

"Maybe what you want to do after you retire. Or we could talk some more about what you do now. Or not. Your choice."

Instead of answering she picked up her purse. "What do I owe you?"

I told her. She took out some bills, placing them carefully on my desk, one at a time, so I could see she was giving me the right amount.

Shortly after she left I took the elevator down to the lobby, where Starbucks had taken a corner from which it dispensed smooth jolts of caffeine to young and old and anyone else whose nervous system needed a little jazzing up. I found a table between two college age women who where typing away at their laptops. A couch in a little lounge area in the corner had some room but I preferred the solitary space of my own table.

I nursed my Grande Latte, which bore the same resemblance to my homemade coffee as pheasant under glass to corned beef hash, while I gazed out the window and watched the passing parade of busy New Yorkers. Everyone seemed to be in a hurry. The best and brightest gravitate here. Most think working harder and faster than the next guy is all it takes to win the game. But it isn't a game and that isn't all it takes. The kind of person you make yourself into matters even more, but most don't understand that. If they can make it here they can make it anywhere, and they all think they can make it here. Well, plenty of them will, and that's a good thing.

I sipped my drink and consulted my watch. Twenty minutes to my next appointment. The woman at the table to my right stopped typing and looked up at me. Feeling friendly, I smiled. She stared at me stone faced and went back to her typing. I'm not even sure she saw me.

So, making it. Am I making it, I asked myself? Not in their terms, certainly. I'd never have a lot of money or a big house or even a fancy car. The watch on my wrist was a Timex.

So if not in their terms, in whose?

Mine, of course. Most people would probably think me a failure. Could I be sure they were wrong?

I'd better be. After all, I affected peoples' lives. I'd better be sure that what I did added meaning and value to my life as well as to theirs. Otherwise I'd be defrauding both them and myself.

Having settled that, I drained the last drops of my ambrosia and headed back to my office.

11

I have a friend, Burt Lidsky. We found one another in high school and became best friends. In school we'd been rivals for Sheila's affections. After a couple of months' hesitation she decided on me and we'd gone together during our junior and senior years. We all went to the same college, where Sheila studied drama and I took philosophy. After graduation she decamped for Los Angeles and I found a small apartment in the capital of the world. New York. Sheila and I never lost touch, but after Burt got married he and Sheila drifted apart. Now he had a wife, two kids, a German shepherd, and a house in Stamford. He commuted to New York, where he ran a hedge fund.

He never forgot Sheila.

A few hours following my session with Valerie I met him in a Greenwich Village café on West Ninth called Symphony, where we sometimes played chess. Although our life experiences had diverged over the years we never stopped enjoying each other. The halo effect of the old days still lingered. I hoped it always would.

"So, have you seen Sheila lately?" Burt said nonchalantly. He asked this question or some variant of it almost every time we met.

"She was in town a while ago. Right now she's back in L.A. making a film."

He made a noncommittal noise. "She really knows how to pick scripts."

"Acting is pretty good too."

Burt stared at the chessboard. "And with her looks, she's got the whole package. The whole world loves her."

"A big enough chunk of it anyway."

He nodded. "Big box office."

My turn to nod.

"Big." He made a move on the chessboard. A middle–aged man with baggy pants and a cap that looked like a vanilla and chocolate cookie with a visor attached wandered over to watch the game, but seeing Burt's move he thinned his lips and wandered away. Well, maybe he was a grandmaster. What had he seen? I studied the board, and in a couple of minutes I saw it. In three moves I could trap Burt's queen. I made the first move.

Burt studied the position. "Shit."

"Is that a command or just a suggestion?"

He tipped over his king and started setting up the pieces for a new game. "She's really really rich," he said without missing a beat. "Did you know she gets a piece of the gross on every picture?"

I nodded.

"She must have a fortune," he said.

I made my first move.

"How come you guys never got together?"

I shrugged. "We tried."

"I mean after college. What happened?"

I looked up at him, then out the large window fronting the street. Village types jammed the sidewalk. Young, old, and in–between. Everyone mixed freely. Everyone wore jeans or khakis. In one of life's little disappointments, I didn't see any skirts. Lots of sandals, running shoes, and jackets over T–shirts.

"Different goals. Different ways of life."

"Like, movie star versus philosophy teacher?"

"Close enough."

"So what's the glitch? She doesn't like philosophy, or you don't like sexy famous ladies?"

"It's kind of complicated."

"How complicated could it be? Is it her money?" He slid his knight to F5. Bad news for the good guys.

"Her money's not a problem."

"Maybe it's a problem for her. The disparity."

"No."

"Then what?"

"Just different outlooks, Burt. We're still working it out."

"Okay, you don't want to talk about it." He took my g7 pawn with his knight. A sacrifice. Bad for me if I took it, bad for me if I didn't. I tried to figure the least bad option.

"Anyway, I don't see how you can work anything out with her living in L.A. and you in New York."

"There are planes. And phones. And e–mail."

He shrugged. "Good luck, pal." He looked up from the board.

"Hey, I really mean that."

"I know. Thanks."

He gestured at the game.

"But luck ain't gonna help in this position."

Too true. I resigned and we began a new game.

"How's Nancy?" I said.

"Fine, I guess." He shrugged. "Yeah. Fine."

We played a few more moves.

"She wants us to join a country club."

"Is that a problem?"

"Yeah." He raised a hand to signal the waitress.

"How come this place has no liquor license," he said to me as she approached.

"Ask her."

He asked her. She had a perky smile and a blonde page cut. Probably an aspiring actress waiting to be discovered. She gave him a blank look.

"Never mind. Sorry," he said. "Double cappuccino, please."

She went off to get it, swinging her hips a little. After all, we could be agents. Or producers. A girl never knew.

"I asked her about the club's activities. She said mainly they play sports. So I said yeah, mainly they try to hit a little white ball into a hole in the ground."

The waitress brought Burt's cappuccino. I nursed my first drink, which was eight ounces of iced coffee, black.

Burt reached out to move a bishop but drew his hand back. He looked over at me. "Nancy likes golf."

"Lot of people do."

"Waste of time. Tennis too. Hit the ball into a hole in the ground or hit it back and forth over a net. I'll watch it sometimes, but I'll never play it. I don't know how anyone can waste their time like that." He took a swig of cappuccino and dabbed at his lips with a napkin.

"Problem there," I said.

"Like what?"

"If they're worth watching they've got to be worth playing."

"Not by me."

"Okay, but you can't fault the players. Besides, people could say the same about chess. Lot of people would think spending hours at a time moving pieces of wood around sixty four little squares is pretty crazy."

"Chess is mental exercise."

I smiled at him.

"Yeah, well. Maybe you got a point."

"Thanks."

He grinned. "I said maybe."

We played a few more moves and called the game a draw. We put some money on the table. I offered my hand.

"Always a pleasure."

"Always."

I didn't tell him about the gun lady, and I realized I didn't want to. It seemed like an imposition on our relationship. People have different friends for different purposes, and most of the time the purposes don't cross.

So we went our separate ways.

***

The first piece of mail I received after moving to my new office had been slipped under my door. It had no return address, a first–class stamp, and PLEASE FORWARD written by hand in the lower left–hand corner and underlined in thick India ink. Inside, three words slashed diagonally across a piece of heavy cream–colored stationery. I'LL FIND YOU. Nothing else.

Brief. To the point. If I taught composition I'd give her an A. Not just for style, but also because the note had the desired effect. She wanted me to know she still had me in her sights. She wanted to upset my routine, to the point where I'd always be looking over my shoulder for her, unable to fully focus on my normal daily life.

As a child, I'd found and loved Henley's poem, the one that ended *I am the master of my fate, I am the captain of my soul*. Well, I had no problem with the second part, which I dealt with every day in my professional capacity. She wanted to undercut the first part, and so far I had to admit she'd succeeded.

***

"My banker recommended you. Bernie Feld," Martin Marks said.

I did my best not to show my surprise.

Martin occupied the middle chair of my three client chairs, flanked by his wife Dorothy and his adolescent son Joel. All three had on jeans, sport shirts, and Nike running shoes.

Martin led off. "Mr. Feld is my personal banker." He was tall, dark, and clean–shaven. About a foot shorter, his red–haired wife seemed subdued. Joel looked somewhere in between. Even his brown hair represented a middle ground. Slight pockmarks pitted his face. He wore a chrome or silver earring in or on his left ear, a statement of some sort that completely passed me by.

"A good personal banker can help you with anything these days," Martin continued.

"So how can I help you?" I stressed the "I."

"Not me. Joel." He indicated his son with a jerk of his thumb.

I looked at Joel. So did Dorothy Marks. Martin looked at me. Joel's expression never changed.

"I don't need any help."

"Now, honey," his mother said. She had a soft voice tinged with a slight southern accent.

"Tell the man about college," Martin said to his son.

Joel looked at his father. "I'm not going to college. I told you that."

"Don't tell me. Tell him. Tell him why."

Joel's face remained devoid of expression. He looked at me.

"There's no point."

I tried to look encouraging. "Not a problem of grades?"

"Oh no, his grades are fine. In fact he's in the honor society. What's it called, honey?" Dorothy asked brightly.

"Arista."

Martin looked at his son for the first time.

"College," he barked. "Tell the man."

Joel looked at me. He fingered his earring.

His mother leaned forward. "Go on, honey."

Joel took a deep breath.

"I look around at the world. I see how it works. People work from nine to five, that's eight hours a day. They sleep eight hours, so the eight they spend at work is half their life. Half their life cooped up somewhere, doing something they don't want to do, taking orders from someone. And they do it all for money." His voice rose to a pitch of incredulity. "They sell half of their life."

He looked straight at his father. "That's what my dad does."

He paused and touched his earring again. "Not me. No way. It's my life and I'm not selling half of it to anyone. What are they going to teach me in college? People go to college so they can get a good job. But I'm not selling my life. I don't want a job. So I'm not going to waste my time."

"You see," Martin said to me, "his poor deluded father works at a law firm from nine to five. Sometimes longer. That makes him a failure as a role model."

No one spoke. I leaned forward. "Joel, what do you enjoy doing? What do you do with your free time?"

He shrugged. "I like reading. I like learning stuff."

"They do a lot of that in college."

"Yeah, but I want to read whatever I want. Not what they tell me to. I don't need them."

"Anything you especially like to read?"

"A lot of stuff. Novels, science magazines. Psychology books. Economics books about how the world works. Computer stuff."

"Anything you like better than the rest?"

"I like it all. The stuff I like to do depends on how I feel that day."

I leaned back. Dorothy Marks watched me, alert. Martin frowned. I pushed on.

"Joel, you know why people sell their time. They have to make a living. You'll need to make a living too. Have you thought about how you're going to do that?"

"Yeah."

"Any answers?"

He shook his head and looked away, out the window. He shifted back at me. A fire engine blared by outside. "I don't belong here."

"Where?"

"In this society. In this world. There's no place for me." His voice went flat.

"I don't think that's true. I know it's not. I think I can help you."

"I don't need any help."

Martin rose. His family rose with him.

"That's a laugh."

He handed me a check made out for the correct amount. It seemed Bernie Feld's briefing included the amount of my fee.

Martin started to leave. "We'll be back."

His family followed him out, Dorothy first, then Joel.

I flashed on that famous photo of Konrad Lorenz and his ducks.

12

Demand for philosophical practitioners had yet to blossom. I had no more clients that day, so I grabbed a quick lunch of bratwurst and sauerkraut on a bun from a corner hot cart and took the subway home. One day my cholesterol would catch up with me if the gun lady didn't get me first. Until then I consoled myself with the quality versus quantity theory of living. A short happy life is preferable to a long muted one. But does that really hold as a general principle? Within reason, I thought. Always within reason. Otherwise the obvious question of how short is short could shoot down the whole thing. Not to mention that the argument risked posing a false alternative. Why not a long happy life?

When I got home I found another message from Sheila. I called her back and she picked up on the second ring.

"It's your favorite philosophical practitioner."

"What makes you think none of the other p.p.'s made the grade?"

"P.p.'s?"

"You can't expect anyone to keep saying philosophical practitioner all the time."

"I'd be happy if some people said it some of the time. I'd even settle for once."

"Your profession needs a PR person."

"Tell me about it."

A pause. I always felt a little awkward getting down to the basics with Sheila, as if each of us had to reacquaint ourselves with the other in the first few minutes of a conversation before we could feel comfortable. I wasn't sure why.

"I called to make sure you're safe," she said. "You haven't heard from that woman again?"

"The post office forwarded a note from her telling me she'd find me, but so far the address change and the unlisted phone seem to have worked."

"Are you still carrying that gun?"

"Yeah."

"Playing it safe."

"Yeah."

"Good."

"So," she said. "You were going to tell me what was missing in your life."

"I was?"

"Well, I think you were. It sounded like you were. Or come on down for a visit and you can tell me in person."

"You done shooting?"

"You know I'm not."

A silence.

"So answer the question, fella."

"Well." My fingers tightened around the phone. She'd asked a straightforward question, one in fact that I had asked of her. What harm could there be in answering it, beside feeling naked at the thought?

I decided that wasn't a good enough reason. I took a deep breath.

"I love my work. I love this city. It makes me feel like I'm twelve feet tall, standing on a mountain top in the center of the universe. I've got my apartment and my practice. As far as I know, there's only one thing missing."

"I know it isn't money. You don't care about money."

"Not true. Money is survival. And freedom."

"But you don't care about it beyond that."

"Not much."

Another silence.

"Sorry. I interrupted you. Only one thing, you were saying."

"No big surprise. Sharing. I'd like to be able to share my life."

Some seconds passed. Then, "That's it?"

"I think so."

"Nothing else?"

"There are other things, but I think sharing covers them all."

"Not to be difficult, but you don't think that's a little simplistic?"

I thought about it.

"No."

"What if you had a client who told you that sharing was the only thing missing in his life. Would you leave it at that?"

"No."

"What else would you ask him?"

"I'd ask him to unpack it. Tell me all the things it covered, all its conditions, all its qualifications, what it did for him."

"So why don't you do that for me."

"I'm not sure I can. At least not now over the phone. That's a very long conversation. Besides, it's your turn."

She laughed. It made my teeth tingle. I wanted her to do it again.

"Not now," she said with a lilt in her voice. "That's a very long conversation."

I switched the phone to my other ear. My left ear heard better than the right. I used a couple of seconds to consider the totally irrelevant question of whether that could mean I was right–brain dominant, taking into account the crossover effect.

No way. Words were my thing, not pictures.

The next irrelevancy that occurred to me was wondering what it could be like to not have irrelevancies occur to you in the middle of sober conversations.

"How's the picture coming?"

"Would you believe we still don't have an ending? I keep telling Conrad it's hard for me to know how to play it if I don't know where it's going. All I get out of him is 'I know, sweetheart, I know.'"

"Still on schedule?"

"Amazingly, we're one day ahead."

All during this conversation I'd been stroking Circe's head and neck, installed comfortably in a reclining armchair in my living room with the cat curled up on my lap.

"Want to say hello to Circe?"

"Hello, Circe."

"No, wait, I'm going to put the phone to her ear. Okay, now."

"Hello, Circe," Sheila said into Circe's ear.

Circe jerked her head away and stared at the phone.

"Again," I said into the mouthpiece.

"Hello, Circe. Hi there. He treating you all right, honey?"

Circe looked at me and looked back at the phone. Then she let out a long, plaintive meow.

"You hear that?"

"Sure did," she laughed.

"She misses you. Me too."

"Yeah. Well. We still need to talk. We didn't get very far today."

"I know."

"Call me."

"Is there a best time?"

"With my crazy shooting schedule?"

"Potluck?"

"Works for most people."

"Talk to you soon," I said.

✳✳✳

"He asked me out," Diana Rogers said at the start of her lunch hour the next day. She twisted her hands in her lap. Today she had on another sweater–skirt combination, in a shade of red that matched her lipstick and made a wonderful contrast with her dark hair. She looked delicate and classy. I didn't find it hard to empathize with whoever had asked her out.

"For Saturday," she went on. "I'm scared to death."

I nodded. She picked up right where she left off last time.

"Okay, let's talk about it. What are you afraid of? It's clear he likes you."

"No!" she cried. Her soprano voice skidded to the top of its range. "He doesn't like me. He doesn't know anything about me. What he likes is my format. Not me."

"Your format?"

"This." She indicated her breasts and swept her hand downward. "Not this," she added, tapping her forehead.

"How do you know that?"

"We never talk about anything important."

"What do you talk about?"

"Computers. Programming. Other stuff. We're both programmers. We work for the same company."

"Do you enjoy talking with him?"

"Oh, yes."

"Do you think he enjoys talking with you?"

"I don't know. He never asks me questions about myself."

"Have you asked him personal questions?"

"No. I can't. The man has to go first."

"We touched on that last time. Those rules don't hold any more. If they ever did."

She dismissed that with a wave of her hand.

"You have to help me. What should I do?"

"Just be the same person he's gotten to know and like up till now."

"But he hasn't gotten to know me. I told you that. All he knows is the outside. The woman shell. Not the real me."

"What would you say is the real you?"

She stared at me. She crossed her legs and licked her lips. She angled her body away from me and shifted it back again. She made an unneeded adjustment to the hem of her skirt.

"I don't know. I'm a woman. I'm a computer programmer. I like to read. I like to cook. But none of that's the real me. I don't know what's the real me."

"You're still getting to know yourself."

She gave a quick nod.

"Would you say getting to really know yourself takes a long time?"

"Yes." Her hands were a little calmer now.

"People are still working on it in their seventies and eighties," I said. "Right up until the day they die. Those are some of the best people."

"Why does it take so long?"

"I'm not sure I can answer that. Neurologists tell us there are as many neurons in the brain as there are stars in the Milky Way galaxy. Each neuron connects to maybe ten thousand others. Think of that enormous complexity and all the memories and hopes and fears and ideas stored there. There's a whole lot to get to know. And each person is unique. No one else ever had or ever will have your particular experiences and your particular take on the world. There's no one like you. There never will be."

She appeared to mull it. "So people are complicated. Computers are complicated too, but you can find everything in their memories. You can know anything you want about what's inside them."

I smiled. "Wouldn't it be great if we could access our own minds that way. Just type in a keyword and hit search."

She didn't respond.

"But even if we could access all our memories with a single click of some mental mouse, that wouldn't tell us what our talents are, or what our needs are, or what we should want out of life, or how hard we should try to get it, or how we should act toward other people, or what we should want and expect from them."

She responded without hesitation this time. "That takes a long time to find out."

"It does."

"So you're saying I shouldn't be too upset if I can't answer your question. About who I really am."

"If you can't answer it immediately. And I'm suggesting you give your friend – what's his name? The man who asked you out?"

"Bruce."

"I'm suggesting you lighten up and let Bruce get to know you at his own speed, in his own way."

Silence.

"And Diana – cut the guy a little slack about the way he looks at you. Men love to look at women. That's not only a good thing for the human race, it's a good thing for you and Bruce."

Diana smiled a small, shy smile. She dug in her purse and handed me a folded check. "Thanks," she said in her small high voice, and she walked out, giving me a wonderful view of her format.

***

Following my limited success with Diana I went down to Starbucks again for a quick Moccachino before my next session. While waiting for the barista I scanned the usual motley assortment of secretaries, housewives, lovers, masters of the universe, students, and unclassifiables, and I realized my subconscious kept a sharp eye out for the gun lady. She wasn't there, which hardly surprised me. She specialized in direct confrontation, not cooling her heels. I had twenty minutes to savor my concoction, and I used every one of them. Savoring is a dying art in adrenalized Manhattan, but the Starbucks chain provided a haven from freneticism for those who wanted one. When the twenty minutes passed I was behind my desk again.

"You were going to tell me how those happy people managed to ignore all the crap that goes down in the world," Bernie Feld said as soon as he was seated.

I noticed he had on polished black loafers with little tassels that flopped around whenever he moved his feet. The flopping clashed with the sophisticated look he always tried for. I wore my standard tweed jacket and pressed khakis. I felt comfortable except for the annoying weight of the gun under my arm, about which I felt more ridiculous every day.

"Hello, Bernie. How've you been?"

He shrugged. "How do they get like that?"

"Partly, they do it the same way you do when you're feeling good."

He shook his head. "You said they feel that way all the time. Or nearly."

"Sometimes they do it the same way you do," I repeated. "There are two main ways. The first is to ignore all the bad stuff. Just push it away. Don't focus on it. Forget it."

"Doesn't work."

"Not very well and not for long. The second way is better."

Bernie waited.

"It's a lot harder, and not many people can do it," I continued.

Bernie twitched a leg. His tassels jumped.

"These people are able to maintain a certain perspective," I said. "They see all the bad stuff, but they see it as not that important. They think about it, but only long enough to deal with it. Otherwise they focus on the good things in their lives."

Bernie shook his head in wide arcs. I noticed for the first time that his nose looked pushed toward the right side of his face. Maybe he'd boxed a little on his way to his MBA.

"No, no. That might be okay if you're talking about everyday life. But what about the stuff you read about in the papers and see on the news? The murders, the rapes, the bombings, people blown up, body parts flying all over the place? How do you deal with that?"

"You don't ignore it. You're aware that there's lots of bad stuff going down and lots of bad people out there. But you hold on to the knowledge that there are many more good people."

"You really believe that?"

I nodded.

Bernie got up and went to the window. He motioned me over, and since I couldn't think of a good reason not to, I stood with him looking not at New Jersey in the distance but at the animated people on the sidewalk. The brilliant sunlight lent heightened reality to everything – trees, buildings, cars, and people. Distant New Jersey, in contrast, looked gray and unreal, far removed from the hot concerns of the big city.

Bernie gestured at the street below.

"How many of those law abiding citizens would stay honest if they thought they could steal and get away with it?"

"Most people are honest," I said.

"Yeah, because they're afraid of getting caught."

"I don't think so."

"I do."

I walked back to my desk and Bernie went back to his chair.

"So there's no way I can keep that perspective, as you call it. I think those people you talk about have their heads in the sand. The reality is the world is a rotten place."

"Is that what you really think?"

He gave me a smirk. "Nah, the world is okay. The problem is just the people in it." His smirk faded. "So, counselor. How do I get from here to there? Without fooling myself like those happy people with their heads in the sand?"

"As long as you think they're fooling themselves, you can't."

Bernie gave me the Bernie version of a Mona Lisa smile. It bore a striking resemblance to his smirk. Just a little less wattage.

"Great." He extended his arms over his head and stretched. "Look, when bad stuff happens, no one's gonna be okay with it. If things are going fine, that's one thing. Don't worry, be happy. But no one can turn shit into gold."

I took a diet coke from the fridge, poured some into a styrofoam cup, and left the bottle on the desk with another empty cup. Bernie ignored them.

"Always thinking about the ills of the world is self defeating. Of course there are things in life that are very hard to deal with. But for normal everyday things, and even for the kind of events you described, the right perspective does go a long way," I said.

"Why did I know you'd say something like that. I don't know what the hell it means. All I know is good stuff makes people feel better than bad stuff. It's a no brainer. That's all the perspective there is."

He slumped in his chair. I never saw him do that. "Well, except in my case. "You know why I'm not happy?"

I said nothing.

"Because everything is so good."

He paused for effect. After a few seconds he continued, the words rushing out of his mouth now.

"You know I'm a banker, right? What you don't know is I'm a First Vice President. I manage my entire branch. We borrow short and lend long, and since the spread between long and short rates is real good right now, and because I watch over credit risk, we're making a ton of money. I get a big salary, a big bonus, even some stock options."

He straightened up in his chair, looking more like a successful banker.

"It's what I worked for all my life. And now it's here. I've got it all."

He jacked himself out of the chair and started pacing. Up and down, back and forth between his chair and the window. He didn't stop to look outside.

"So if people are happy when good things are happening in their lives, how come I'm not?"

He stopped moving and fixated on me.

"Sit down, Bernie." He did.

"Not to trivialize it, but you know it's a pretty classic problem. It's so common, every comic has a file of jokes about it."

"Jokes?"

"You know, the ones that start, 'Guy comes into a psychiatrist's office, says doc, I worked hard all my life, I've got ten million dollars, but I'm not feeling the way I thought I would, so I'm looking around at the world and I'm asking, is that all there is?'"

"That's not funny."

"That's the intro. But you're right, the setup is not funny. Because for the guy asking the question, it is all there is. At least up to now. Up to his asking the question."

"So you're saying I'm overlooking something. I doubt it. I've got what everyone I know is working for every day of their lives. The people I know, that includes weekends and holidays. But I'm listening. Tell me what I'm not seeing."

"We already talked about it. Perspective."

"Yeah, we did. We're going around in circles."

"Not quite. I think you'd agree that knowing what's important and what isn't is a pretty fair definition of wisdom."

Bernie cocked his head at me, like the dog in the old advertisement listening to a voice coming out of an ancient gramophone.

"The big question is which things go in each category," I said.

"That's what you mean by the right perspective?"

"A good part of it, anyway. Call it a way of looking at the world. Everything bears on it. And it bears on everything."

"I don't see how there can be one right perspective. The world is too complicated." He sat for several seconds. Then he gave a sudden jerk.

"Whoa. I'm gonna be late."

He handed me a check and left. No social niceties for Bernie. I had no idea whether he would return for another session.

13

"The reason I don't want you to know my real name," non–Jeremy said later that afternoon, "is that I'm very well known in business circles."

I spent a couple of seconds trying to figure out why he thought this non–sequitur was a sequitur. Failing, I said nothing and waited for him to go on.

"People in my position can't go to shrinks."

"I'm not a shrink."

He made a gesture.

"Same thing. People talk to you, you help them with their problems. Only difference is you have a degree in philosophy so you maybe have a different perspective."

"Tell me why you think people in your position can't go to shrinks. Or to practitioners like me."

"Isn't it obvious? I am where I am because of competence. I'm a leader. People look to me for answers. I have to maintain the perception of strength."

"Strong people have all the answers?"

He shrugged. "Perception is everything."

"Well, no."

"I really don't want to talk about that. I only brought it up because I thought I owed you an explanation. About not telling you my name."

"Okay."

He took a studied sip from his cup, swallowed, and looked up.

"I'm leaving my wife."

I waited.

"There's nothing left but sex. And the kids are not that bright. Maybe a little above average, but that's it."

"You love them less because of that?"

Another shrug. "I'm realistic about them, that's all."

"Not an answer, Jeremy."

"Do I love them less? Well, let's look at it. What do people love the most? Want the most? Beautiful things. Functional things. Things that are best in their class. That applies to everything. Cars, houses, refrigerators, mousetraps. So why shouldn't it apply to people?"

He worked his lips. "Do I love them less because they're not exceptional? I might wish it were otherwise, but the answer has to be yes."

"Has to be, or is?"

He looked straight at me.

"Is."

I held his gaze, trying to think of a way to reach him. If possible.

"I wish it were otherwise," he repeated.

"Why?"

"Why what?"

"If you believe your argument, why should you wish your feelings toward your kids were different?"

"Because they're my kids, dammit."

Maybe he could be reached after all.

"You're saying it seems wrong to feel as you do."

He shifted in his chair and pursed his lips but didn't respond.

I steepled my fingers. "Why do you think it seems wrong?"

Jeremy spread his hands. "You have a theory?"

"Let's start with what we know. Like people are not refrigerators or mousetraps."

"I was making a point."

"You made it through an analogy. Analogies can be tricky. You want to make sure the items you're analogizing are similar in the right way. Refrigerators and mousetraps are not moral agents."

"Of course not, but what has that got to do with it?"

"Could you love a really clever embezzler or murderer who was the best at what he or she did? I don't think so. Only one kind of person deserves to be loved. In fact only one kind of person is the best kind of person, to put it in your terms. The person who is good. And I'm not using 'good' in any obscure or argumentative way here. I mean a person who tries his best, who is kind, who doesn't lie, cheat, steal, or force himself on others. I'm guessing that your children are good kids. True?"

He let the question hang.

"You think ability and talent are irrelevant?"

"Think about a very able, talented artist or business man who beats his wife. Is his talent relevant?"

"There's something wrong with that argument."

I unsteepled my hands. "The icing is not the cake."

"It's the best part."

I sipped some coffee while I considered my answer.

"Where did you go to college?"

"What?"

I sipped some more.

"Harvard," he answered with some pride. "I went to Harvard."

"How did you make out? Were you first in your class?"

He frowned. "I was in the top quartile."

"So there were, what, maybe a hundred people ahead of you? More?"

"What has that got to do with anything?"

"Do you think all those people were more worthy of love than you? After all, they got better grades. Maybe at least some of them were smarter than you." I paused. "Better than you."

His face darkened to a red several shades deeper than a blush.

"Define worthy."

I looked at him. "Don't do that."

He stared at me. His color slowly drained to a pre–dawn pink.

"I take your point," he said at last.

"Why don't you think about it some more."

Jeremy pressed his lips into a thin white line. He gave a curt nod.

"Would you like to talk about your wife now?"

"Not really."

"She was the first thing you mentioned the first time you walked in here."

He crossed his right leg over his left, holding the crease on his left thigh to one side. Did that mean he was right handed? Right–handed people come down harder on their right foot when they walk. Are they also more likely to cross their right leg over their left? Or is it random? And why did I care?

"Yeah, okay. What about her."

"Are you sure you want to leave her? It's a big step. You want to be sure."

"Well, I'm not. But I'm leaving her anyway."

"Does that bother you? Not being sure?"

"Why should it? I make decisions I'm not sure of in my business all the time, and I've done okay."

"A mistake here may have more important consequences. Four lives are involved."

"The kids will be fine."

"Maybe. Do you care how it will affect your wife? Does she love you?"

"She says she does."

"Do you believe her?"

He gave a slow, minimal nod. "She'll be hurt."

"Hurt a little? Or hurt a lot?"

He didn't answer right away. "A lot." He hesitated.

"I'll give her a good settlement."

"Will that make it hurt less?"

He turned his head and stared out the window. Then he spoke in a near whisper.

"No."

"Understand, I'm not suggesting you stay in the marriage if you're miserable."

He looked at me. "You could have fooled me."

"Look, you loved your wife once. By the way, do you want to tell me her name, or is that a secret too?"

"Alice."

"Last time you said she wasn't interesting any more."

"Right."

"But she was interesting once."

"I guess. Yes."

"Is it possible she still is, but you don't know it?"

"What do you mean? No. How could I not know it?"

"These books you say she reads. Have you ever discussed them with her?"

"I don't have much time. Most days I come home late. On days when I'm home in time for dinner, it's all about the kids. Their problems with their schoolwork, their problems with their friends, their problems with their clothes and their looks. Weekends I do golf. A lot of deals get done on the golf course."

"So you don't talk to her about your business either."

"No."

"Ever try?"

"Once or twice. In the beginning."

"She seem interested?"

"I don't think so."

"You're not sure?"

"She couldn't have been. She never asks about it. She never brings it up."

"Jeremy, if she were here now, and I asked her why she doesn't ask about your business, what do you think she'd say?"

He looked up at the ceiling and stared at it for a while. "Probably that I don't want to talk about it."

I waited a little. Jeremy didn't continue. Then he nodded, more to himself than to me.

"All right." Without further elaboration he stood, dug in his pocket, handed me some bills and walked to the door. No goodbye, no mention of his next session. Maybe, I thought, I should introduce him to Bernie Feld.

What was it with these clients of mine?

14

Back in my cave, I did further violence to my cholesterol with a ham and cheese sandwich from the fridge, bought ready–made along with an egg salad and a tarragon chicken sandwich from the corner supermarket. I'm a confirmed sandwich–buyer. Time, a little dollop of which is all we have on this earth, is my enemy, or at least its passage is, so convenience is one of my catchwords. I love instant meals. Cans fill my entire pantry. Sandwiches are a treat because other than the occasional restaurant meal they are the freshest food I ever get to eat.

I washed the ham and cheese down with some bottled tea and fired up my laptop to check my e–mail. The usual assortment of ads had somehow made it past my spam filter. Nothing from Sheila, but a message from a Lady57. Since curiosity is one of my most persistent weaknesses, I opened it. A large bunch of shriveled flowers lying on a small patch of dry, cracked earth filled the screen. Tied in a loose bunch with a blood–red ribbon, they looked as if someone tore them out by the roots and left them to bake in the sun. I had no doubts about the identity of that someone.

Several broken husks stuck out from the bunch at awkward angles. Beneath the photo three words in thick black caps spanned the margins of the page.

SEE YOU SOON.

She had escalated. First the forwarded letter, which in spite of its threat meant she failed to find my new address. Now she had found at least my e–mail address. How, I had no idea, and it probably didn't matter because she couldn't use it to find where I live without hacking into my ISP's computer systems. Could she do that? Did she know it could be done? From everything I'd read, that would be very difficult even for an experienced hacker. Given the number of people with those skills compared to the total population, she most likely didn't have that capability. Or so I hoped.

I rubbed my eyes, logged off, and sat for a moment until my breathing returned to normal. I craved normalcy now. I called Circe, who padded in, sprang onto my lap, curled up, and began purring even before I started petting her. The powerful purr vibrations travelled along my veins and tickled the spot in my brain where calm lived. I picked up the phone and dialed Sheila. Her voicemail came on. I left a message telling her what had happened and not to worry, which brought to mind my mother's rejoinder one day when I went swimming in Coney Island with friends for the first time. "Don't worry? Don't worry? What do you mean, don't worry? That's what a mother does!"

I started off to the fridge when the phone rang.

"I was in the shower," Sheila said. "Dead flowers?" Her voice was ragged. "She's threatening you!"

"Not as if she hasn't done it before," I said. "How are you?"

"Never mind how I am. This is about you. This woman is serious."

"I never thought she wasn't."

"How can you be so calm?"

"How upset do you want me to be?"

"If you're upset you'll be careful. I want you to be careful."

"Not to worry."

"You said that in your message. How can I not worry?"

I smiled a private smile. "I ever tell you you remind me of my mother?"

Her voice came back to normal. "You loved your mother."

"I did."

"You told me she always took your side. Against your father."

"Mainly when I wanted to do something he didn't consider manly. Like play chess. Or read."

"Anyway," she said in her normal voice, "please be very careful. I have to go now. I have a meeting with my agent. Call me later if you want to talk?"

As soon as we hung up I checked my e–mail.

Nothing more.

***

Still in search of normalcy, I tried relaxing with my feet up on the desk the next morning with a newly acquired copy of some recollections of Socrates written by a friend of his named Xenophon. Socrates himself never wrote anything. Most of what we know of him we have through Plato, but since it's hard to know which ideas really represent Socrates and which are Plato using Socrates as a mouthpiece for his own ideas, it's useful to read the accounts of someone else in Socrates' circle. I was enjoying Xenophon's account of Socrates' explanation of why he married his wife when I heard a tentative knocking on my door. I checked the camera. Valerie Marsh stood on the threshold.

"I didn't expect you back."

"I didn't expect to come back," she said as she sat down.

"So why did you?"

"I figured out what I want to talk about."

I waited.

"I wish I could smoke in here."

When I didn't respond she said, "I'm going into business for myself."

When I still didn't reply she added, "I've been working out of a suite of rooms, me and four other girls. We work for a madam who gets half of what we make. We get to keep all the tips, but still. I got nothing against the madam, but half is too much to give away. I start my own business, I get to keep whatever I make. Plus half of what my girls make."

She tucked her skirt under her. Her outfit today, a blue business suit of some knobbly material, appeared more assertive than last time but still tasteful, if I was any judge. Well, I wasn't any judge. But I knew what I liked.

"So the difference is, since it'll be my business, if I get busted I'll go down harder. But I'm willing to take that chance."

A thought born of my experience with Jeremy occurred to me.

"Let me ask you something. Is Valerie your real name?"

She smiled. "Of course not."

So I was a slow learner, but at least I was a learner.

"I gather you want to keep using that name here."

"How do you feel about having someone who's starting an illegal business as a patient?"

"Client."

"Whatever."

"Victimless crimes don't bother me. Legally, they're crimes, but that's because we have some bad laws."

"Well I'm glad that's settled. Now I want to get to another subject."

She crossed her legs and then uncrossed them. She sat up straight against the chair back, knees pressed together, looking as prim as Whistler's grandma, if his mother was any indication.

"Before you said you thought I was beautiful."

I nodded.

"Did you mean it?"

"Sure."

"Do you like sex?"

I stared at her.

"Well then I have a proposal for you. Try me out. No charge. If you like me, maybe you'd recommend me to your friends. Maybe your clients too, but that's up to you."

I thought my jaw dropped and my mouth hung open, but when I checked it hadn't and didn't. I tried to think of how to respond when she said, "I'm a businesswoman giving away a free sample to build my business. Any problem with that?"

I thought about it. She hadn't asked me what I thought of prostitution.

"I guess not."

"You don't sound too convinced."

"It's not the kind of proposition you hear every day."

"You're a philosopher. You're not supposed to care what everyday people say."

I let that pass.

"I can't take you up on it, but thanks for the offer."

She shrugged. "Mind if I ask why?"

"I'm sort of involved with someone."

"And you love her and want to be faithful." She laughed humorlessly. "I don't come across that very much. In fact, I don't come across it at all. I've read about it though."

Not about my situation she hadn't. Or maybe she had. What was so unusual about being involved but not yet involved? Nothing really, if you were a teenager.

"Anything else you want to talk about?"

Her head came up. "Like what?"

"How about what we touched on last time. What you do. How you want your life to change when you're not doing it any more."

She gave a rueful laugh.

"Not right now."

She snatched up her handbag, fished in it, took out a small pad and a pen. She scribbled something, tore the sheet off, and placed it carefully on my desk.

"My number." She gave me a blunt look.

"In case you change your mind."

***

After recovering from my first–ever offer of free sex from a prostitute, I checked my e–mail. Nothing more from Lady57. Maybe she was through with me.

Maybe there was a Tyrannosaurus Rex tearing up Fifth Avenue.

Dorothy Marks came in with Joel but without Martin, who I supposed couldn't fully control the amount of time he could take off from the office. Dorothy wore an olive business suit and a plain gold necklace, both of which complemented her red hair nicely. Joel had on blue jeans and a tie dyed T–shirt with jagged black lettering that said Einstein Rocks.

"Martin couldn't make it today," Dorothy said.

I nodded and looked at Joel.

"Einstein rocks?"

Joel shrugged. He wasn't happy to be here, and he wasn't going to pretend.

I planted my elbows on the desk. Bad etiquette for dining, but Emily Post hadn't gotten around to philotherapy sessions yet.

"Are you into physics now?"

Another shrug. "Physics is cool."

I looked at him encouragingly. After a short silence he said, "How the world works. Cool stuff."

"Yes it is. If you want to learn more about it, I can recommend a few books."

Dorothy snapped open her purse. She took out a pen and held it poised over a credit card sized notepad. She was smiling at me.

"This guy," Joel said, pointing to the lettering on his chest, "he figured it all out. What's cooler than that."

Einstein as the epitome of cool.

"Have you taken any physics courses?"

He shook his head. "Next year."

"If you want to start reading about it now, I can recommend some introductory books," I said again.

"I can wait till next year. But I wouldn't mind reading about this guy." He pointed to his chest. "Einstein."

"Biography?"

"Maybe. Yeah. How he did it. I mean, what kind of guy could do that, figure all that out, when no one else could, you know?"

"There are lots of good biographies of Einstein. One you might like is the Abraham Pais book, although some of the newer ones claim to have found additional material."

"Can you spell that?" Dorothy said.

I spelled it. She wrote it down and looked up at me brightly with an air of accomplishment.

I looked at Joel. "Any more thoughts since last time about what you might want to do with your life?'

Joel slouched in his seat. "Hey. I'm sixteen years old. I got plenty of time. I don't have to know that stuff now." He fingered his earring, the same silvery one he had on last time. Years ago I wondered what kind of strange urge could make a guy want to wear earrings, but when it became fashionable I stopped wondering. Fashion has its own logic, much of which has to do with fitting into a peer group, and it didn't much interest me. Why a person wanted to be counted as a member of which peer group, however, did.

"Why do I have to do anything with my life? I don't even know what that means. I don't want to do anything with it. I just want to live it."

"Do you think you can live without goals, Joel? Do you think anyone can?"

He gave an elaborate shrug. "Why not?" He sat up straight.

"I don't need goals. I just want to learn."

"Learn what?"

"Stuff that interests me. I don't know. Whatever comes along."

I debated whether to point out that that was a goal. Decided against it.

"A lifetime of learning," I said.

He gave a short nod, waiting for my next Babbit–like pronouncement, which I duly provided.

"You'll need a lot of free time."

He didn't reply. His mother watched me with a look I couldn't decipher. She had put the notebook away.

"You'll need to make a living, but last time you said you didn't want to sell eight hours a day of your time."

"Right."

"Have you ever thought of buying your time back from the open market?"

Joel just looked at me. Dorothy frowned with the lower half of her face. Her forehead remained perfectly smooth. Botox.

Joel said, "What?"

"As things stand now you have to make a living, so you have no choice. About selling your time."

Dorothy's forehead remained untroubled. "I don't understand."

"Someone, I forget who, once said the stock market is the last refuge of a dangerous mind." I smiled. "Are either of you familiar with the stock market?"

They looked at me blankly.

"It's just what it sounds like. A market for stocks. A place where people buy and sell shares of stock, which represent ownership of a business. The more shares you own, the more of the business you own."

No reaction. They both looked at me as if I were speaking an alien language, which of course I was.

"See, over a long period of time, stocks tend to go up. A lot of people have made a lot of money by buying the right stocks and holding them while the companies' earnings increased. The stocks of those companies went up in price. Sometimes a lot."

Still nothing.

"Some people have made enough money that way so they don't need to hold down a job any more. Of course, it's not guaranteed because you can lose money too. Sometimes very fast when the economy or the company goes bad. And even if you succeed it could take a long time. There's no way to tell in advance. But the people who do succeed have done what you want to do, Joel. In effect, they've bought back their time from the open market. That's an extra eight hours a day they can use however they want. Not counting commuting time."

Joel tilted back his chair and brought it down again. "I don't know anything about that stuff. Besides, I'm a kid. I don't have any money to buy stocks."

"You could get started buying just a few shares with money you could save from your allowance or from odd jobs."

He thought about it. His mother looked at him, then at me, then at him again. She opened her mouth to speak but changed her mind. She folded her arms across her chest, unfolded them a second later and sat primly with her interlaced fingers in her lap, a patient woman who was used to waiting.

Joel spaced his words evenly. "It can't be that easy."

"It isn't. Plenty of people lose money in the stock market even though it generally goes up over the years. You might get caught in a long downturn. It's not a free lunch. And you have to find the right stocks. You have to do the work. If you're good at it, you'll probably make money, but you'll get there faster if you get a job first so you can save money to keep investing more."

"Now it sounds hard," he said.

"It does take work. Actually, I've been oversimplifying a little. Finding the right stocks is not really the hard part."

Joel leaned forward a little.

"The hard part is controlling your emotions."

His face went blank again.

"You have to be able to buy when other people are scared. And to sell when everyone wants to buy because everything looks great and prices are high."

He sat back. "That doesn't sound so hard."

I smiled. "It's harder than it sounds."

Joel eyed me speculatively while he thought about it. Trusting me was probably out of the question given the fact that I'd been forced on him by his parents. He had to be wondering whether there was any chance I knew what I was talking about.

"But you said I'd have to get a job."

"In the beginning. And maybe for a long time. Maybe a very long time. It depends on what the markets do, how good you are, and how long it takes you to succeed. If you succeed."

He looked at his mother for the first time. Either he found what he needed in her face or he gave up trying, because he swung back to me a second later.

"How about a book I can read about that." He didn't sound excited, but then I didn't know what excitement sounded like for Joel.

"I don't want to take you away from Einstein," I said.

Dorothy chimed in. "He'll read this one first." Joel glanced at her. She smiled.

"Yeah," he said.

"There are plenty of good investment books. One I like is *Stocks For The Long Run,* by Jeremy Siegel. It's not a beginner's book, but I think you can handle it. If you want to start with a beginner's book, there are lots of good ones. One that got good reviews is *The Wall Street Journal Guide To Money And Investing.*"

Dorothy wrote.

I leaned back. "That's about it for today."

"Thanks," Dorothy said. At the door Joel turned back to me.

"You read this book? The Siegel?"

"Sure."

"And a lot of other investment books?"

"Uh huh."

"But you aren't rich."

"Joel!" his mother said.

I smiled. "I'm working on it."

"Cause, I mean, you still work."

I shook my head. "Can't tell by that. I like my work. I'd do it regardless of how much money I had."

He canted his head to one side as if considering whether that made any sense to him. Then he nodded once.

✳✳✳

When the door closed behind Joel and his mother I had just enough time to check my e–mail again. Still nothing more from the gun lady, alias Lady57. Rather than feel relieved I was more puzzled than ever about what game she was playing and what stage of the game we'd reached. The middle game? The end game? Did she really intend to kill me? I had to assume she did. I had taken countermeasures and needed to stay alert, but I also needed to continue leading a normal life. Well, as normal as possible with a gun banging against my ribcage whenever I moved my left arm.

***

Sally Carter sat with her legs pressed together and her hands clasped in her lap.

"What does my life add up to?" Her voice was low.

"What do you want it to add up to?"

"I want to make a difference. Like I said last time."

"Well, let's see." I had on khakis and a yellow permanent press shirt. My tan corduroy jacket with the brown elbow patches hung on the back of my chair. Sally wore tailored slacks again, olive this time, and an open–necked yellow blouse with only the top button open. Pink lipstick perfectly outlined her mouth, as if it had been applied with a fine brush. Why would a depressed person be so painstaking in putting on makeup? Maybe to hide the depression. From whom? Everyone but herself.

"You brought two children into the world and raised them to adulthood. You made at least one film which brought your message to many people and probably changed the behavior of some. And you've still got plenty of time left to do more."

"Like I said. The drug problem is worse than it ever was. Did my film have an effect? Maybe. Maybe not. Anyway, not that I can see." She leaned back, sucked in her cheeks as if to withdraw further into herself, rested her head on the back of the chair and closed her eyes. "Anyone can pop out a couple of kids."

I shook my head. "The difference is in how you bring them up. Doing that well is a hard job."

She opened her eyes. "I guess the boys turned out okay. They're good boys. Sam's a radiologist in L.A. and Dan's an accountant in La Jolla."

"So you did a good job bringing them up."

"I did my best."

"Sounds to me like you have every reason to be proud of your life so far."

"You really think I've made a difference."

"I do. But whether or not you believe you did, you have lots of time to do more. That's up to you."

"I don't know."

"Don't know what?"

"If I can do it. If I want to do it."

"As I recall you said making a difference is the one thing you did want."

"I also said it's a lot of effort."

I leaned forward slightly and clasped my hands on the desk.

"You're not sure the effort is worth it."

"I guess that's right."

"That's entirely your decision. As long as you know there's no writing in the sky that says how you have to spend your time."

"Maybe not, but everyone wants to make a difference. What else is there."

"I'm sure you know many people are focused on getting money or power or fame. People for whom everything else is an afterthought."

"I thought it was the other way around. That people want those things, but making a difference comes first. Otherwise how do they live with themselves?"

I shifted my position. Sitting for long periods of time is harder than it looks.

"About that writing in the sky. You don't have to make a difference to anyone but yourself unless you decide you want to. If you're financially secure and want to do a lot of reading there's nothing to feel guilty about. The only person who can decide what you do with your life is you."

"I should be putting something into the world."

"'Should' is the wrong word. Besides, you already have. And are."

"Are? How?"

"When you read you learn new things, as you said. Even when you're reading fiction. Think of yourself as a work in progress. You're building a better you every day. That's what you're putting into the world."

She was watching me intently. Now she pulled her gaze from my face and looked around the room. Without looking back at me she said, "You think that's enough?"

"Your decision, but if that's what you want, just continually improving yourself, and you can afford not to work, then yes. If it works for you."

Sally crossed her legs and clasped her hands over one knee. She looked at me again but didn't seem to be seeing me. Looking not so much through me, I thought, as into herself.

"Maybe I don't want what I used to want. Maybe it's too hard."

"Let's go back to a reason to get out of bed," I said. "You mainly read and go to the movies, but it doesn't seem to be working for you. Let's see if we can find out why. You said you read because it lets you feel something. You get emotionally involved. Why do you think that is?"

"Why what is?"

"Why does reading fiction get an emotional rise out of you?"

"Isn't that obvious?"

I shook my head.

She shrugged. "You identify with the characters. When something happens to them you're right there with them. In good books, exciting things happen, and you're always hanging on, wanting to know what happened next."

"Why?"

She stared at me. "I don't understand."

"Nothing happened next. The writer made it up."

"Willing suspension of disbelief." She strung the words together quickly, like a canned response to a catechism. "Everyone knows that."

I had a quick flash of how wonderful the world be if what everyone knew always turned out to be true.

"Suppose you've just finished an exciting chapter and you're about to turn the page to find out what happened next and I come in and say, 'Wait. Don't bother reading further. I've got a better idea. This novel is going to end exactly the way you want it to. The way that'll give you the biggest kick. The most satisfaction. Just make up your own ending. Why settle for the one the author made up?' Don't you think that would be more satisfying? Give you more pleasure?"

She kept staring at me. "Of course not."

"Because?"

"Because if I make it up, that's not the way it happened. The way it happened is the way it's printed in the book."

I tried for a neutral look. Harder than it sounds, as poker players know. You get better with practice.

Sally shifted her legs, pressed her palms together in her lap and stilled. Her mouth made a small puckered moue.

"All right. I'm contradicting myself. Willing suspension of disbelief means I know it didn't really happen. But it feels like it did. With a good book, I really want to find out what happened."

"As if it really did happen, even though you know it's fiction. As if suspension of disbelief doesn't quite cover what's going on," I said.

Sally considered this. I let her take her time.

"I suppose so. Where are you going with this?"

"I want to suggest that when you read an absorbing work of fiction, on some powerful subconscious level that goes beyond suspension of disbelief you're convinced it's real. That it really happened. Your conscious knowledge that the writer made it up is just an abstraction. It doesn't have the convincing emotional power of the concrete book in your hand. The actual words printed on the page. The images they produce in your mind."

She took a few moments to answer. "I still don't see why it matters."

"If seeing real people overcome obstacles to get what they want is what makes you feel alive, what would you say that tells us?"

She looked blank.

"Put it together with what you said about it being the only thing that makes you feel excited. So now we have excited and alive."

Her expression didn't change. It was all too new to her, too abstract and at the same time too personal.

"Maybe you need to reach for something again, Sally. Something that won't come too easily. Otherwise life can end up feeling pretty random."

"Random."

"Dull. Pointless. Unexciting."

This seemed to reach her. She stared off into space.

"You want me to think some more about what I said about it being too hard."

"Is it harder to want something and try for it, or to live without a purpose?"

Sally rose, a tall woman with an attractive, composed face that belied her inner turmoil. She gave me a grin.

"You have a way of putting things."

15

Too many clients with too many problems and too little insight. Even work you enjoy can be wearing sometimes, and I decided that with the weekend coming up I needed a break. Not to mention that with the gun lady rattling around out there with mayhem on her mind I sometimes felt I lived in a fantasy western in the middle of New York.

I needed a change. Sheila and Los Angeles came to mind. It didn't hurt that the airlines were engaged in one of their ruinous price wars. I got a round trip ticket to L.A. for a price that couldn't possibly have covered Continental's costs.

I toyed with the idea of surprising her. Take a cab to her address, knock on the door. Smile. Congratulate her on finishing her film. Dramatic. Romantic.

And dumb. She had a life out there. I had no claims on her. I didn't know whom she might be seeing. She was one of the best–known women in the world. Thousands of men, maybe millions, had fantasies about her. She probably knew all the leading men in Hollywood. Not to mention producers and directors. I had no idea what I might be walking in on.

So I called her and asked her if she was free and she sounded happy and said she'd meet me at the airport. When I deplaned I spotted her at the gate a little off to the side of the crowd, wearing big square sunglasses too big for her perfect oval face but easily big enough to hide her from anyone who didn't look too closely. When she saw me she flashed me the smile that had lit up thousands of big screens and millions of small ones. As I came toward her she ran to me and hugged me, then stepped quickly back.

"Photographers," she murmured.

Apparently she thought less of her camouflage than I did.

On the way to her car she took my arm.

"Who'd you find to watch Circe?"

"There's a woman in the apartment below mine, has a sixteen year old daughter. I pay her to feed Circe and make sure the water dish is full. She has to play with her for at least half an hour. If she plays with her longer, she gets more."

"You trust her?"

"I've used her before."

"Here's Betty," she said.

I looked around. We were in a parking lot. A man was climbing into a light blue Subaru five cars away from us. Another man two cars down from him was beeping a black Toyota. Neither man looked like a Betty.

"The car," Sheila said. She stopped beside a two door sliver Lexus hardtop convertible. She pressed the button on her key and Betty flashed its lights at her.

"You named your car?"

She smiled. We got in. As we pulled out she said, "Cars are special out here. You have a relationship with them. You depend on them." She turned on the radio. A woman was singing a tune from South Pacific about washing a man out of her hair.

"They'll even sing to you."

"How come the car is feminine?"

"A car is a friend, not a sex object."

"Men are not friends?"

"It's harder."

She had on a navy blue tailored shirt with the top two buttons undone. Her skirt was a lighter blue and rode up just above her bare knee as she drove. I watched the palm trees flash by. To me, they were exotic. I associated them with perpetual sunshine, tropical paradises, carefree natives eating coconuts. The fact that I knew better didn't seem relevant. I think she saw some of it on my face.

"Want me to put the top down?"

"Sure."

She pulled over and pressed a button. Magically, the metal top of the car lifted and folded into the trunk.

"Sunscreen in the glove compartment."

I shook my head. "Nah." The wind eddied around the windshield, billowing out my shirt. And hers.

"Sunscreen is for sissies?"

"I don't do this that often. Make that never."

"Sun doesn't know that."

I gave a mock sigh and opened the glove compartment. Sprayed the stuff on my face.

"Smells good," I said.

"Like a sea breeze on the beach?"

She nailed it. I glanced at her. "That's right."

She smiled. Even in profile that smile produced heat in my chest.

"Your choice of where to eat," she said as we left the freeway. "You want to see and be seen, or you want privacy?"

"I have a choice? I thought those big sunglasses were for privacy."

She nodded. "I take them off for special occasions. Like restaurants where I know the clientele. Strictly A–list. And whenever else the mood strikes me."

"They come over to your table to say hi? Or do they just wave?"

She glanced over at me.

"Yes to both. Is that so bad?"

"How about a place with privacy and good food. You and the night and the music."

"Done."

She turned off Rodeo Drive and went another four blocks, then hung a left and parked in front of a small Italian place tucked away three steps below street level between a pen shop and a bookstore that specialized in Eastern philosophy and religion, according to a small black and white sign that would be clearly visible only to someone within three feet of it. I wondered why the owners had bothered. Two women and a man browsed the shelves. The pen store was empty.

"I'm assuming Italian is okay," she said as we went into the restaurant. The place was about as big as my living room and had only five tables, with tablecloths in a purple and white checkerboard pattern. Three of them were occupied, which was surprising given that it was only six o'clock.

"How'd the film turn out," I said when we were seated.

"Well, I don't know how the editing will go and I haven't heard the music yet. But I like it. I think it'll be pretty good."

"You okay with the ending?"

"Yes. The guy who seems to be the good guy turns out to be the bad guy, and the guy who seems to be the bad guy turns out to be the good guy. I end up marrying the good guy."

"What happens to the bad guy?"

"He cheated on his wife, lied to me, and stole from his boss. His wife leaves him, he gets fired, and he loses me. And his two kids. And his dog."

"Who gets the goldfish?"

She smiled. "No goldfish."

"An unforgivable oversight."

The waitress who took our order didn't seem to recognize Sheila. Neither did anyone else. Her disguise apparently worked. Wearing sunglasses indoors didn't attract any attention around here.

"The story doesn't sound too original. From what you've told me."

"Ah, but it is. This is a romance."

"So?"

"In romances the good guy is poor and the bad guy is rich. In this movie it's the reverse. The good guy is rich, and he gets me."

"Wow."

The waitress brought the house Chianti and Sheila took a sip, nodding her approval.

"That should appeal to you, as a philosopher, right? Justice."

"Appeals to everyone. Almost."

"That's a strange thing to say."

"Why? Justice is just getting what you deserve. Reaping what you've sown. Cause and effect. Everyone likes cause and effect. Well, except for some philosophers."

"Hmm. And criminals. How about criminals."

"Yes. Criminals too. They want effects without causes."

"They wouldn't like my movie."

"Some might. They're pretty good at lying to themselves about who they are. At least for a while. They try hard to think of themselves as good guys."

"I'll tell the producers we've got a box office problem. Not enough criminals or philosophers are gonna buy tickets."

The waitress delivered an avocado salad for Sheila, veal picatta for me.

"How do you survive on that stuff," I said.

"Barely. But it lets me keep my figure and the big box office."

"Don't have enough money yet?"

She shrugged. "Not the point. I get a piece of the gross."

I tried a mouthful of the veal. Delicious. "Hard to give up."

She smiled and dug into her salad. "Not to mention the stuff you don't like. The recognition."

"I think you've got me wrong."

"I don't think so."

"I have nothing against recognition. It's a natural human desire."

"But?"

"A matter of degree. How much you need it, what kind of things you'll do for it, what kind of people you need it from. Nothing wrong with wanting credit for something you're proud of. Needing to be known and admired by the whole world, that's something else again. We've talked about this."

"You don't think being admired by the whole world would be, um, pleasant?"

"Needing it desperately wouldn't be, no. And there's other stuff that's not too pleasant either." I indicated her oversized sunglasses. "How often do you have to hide your face?"

She shrugged. "It's worth it. Besides, I don't do it all the time."

"Kind of defeats the whole purpose of the fame thing though," I said mildly.

"Sometimes you want privacy."

"Ah."

"Don't 'ah' me. If I want privacy I cover up. If I don't I don't. I'm fine with it."

"The need just comes on you sometimes."

"Which need are we talking about here?"

"Either one. Both. Privacy and public recognition."

She took a forkful of her salad and appeared to think it over.

"I'll just sometimes feel like privacy, sometimes like being seen."

"Is it random? How about when you go to the supermarket or the cleaners?"

"I don't often go to the supermarket or the cleaners, and I'm getting a little tired of talking about this."

I nodded. "Then we'll stop."

The door dinged open and a man ambled in, pausing when he glanced at our table. Tall, tan, and well built, he wore a short sleeved brown silk shirt and khakis. In an instant he made his decision and came over to our table.

"Sheila!" he boomed, demonstrating the imperfection of her disguise. His mouth stretched in a smile that showcased a set of perfectly capped teeth. "Gorgeous as ever."

Others were staring now. He had given them enough of a hint to figure out who hid behind the glasses. Or at least make a good guess. This was Hollywood, after all.

"Clay," Sheila said, her voice flat. "What are you doing here?" She motioned towards me. "This is Eric. Eric, Clay Brock."

"Hi," I said.

"I was just passing by and realized I was hungry," he said to her. He still hadn't looked at me.

"Mind if I join you?"

Sheila indicated her depleted salad. "We're almost through."

He started to pull over a chair from an empty table. "I don't mind."

I placed my hands on the table's edge. "Clay. We kind of came here to be alone."

He turned and looked at me for the first time. When he spoke his voice was soft.

"That's not very hospitable." He stood there staring at me. I stared back. He didn't know what to do. Should he make an issue of it or should he let it go. He had already started to make an issue of it, but there was nothing else he could do.

"Clay. Another time," Sheila said.

It gave him an out. He flashed her a blinding smile.

"Sure. Ciao, baby. I'll call you," and he exited with a hand wave that took in the entire universe.

The other diners watched us covertly. Or watched Sheila. She leaned close to me.

"Let's get out of here."

"We haven't had dessert yet."

"Let's go."

I signaled for the waitress who came over in an instant. I handed her a credit card and she left.

A moment later she was back. I left her a big tip and we went outside. Sheila drove the first couple of blocks in silence. At the first stoplight she turned to me.

"He was upset."

"I got that impression."

"He's got a temper. Got hauled in for starting a fight in a bar near here a few months ago. He said the other guy was staring at his date. You might have read about it."

I shook my head.

The light changed. She said, "Would you have fought him?"

"What?"

"Would you?"

"Where did that come from?"

"Do you know who he was?"

"Should I?"

"You didn't recognize the name?"

"No."

She chuckled. "Clay Brock. He'd be crushed if he knew that. He's a big action hero. Came out of a TV series three years ago. They took a chance on him and starred him in a film about a comic book hero. Captain Marvel. You never saw it?"

"Afraid not."

"Well, it grossed over 250 million worldwide so they did a sequel that did almost as well and now he's got a franchise. And big bucks."

"He a friend of yours?"

"I dated him. Once. Would you have fought him?"

"I don't start fights. A guy wants to fight you, sometimes you have no choice."

"Could you beat him? He's much bigger than you."

"Probably not."

"But you would have fought him?"

"If I had to."

"Do you even know how to fight? You're a philosopher, for God's sake."

"Everyone knows how to fight, a little. But no, I haven't developed any skill." I faced her. "Sheila, what's this all about?"

She shook her head and blinked rapidly. "I don't know. I just wanted to know if you'd have fought him."

"Why?"

"Maybe because I'm trying to understand you. And I don't. For example, I don't understand why you'd fight a guy who's bigger and stronger than you."

"Sure you do."

"It's some stupid macho thing, right? Only you're not stupid. You're the smartest man I ever met."

"Nothing macho about getting beat up."

"But a man's gotta do what a man's gotta do, is that it?"

"Close enough."

"You don't call that macho? That's what macho is all about."

Our freeway criss–crossed another one below it which was jammed with traffic. Horns blared and as we shot over the other freeway we were treated to a sort of modified doppler effect. I had a choice of looking at the palm trees and houses whizzing by or looking at Sheila. No contest, even with a frown on her face.

"All depends on what a man thinks he's gotta do," I said.

Her frown deepened.

"What's the point if you can't win?"

"Isn't always about winning."

When she didn't reply I said, "This something you want to talk about?"

She was silent for a moment. Then she shook her head once.

"Where are we going?" I said after a while.

"I thought you'd like to see my house."

***

Sheila's street curved so sharply I couldn't see more than two houses from any particular vantage point. She turned between two high hedges onto a long graveled driveway which snaked around dramatically, finally revealing a long, low, modern concrete house with a round turret at one end. Except for the mahogany door, the entire, stark white house, even in the fading light, gleamed with the brilliance of a cut diamond.

"Sheila, it's beautiful."

She flashed a delighted smile, looking like a teen just asked to the high school prom.

"You really like it? Oh, you do, of course you do. You don't lie." She pulled into the garage.

By New York standards, the living room was huge, but divided up nicely into several conversation areas defined by groupings of modular gray sofas. Woolen broadloom with speckled black and white tufts underlay it all. Several spectacular nature photos, all in black and white, hung on the walls. Except for one, the biggest, positioned over the fireplace and featuring a blazing red sunset.

"Wow."

She grinned. "Can I get you a drink?"

I shook my head. She went over to the bar and came back holding a glass. After a couple of sips, she abruptly turned to me.

"Is it the money?"

"What?"

"We never talked about this, but we have to sometime. I have a lot of money. I make a few million every time I do a film. Does that bother you?"

"Sheila, if I wanted to go after money, getting a Ph.D in philosophy wouldn't have been high on my priority list."

"I know. I know you don't care about money for yourself, not in the way people I know care about it. But what about the difference between us? What about the fact that I'm the woman and you're the man?"

"Me Tarzan, you Jane. Tarzan know difference. Tarzan not confused."

"Don't joke. You know what I mean."

"I'm not upset by your having more money than I have."

We were silent for a while as she sipped her drink. She swirled it around in the glass and sipped some more. When she spoke her voice was lower.

"I know you know I want to get back together with you, and something's holding you back, and it isn't that fame issue you're always bringing up. So I'm thinking something about my having money bothers you."

"I told you..."

"I know what you said. But it might be something else about the money."

"Something else?"

"Yes. Like my wanting it. Like my liking it. Maybe you think I like it too much."

She rose and crossed to a sideboard against the wall. She took out a coaster, came back, and placed her glass on the coaster without looking at me.

"You're entitled to want what you want," I said.

"Don't make this hard." She took another drink. "It's hard enough as it is."

"All right. I do think you're a little too caught up with money and fame. Maybe not so much with fame any more. I don't know."

She gave a short laugh.

"A little?"

I said nothing.

"So what? Let's say you're right, although I'm damned if I know how you come up with how much is enough and how much is too much. But let that go. What difference does it make? On an ordinary, day–to–day basis. On the level of two people getting along. Sitting down at the breakfast table. Going out to dinner and a movie. Playing with the cat. Taking a drive in the country. Life. Not theory."

A window wall with sliding glass doors took up one end of the room. The windows afforded a view of the pool, which was surrounded by flower beds. I went over and stood looking out at the pool, now in shadow but for the lingering last rays of the sun infusing a small blue triangle with deep gold.

"It's not that simple."

"Yes it is. It's hard for me, saying these things. Being the aggressor. It's not how I was brought up." She moved closer. Our arms touched. "But I know you want me. Physically, at least."

My body was letting me know how much it agreed with her.

"Any man would." I didn't recognize my voice.

"We could go upstairs."

I stood there like an idiot. If we resumed a sexual relationship now with little things like how each of us wanted to live our life still unresolved between us, would it hurt our chances of ever resolving them? Would it introduce an intimacy that wasn't really there yet and create tension and ambiguity in our relationship? Or was I over intellectualizing a simple, basic matter that men and women have known how to cope with for thousands of years?

She stepped around to face me. "No promises. No contracts. No expectations."

I lifted her, hefted her small body in my arms.

"How about if I carry you up."

She nestled her head against my shoulder and clasped her arms around my neck.

"That would be nice," she whispered.

16

Before she took me to the airport the next day Sheila wanted to go to the L.A. zoo. We watched the seals with their sleek black torpedo bodies as they leapt into the air when their keeper threw them a fish. We watched a polar bear try to hold a buoyant green ball underwater. Every time it popped up some kids, leaning on the railing a few feet away, let out a collective giggle. Sheila suppressed a giggle of her own, not wanting to call attention to herself. She hid behind her trademark sunglasses and a wide straw hat. She took my arm and we went into the reptile house and stared at the coiled muscles of the thirteen foot reticulated python whose pitiless black eyes stared back at us from behind what we hoped was a very thick sheet of glass. We saw monkeys and cheetahs and gorillas and a black panther which paced back and forth on its stubby legs and paused now and then to direct a yellow–eyed challenge at the crowd outside its cage.

Sheila's grip tightened on my arm.

"What do you think it's thinking when it looks at us like that?"

"It's thinking, mmm, lunch. How do I get it?"

She gave a mock shudder and grasped my arm harder. We had time for an early lunch at the zoo's restaurant, an open air area which served the only food I can recall worse than airline food. We didn't mind. We were there exclusively for the pleasure of each other's company. Our location or our particular activity were beside the point.

As we finished our sandwiches Sheila said, "The gun lady?"

"What about her?"

"You haven't seen or heard from her recently?"

I shrugged. "Maybe she changed her mind. Or gave up."

And then there was that Tyrannosaurus...

"Do you believe that? I didn't think wishful thinking was one of your strong suits. I thought you always planned for the worst case."

I stood up and held her chair. "Plan for the worst, hope for the best."

"Yes, but the worst case here is unacceptable."

We walked toward her car in the zoo's parking lot.

"In the worst case she kills you."

We kept walking.

"Are you really that cavalier about dying?" Not that it's going to happen."

"I don't think cavalier is the right word."

We reached the parking lot. The cars broiling in the sun gave off shimmering heat waves that distorted the trees lining the lot.

"We never talked about this," Sheila said.

"What?"

"Dying. How we feel about it."

"I'm for postponing it as long as possible."

"Yes, but it'll happen some day. How do you feel about that?"

"What kind of question is that?"

"I don't mean to be morbid. But I have to tell you, I'm terrified. I've always been terrified. I try not to think about it, and mostly I succeed. But sometimes, especially when I wake up in the middle of the night, I can't help myself. How do you handle that?"

"Besides postponing it as long as possible and trying to avoid the gun lady?"

"Besides that."

We settled into the car. Sheila switched on the air conditioning.

"You're probably afraid of what you'll be missing," I said.

"Of course."

"But there'll be no you. So you won't be missing anything."

She didn't look convinced.

"Look at it this way. You don't beat yourself up about all the things you missed before you were born. Why should your feelings about what happens after you're gone be any different?"

She was still not convinced, but she looked thoughtful.

"So you're not scared?"

"I moved my office. There's a camera outside my door and a gun under my jacket."

"I don't mean that. That's a precaution against a crazy person. Anyone would try to protect themselves. I mean the whole idea of being...non–existent. Of being nowhere. Of not being." She shook her head in frustration. "I'm not saying this right. Anyway, does that scare you?"

"I don't think about it much."

"Does anything scare you?"

I laughed. I didn't think it was worth continuing the dialogue to convince her that I wasn't Superman. Maybe another time.

"Drive," I said.

At the airport we kissed with the hungry remembrance of the previous night. Aside from that, we managed to stick to last night's bargain. No promises. No expectations.

Or none spoken.

17

I had purposely scheduled only one client for the day after my return to New York so I could sleep late, recover from jet lag, and generally slow down a little. Diana Rogers was not due until late afternoon. I went to the office to wait for her, made some coffee, and poured a cupful for each of us. I placed hers near the edge of the desk closest to her usual chair. I had time to finish mine and pour myself another by the time she arrived, exactly on time as usual. As always, she was dressed immaculately, this time in a straight pink skirt and a simple white blouse. She had on pendant earrings and tan and white pumps that had cost the life of some unlucky reptile.

"Good morning." She placed her handbag on the chair next to her and flashed a brilliant smile.

"Well, good morning to you too. I see you changed your hair. Nice bangs."

Nice was probably the wrong word. Women liked superlatives when referring to changes in their appearance, and who could blame them? But nice already hung out there between us. I'd be more careful next time.

"I take it things went well? With Bruce?"

Her smile got wider, which I hadn't thought possible.

"He likes me. He really likes me. You were right."

"Not just your, ah, format?"

She laughed. "Well, he likes that too. He likes that a lot."

I smiled back at her and waited.

"But it isn't only that. We talked a lot. About a lot of different things. Books, and music, and our plans. Where we wanted to be. What we wanted to do. He was really interested in what I had to say. I could tell."

She leaned forward and picked up the coffee. "Is this for me?" She took a sip and replaced the cup on the desk.

"I don't know what I was so afraid of."

"Sounded to me like you didn't think anyone could get past your looks. That no one would like you for what you really are."

She inclined her head. "And I was not including my looks in my idea of who I really am."

"You weren't."

"Well I don't feel that way any more. Bruce likes me and my body makes him like me even more. Or maybe it's the other way around. But I don't think it matters. Do you think it matters?"

"No."

She nodded several times, satisfied.

"Well," she said. "That's it, then."

"One thing, Diana. You've said he likes you, and I'm glad. But you haven't said, now that you know him better, whether you like him. And trust him."

She looked at me as if I were crazy.

"Oh, I do. Of course I do. It would all be for nothing, him liking me, if I didn't."

It would also all be for nothing if she liked him mainly because he liked her. That didn't seem to be what was happening here, and I was glad.

"Just checking."

She uncrossed her legs and sat back in her chair. She seemed content to sit and wait for me to speak.

"Not afraid of getting old and losing your looks anymore?"

She frowned and shifted in the chair. "Everyone gets old."

"But you always knew that. Has your attitude about it changed?"

"How do you mean?"

I took a breath. "Do you think Bruce will still like you when you're old?"

"What? We're not getting married, for God's sake. We went on two dates, that's all." She was getting agitated.

"Why are you asking me that?"

"The question bothers you."

"Yes," she said with some heat, "it does. It bothers me."

"That's why I asked it." I knew I was taking a chance.

She glared at me. I tried to look neutral and non–threatening.

"Look, the first time you were here you were worried that you weren't interesting and men would only like you for your looks. We need to make sure you're over that. Talking about maybe one day losing your looks might be one way to do that."

A few seconds ticked by. She raised her chin.

"Bruce thinks I'm interesting. He wants to know what I think. He likes the way I look. I told you that."

"Yes you did." She was not going to pursue it, and I was not going to force her.

"So you've decided you're an interesting woman after all?"

Her eyes widened. "I guess I'm as interesting as the next person," she said slowly. She was not going to address her previous fears. Now she stood abruptly and scooped up her handbag.

"I don't have to use the whole forty–five minutes, right? I want to go now."

Did I accomplish anything, or did I made things worse? It's not always clear in the short term, and the trouble with the long term was that first you had to get past the short term.

***

"We joined the country club," Burt Lidsky said.

We were doing our coffee and chess thing at the Symphony in the West Village again, a couple of hours after Diana's session. The usual assortment of counterculture types occupied most of the other tables. Dressing down was an art here. Aside from us, no one wore anything dressier than jeans, the rattier the better. If they held a contest, I thought the winner would be a dark–haired guy in his early twenties who sat alone at a table near the window. Whenever a woman under the age of eighty–five passed by he followed her progress until she passed out of range. He wore pre–weathered jeans pre–torn at both knees and spattered in random places with red, green, and yellow paint. An ambulatory Jackson Pollock. He also had on a gray sweatshirt with bold red lettering that said OUT OF THIS WORLD, which I thought might well be accurate. At another table a couple who looked to be in their seventies quietly smiled at each other, her hand resting on his. A lot of older couples are afraid to show affection in public, and looking at these two made me smile. At the next table a pair of earnest students discussed the nature of reality and seemed agreed that reality was an illusion between sips of their illusory cappuccinos.

"I thought you weren't going to join."

"Yeah. Well. Some things aren't worth fighting about."

"She really wanted it," I said.

"Yeah."

"So is it as bad as you thought?"

He shrugged and made a move on the board.

"Marriage is compromise."

I studied his move. "Worth it, though."

He smiled and sipped his coffee.

I moved one of my knights to a center square. "What?"

He put down his cup. "Life is funny. Whatever you do, you take your chances. You never know how anything's going to turn out. But you have to live. You have to act."

He threatened my knight with his bishop and looked up. "Sometimes I think that's all life really is. You have a certain amount of time, and you have to use it to act, and every time you do it's a risk." He shrugged. "In my marriage. In my work. When I make a move in chess. When I cross the street. Risk. Risk is all there is."

"This all coming out of a question about your country club?"

The students at the next table stopped talking and listened to us. They tried not to show it. They probably didn't realize that according to their previous conclusions they had only an illusory interest in an illusory conversation about illusory problems in an illusory world. Which was fortunate for their sanity.

"I've been thinking about it for a while. It's like my investment business, only it's not like it. I'm in business to make money. If I do, I can save it. I don't have to spend it. I can save it up and feel secure. But it's not like that with my time, is it? I've got, what, eighty years, if I'm lucky? Eighty–five? Who knows? But what I do know is that I have to spend twenty–four hours of it every day. No choice. If I think tomorrow is going to be a boring day, like maybe a day at the country club, I can't say, 'hey, wait, I don't want to spend this day, put these next twenty–four hours into my savings account and I'll spend them later.'"

I sat back. "You could not go to the country club."

He tilted his head and drained the last of his coffee.

"A lot of the guys I know, older guys, they've got a lot more money than they'll ever need in a lifetime, or in their kids' lifetimes. But they keep scrabbling as if money could hold back time."

The boy and girl at the next table abandoned all pretense of not listening to our conversation. They stared at Burt, who didn't seem to notice. I leaned over toward them.

"Would you like to join our conversation?"

The boy looked startled. He flushed a bright red and stood up hurriedly.

"Uh, no, man."

He dug into a pocket of his jeans and took out some bills which he threw on his table.

"We gotta go," he said, taking the girl's hand. They left without another word.

"What was that all about?" Burt said.

I shook my head. We made a few more moves, but the game had degenerated into a stupefyingly dull position.

"Tell Nancy I said hello."

Burt nodded. His eyes had a faraway look. His mind was clearly somewhere else.

We left the game unfinished.

18

As soon as I got to the office in the morning I powered up my laptop and found another e-mail from Lady57. Should I open it? Why bother? How did it enhance my life to know what sick picture or particular threat she had chosen this time? I'd already done what I could do. Moved my office, got an unlisted number, bought a gun, gone to the police, tried to find out her identity. Which I'd continue doing. But what could I gain by subjecting myself to her latest intrusion on my life?

It might reveal something about her. Unlikely, but possible. The title was YOU CAN RUN. The body of the message said, "BUT YOU CAN'T HIDE. A president said that once. He was wrong. BUT I'M NOT."

A photograph of an American soldier in full battle dress holding an M–1 rifle on a prisoner took up most of the screen. The prisoner had no uniform but looked vaguely mid–eastern. In the far background several small white houses clumped together as if squeezed by some giant hand.

All at once I felt very tired. Why did I open this? What did I learn? Nothing. Well, maybe something. Maybe that she thought of herself as a soldier. Of course she did. The thought didn't have to be conscious, but she had a cause, whatever that might be. Soldiers fought for a cause, and that's how she saw herself. Fighting against the enemy. Me.

I patted the gun under my armpit. It felt bulky.

It should have felt reassuring.

I saw no way to avoid her forever. One day she'd find me or I'd find her first, but one way or another I had the feeling that this would come to a head soon.

***

"I don't know why I keep coming back here," Valerie Marsh said. She took out a cigarette, tapped it on the pack, and glared at me. She held the cigarette between her forefinger and her index finger but made no move to light it. Her lipstick was bright red. To me. To its marketers it was probably something like Jungle Red or Passion Fire or Flaming Desire. It had bled into tiny hairline cracks just above her upper lip.

"I'm in business now. We already have thirteen steady clients. You could have been the first, if you weren't such a prig." She laughed. "Then you could have used that line, 'madam, I'm Adam.' You could have had me backwards and forwards." She laughed again. "Get it? Madam I'm Adam. Backwards and Forwards."

I didn't smile. Valerie tried a puff on her cigarette, remembered it wasn't lit, gave a disgusted grunt and shoved it back into the pack.

"This is crazy. I shouldn't even be here. I have work to do."

"So why are you?"

"Damned if I know. Look, this is crazy. I'm going." She shot to her feet, walked to the door, put her hand on the knob. And stood there. Then she gave a great heaving sigh, turned around and came back.

Without preamble, she said, "There was a man once. A long time ago."

She dropped her gaze to the floor, then looked out the window for a while. When she spoke again she kept her eyes on the window.

"I was sixteen and he was twenty two. I thought he was the greatest." She swung her eyes back to me. "He was the greatest."

"Tell me about him."

"He was six two with chestnut brown hair that he wore long. Big bones. Big ideas, too. He was very smart. Graduated at the top of his class. He wanted to be a doctor, but he could have been anything. He was so smart."

"What happened?"

She shrugged. "We went out for a while, but I was too young for him. A six–year difference at that age. It's like a whole lifetime."

"You're not sixteen any more. Have you tried to find him?"

Her large hazel eyes regarded me thoughtfully. "He wouldn't sleep with me. Said I was too young to know my mind. The only man I ever knew who said no to me. Until you." She seemed to gather herself up and sat straighter. "And no, I never tried to find him."

"Why not?"

She turned away and looked out the window again. From her seat she could see the rows of windows on the office building diagonally across the street. You couldn't see inside the offices because of the angle of the sun, which turned the squares of glass into a series of mirrors. She stared at the mirrored glass for a while. Then she faced me again.

"What would be the point? He went away and didn't tell me where he was going. Wherever he is, he knows where I am. I still live in the same city. If he wanted to, he could find me."

She started to speak again, caught herself. Her lips thinned.

"He doesn't care. Didn't care then, doesn't care now. He doesn't want to see me. So there'd be no point in looking for him, you see? Because it takes two to tango. And he doesn't want to dance." She glanced down at her hand in her lap. I thought she was checking the time, but she was examining her nails. "At least not with me."

"You must be curious about what happened to him."

She stopped inspecting her nails. "Oh, sure. Of course. I loved him."

"You could find out what happened to him without contacting him. Have you tried Google?"

She shook her head several times, a sad smile on her face.

"What would be the point?"

She lifted her chin. "There are a lot of stories like this. Millions.

Hundreds of millions. Always have been, always will be. One person falls in love with another but the other doesn't care. Just doesn't care." She smiled her sad smile again.

"And you know what? None of it really matters, when you think about it. Oh, it feels like it matters at the time. It feels like it's the only thing in the world that matters. It feels like you're worthless and the pain is so bad you're gonna die. But time passes, and you don't die, and more time passes and the pain gets less and when enough time passes you don't want to die any more and when that happens you've survived."

She looked fixedly at me, putting her thoughts together. "The same old story since the human race began. The race has survived. So have I."

I considered whether to pursue her reasons for not getting in touch with this man or to try another tack.

"Any of this have anything to do with the profession you chose?"

Valerie crossed her legs and leaned back. "That's bullshit," she said calmly. "I loved a man, he's gone, that's it. His choice. Doesn't mean he's a bad man. Sure as hell doesn't mean all men are bad. What, you think I'm trying to get some kind of revenge on men? Is that it? How? By giving them pleasure? What kind of revenge would that be?" She paused. "All that psychological shit. I thought you were, I forget the name you called it, some kind of philosophy guy, not one of these people who are always poking around in someone's head and not believing their reasons for things. Next thing, you'll ask me about my relationship with my mother and did I want to sleep with my father." She regarded me steadily.

"Please don't."

"There's not as hard a line between philosophy and psychology as you might think," I said. "There's quite a bit of overlap."

"Whatever. As long as we stay away from my childhood, which by the way wasn't special one way or the other."

"Valerie, I can't force you to talk about anything you don't want to talk about. Not that I'm particularly interested in your childhood. But I want to remind you that you're paying me to help you the best way I know how. You're relying on my knowledge, including my judgement of what questions to ask and what to leave alone."

She glanced at her wrist. "I have an appointment." She took some bills from her bag.

"You know, you sort of remind me of him." She read my surprise in my face. "Oh, you're not six–two. You're not a big man. But there's something. You remind me of him."

"Thank you," I said carefully.

"I mean, when Courtney first recommended you all that time ago, I had no idea what to expect, not really. I was going to ask her, but the next day she disappeared. Just left. I never saw her again."

Courtney. I thought hard, but came up with nothing.

"I'm at a little bit of a loss here. I don't know any Courtney."

"Courtney Felton. At least that was the name she went by with the Johns. She didn't want them bothering her after work. Of course none of the girls in the business give out their real names. They need to keep their private lives separate."

She got up and walked to the door. Opened it. Started to leave. I called after her.

"You never knew her real name?"

She looked back over her shoulder. "Oh sure. We were friends, after all. At least I thought we were, before she disappeared without a word. Her name was Clara Thompson." The door closed behind her.

Clara Thompson. The name the gun lady had thrown at me.

And now I had a lead. I would speak with Valerie again soon. Very soon, regardless of whether she came for another session. But the weekend started tomorrow, and I had to take a quick trip.

19

On Saturday I flew down to Fort Lauderdale where my father lived in a nursing home. He liked warm weather and besides he had friends living there, so when he crossed eighty and the time came when he felt it was too hard for him to live alone, he asked me to help move him from New York. Now he was eighty–six and fading fast. He had good days and bad days and I never knew which I'd encounter when I visited. Even on the good days his awareness flickered in and out unpredictably. Sometimes he forgot his name. Sometimes he forgot he had a son.

Today was a good day, at least so far, according to the white–coated male attendant who walked me through the main lounge where several residents watched TV. Three women and one man slumped in faded red armchairs that seemed as old as their occupants. One woman sat alone on a black faux leather sofa. Several hardback chairs scattered around were all empty.

"How do they decide what to watch? Do they take a vote?" I asked as we reached the elevator.

He laughed. "Vote? Yeah, sometimes. Sometimes it's whoever has the loudest voice, you know?"

"You let that happen?"

He shrugged. "It happens. Just like everywhere else," he said. "This place is no different."

We got off on the third floor. "The ones like your father, with their own room and their own TV, they don't have to worry about that. Some of them don't even want their own TV. They like coming down and watching with other people."

After he had gone I knocked on the door. No one answered so I knocked again.

"Pop, I'm here," I said loudly. Still no answer, so I went in.

He sat on the bed, his hands on his knees, staring at the floor. He looked up as I came in, and I saw recognition in the faded gray eyes.

"Hey, pop." I sat in the brown naugahyde recliner opposite the bed. "Why didn't you answer the door?"

He looked up at me. Some moisture had leaked from one eye to the left side of his nose. I took a tissue from a stand near his bed and wiped it away.

"I know who you are."

"Of course you do, poppa. I'm your son, Eric."

"Eric. Yes. And I'm Scooter, right?"

"Right, poppa."

"That's what your mother called me."

"Yes."

"But she's dead."

"Yes."

"Why did she call me that?"

"You know why, poppa. Because you had all that energy. She said you were too much for one woman to keep up with."

He shifted his gaze to the window twelve feet away at the end of the room. Palm trees took up most of the view. Far in the distance, too far away to see but not too far to smell when the breeze was right, stretched the ocean.

He looked back at me and his face took on a puzzled look.

"Who are you?" he asked querulously.

I closed my eyes. The picture I had of him in my mind's eye was of a big, capable man. He had been good with his hands and worked at various jobs where that was an asset. He fixed cars, tractors, outboard motors, even aircraft engines at one point. But he never lasted long at any one job. It wasn't that he didn't get along. He was just restless. "It was boring," he would tell my mother when she asked him why he quit the latest job. "I'm better than that."

Now his big frame, that giant I once knew, had collapsed and squeezed down onto itself. The shrunken result peered at me, no longer fully in touch with the world he was in.

"I'm your son, poppa. Eric," I said once again.

His face didn't change. I wasn't sure he'd heard.

"How have you been, poppa? Is everything okay? Do you have everything you want?"

With effort, he pushed himself up from the bed, shuffled over to the window, and stood looking out. I went over and stood beside him. "Pretty trees."

He looked at me and his eyes cleared again.

"Why am I here? I did everything right."

"You're here because you wanted to be. Your friends are here. Remember?"

He gazed out the window some more.

"Hungry."

"Let's go downstairs and get you something to eat."

As we left the elevator on the ground floor he stopped and grabbed my arm with surprising strength.

"I was afraid."

"What?"

"I could have done more."

We walked a few more steps to the dining room. Apparently it wasn't time for dinner yet, but half a dozen octogenarians were seated at a couple of the tables in anticipation. A woman in a green cardigan and red and green plaid slacks greeted my father as we walked in. He turned to me, still holding my arm.

"Don't be afraid. Never be afraid." He blinked, dropped my arm, and walked away from me.

***

Valerie Marsh worked out of an unobtrusive brownstone in the west seventies between Columbus and Amsterdam. The façade and the brick–colored stone stairs leading to the front door looked clean and well cared for.

Valerie had been surprised when I called, which I did the night I returned from Florida, and she'd sounded less than pleased when I explained that I just wanted to talk.

"Will there be a charge?" she'd asked. I couldn't tell if she was being sarcastic.

"No charge. This isn't about you."

She answered the door in a dark blue blazer with brilliantly colord mallard ducks on its enamel buttons. She led me to the living room, which was furnished in low black modern. A four cushion sofa, three semicircular swivel chairs and two of those chrome and leather jobs with the uptilting seats and the movable backs filled the room without crowding it. Valerie took a seat on the sofa and motioned me to one of the swivel chairs.

"Okay, I'm curious. Why this visit? I didn't know you made house calls."

"I like your living room."

"It's where I live, not where I work, if you're wondering. Except in very special cases. Like for instance, if you've changed your mind about my offer."

"It's about something you said at the end of our last session. You mentioned a Courtney Felton. You said her real name was Clara Thompson. I'd like to know more about her. Anything you can tell me."

"You could have waited until my next session."

"I never know if there's going to be a next session with you. Besides, you're paying me for your sessions. It wouldn't be fair for me to use up your time that way."

She nodded. "So maybe I should be charging you."

"Okay with me."

She waggled her head as if considering. "Nah. On the house. This time. What's the big deal with Clara? She was just one of the girls. Nothing much different about her. Or if there was I didn't see it. I mean, you don't get to see all sides of a person in the play for pay business, you know what I mean?"

"Let's start with what she looked like. Clients picked her out from a photo book, right?"

"Sure. Her madam's book. But Clara's not in it any more. When she left and didn't come back the madam took her picture out of the book and got rid of it."

"Can you describe her?"

She shrugged. "Hey, you want a drink? I'm forgetting my manners."

"Thanks, no."

"Nothing? Not even juice? Water?"

"I'm fine."

She settled back. "What can I tell you? A nice looking girl, tall, maybe, oh, five nine. Light brown hair, shoulder length. Good dresser. Kept her appointments. The madam never had any complaints about her. A good worker."

So, a generic description. Tens of thousands, maybe hundreds of thousands of women in Manhattan would fit it.

"Do you have her address?"

"No. Nothing like that. We were friends but only work friends. The girls had their appointments in a place on the east side. Or they'd go to the John's hotel room. Clara worked nights only, like a lot of the girls."

"How did the madam get in touch with them? How do you get in touch with your girls? You must have a list of their phone numbers."

"Yes. All their numbers are unlisted, of course. The cops could get the numbers from the phone company if it ever came to that, but you make things as hard as you can for them. And you try to be discreet, stay under their radar."

"So even if you don't have Clara's number, her old madam does."

She spread her hands. "No. Afraid not. I told you, Clara disappeared a few years ago. You can try if you want, but you'd be wasting your time. No one in the business keeps old records. Too dangerous. Besides, it wouldn't help you anyway. After she stopped coming I called her five or six times to find out what was going on. I left messages but she never called back. The last time I called I got a canned message that the number was disconnected. There was no forwarding number."

So either Valerie was being purposely unhelpful or the trail had gone cold with the passage of time.

"Anything else you can tell me? Anything at all?"

She looked off into space. Then she brightened and gave me a wide smile.

"She always had a book with her. Whenever someone was late, she'd take out a book and read. Kept it in her purse. I once asked her why she was always reading. Said she didn't want to waste her time."

"Was it a different book each time, or the same?"

She looked incredulous. "Why would anyone read the same book all the time?"

"Did you ever see a title?"

"I really didn't pay attention. I'm not much of a reader."

"Any friends? Names that you remember?"

She shook her head. "She was a loner. Didn't mingle with the other girls. Don't ask me why."

I stood. "Anything else you remember, call me any time."

She walked me to the door and put her hand on my wrist.

"You don't have to leave if you don't want to. If you want to stay a while."

"I really have to go. And thanks for your time."

"Sure," she said. "Sure."

She turned and walked back to the living room, leaving me standing at the door.

20

"We're not getting anywhere," Bernie Feld said.

After my talk with Valerie I'd caught the subway back to my office in time for his ten–thirty appointment. When it was over he would have plenty of time to get back to his bank before the lunch hour crunch. This left open the question of when he took his own lunch. Maybe he ate late in the afternoon. Maybe he had concerns about his weight and skipped lunch entirely.

Maybe I should give up all hope of ever ridding myself of idle speculation.

"You keep talking about perspective. I don't know what that means. It's just words. In banking words mean something tangible. Like money. Like collateral. Things you can see. Things you can put your hands on."

"How about words like credit? Or foreclose?"

Bernie set his mouth and glared at me.

"Those are pieces of paper. You can see them and touch them. A foreclosure is a legal document. Credit too. A man wants credit, he signs a piece of paper. You can look at it and handle it. You can file it in a drawer."

"Doesn't a man have credit before he signs anything? Don't you know, most of the time, whether his credit is good even if he never takes out a loan?"

Bernie looked uncomfortable. "You're playing with words. The point is, I don't feel like I'm getting anywhere here. I came to you because I've got everything I want, I did everything by the book, but I need something else and I don't know what it is."

I wondered if he remembered the intro to those old jokes we'd talked about. Apparently not.

He stopped and waited for me to speak, but before I could say anything he said, "I mean, if getting what I want isn't the answer, what is?"

"Do you think part of it might be wanting the wrong things?"

"Wrong things? What's that mean? We want what we want. Everyone has a right to live his life whatever way he wants."

"Are some ways better than others?"

Bernie cocked his head to one side.

"Unless you're a junkie or a hit man or something, for most normal people whatever lifestyle they go with is the one that's good for them. That's why they go with it."

"Many people would agree with you."

"But you don't."

"Some things are worth going after. Some things aren't."

"According to who? It's up to everyone to judge for himself."

"Yes it is. But that doesn't make every choice equally good."

Bernie thrust his jaw at me. He looked like Dick Tracy in the old comic strip, but the long hair was wrong.

"Show me. You know what I wanted. Still want. In fact everyone wants. Money. It doesn't just buy you things. It buys lots of... intangibles."

"Only you're not happy."

His voice rose. "That's not because I have money. What, I'd be happier if I were poor? I'd be better off?"

"I didn't say that."

"Then what are you saying?"

"Let me ask you this. A minute ago, before you said there was something else you needed or wanted, you said you had everything you wanted. You also said you want more money, but that wasn't the something else. So I'm not quite clear what you're saying." I paused. Bernie remained silent. I plowed ahead.

"Do you feel you've got enough money, or do you still need to make more?"

He turned and looked out at New Jersey. Then he turned back and looked at me. Through me. After a while he focused again.

"I have enough, by any reasonable standard. But it never hurts to have more."

"So the reason you're staying in your job at the bank even though you don't need to work any more is not because you enjoy the work but to make more money? Or is it both?"

"It's the money."

"Still not enjoying the work?"

"It's the money," he said again.

"Why, when you say you already have enough?"

"I told you. It's always nice to have more."

"Why is it nice?"

"What?"

"What's nice about having more money when you already have all you need?"

"That's obvious."

"If it were obvious I wouldn't be asking."

"Plenty of people have more than I do, and they keep working."

"A lot of them because they love what they do."

"A lot of them do it for the money, like me."

I paused to consider which direction to take. "How do you feel knowing that lots of people have more money than you? Does that bother you?"

I wondered if I would get an honest answer. "Take your time. Don't answer right away."

He sat for a while. He shifted his weight and fidgeted with the middle button on his jacket. Then he stilled himself and sat quietly. His eyes had a faraway look. I hoped he was looking inward, because if he didn't or couldn't, we wouldn't get very far.

He abandoned the button and hooked his right thumb into his belt. "I know it shouldn't, but it does. Why is that?"

"Without getting into the why for now, we need to focus on what it means for your life."

He eyed me, saying nothing.

"Obviously there'll always be someone who has more. You'll never have enough."

His eyes shifted to the wall above my chair but focused far beyond the room on something only he could see.

"A goal you can never reach," I prompted.

Bernie sat. I waited.

He dragged out three words. "A perpetual motion machine."

He glanced at his watch, put his hands on his thighs and sat for a few more moments before leaving. He didn't make another appointment. I got a lot of that. Was it unique to me? I had no way of knowing.

While I waited for my next appointment thoughts of the gun lady assaulted me yet again. I tried to make some sense of what Valerie Marsh told me about her obsession, Clara Thompson, but Valerie hadn't told me much. So little, in fact, that going over and over the few concrete details she gave me left me stymied and frustrated every time.

My mental machinery skittered away from Valerie and Clara, searched its frustration files and seized on another question that always puzzled me, namely exactly what is passing when we say time is passing. In the movies when they want to show time stopping they show all the actors and all motion stopping. Everything and everyone frozen in place. Time as measurement of motion. But couldn't we say an hour passed and nothing moved? If so motion is within time, and time is passing even when there is no motion.

Except in the larger sense motion never stops. Beyond planetary motion, the entire universe is expanding. Motion is forever. So time could still be a measurement of relative motion. Or could time be something in and of itself? And what did that mean?

Maybe I was just too far behind the times and I should be thinking about spacetime.

Sure. Maybe when I had some more time.

My head hurt.

I still didn't know what was passing when we say time is passing, but right now my life was passing as I made no more progress on this question than on previous tries.

Hopefully the problems my next client posed would be more manageable.

***

"I left my wife," Jeremy said. "I'm living in a hotel. I thought it would be a big relief. Not having her around all the time, having my own space. Being able to do anything I want. Not having the kids underfoot all the time."

He shifted his weight, shifted back again. He got up and went over to the coffee machine. Poured himself a cup and sat down again. Gulped down some black coffee without testing its temperature. Luckily for him I had made it an hour ago so he avoided getting scalded, but not realizing his luck he made a face anyway.

"It's no good. I miss her. Maybe even the kids, strange as that might sound. There's a certain energy when they're around, you know? I think I must have gotten used to that. It's too quiet now."

"So you're lonely."

He looked bleak. I leaned back as far as my office chair would let me. "That make sense to you? You don't love your wife or your kids, but you feel lonely without them?"

"Beats me. But if you're trying to say I really do love them, forget it. I know my own mind. I miss certain things about them, that's all. I'm just not used to being alone."

"So what are you going to do about it?"

"I'm not going back, if that's what you mean. I was thinking I might ask Alice to come here with me next time."

"Why?"

He grimaced. His brows beetled and his nostrils flared. Immediately, he pinched the offending nostrils between thumb and forefinger. Choke off the emotion.

"I don't know why. It's a feeling. I don't ask myself for the reasons behind every feeling I have, dammit." He drummed the fingers of his left hand on his thigh. "I just think it might help."

"How?"

He shrugged, drained his cup, tossed it in the waste basket. "Can't hurt."

"What makes you think she'll come? I assume she's still speaking to you."

His eyes widened in surprise. "Of course."

"Well, you did walk out on her. People sometimes take that kind of thing hard."

Jeremy hitched up his trouser leg a bit and crossed his leg. The emotion was gone, and his voice lapsed into pedantic mode.

"One thing I'll say about Alice, she's a realist. Everyone knows relationships are hard. People break up every day. Hell, half the marriages in this country end in divorce, and that's not counting any of the ones where one of the partners is miserable but is afraid to be alone. Or where maybe they're both miserable but agree to stay together for the kids. Or a hundred other crazy reasons. Alice knows all that. She doesn't hold it against me."

"You're sure of that."

"We discussed it."

"And she wasn't angry or upset."

"Well, not at the end. No."

"Ah."

"What's that mean?"

"I'm not sure we should get into it. I'm not a marriage counselor."

"I'm not sure what you are."

I smiled. "Good point. I do what I like to call philotherapy. Sometimes that involves philosophy, sometimes psychology."

"I thought the sign on the door said you were a philosophical practitioner. Whatever that means."

"I just told you what it means."

He shrugged. "Whatever. What's the verdict on Alice? Can I bring her next time or not?"

"I don't see how it will help you."

His mouth tightened. "It's my money."

"Tell you what. If you think of a reason why bringing her along might help you, give me a call. Keeping in mind that I'm not a marriage counselor."

Jeremy had said what he wanted to say, so we called it a day.

***

Maybe I didn't know what time was, but I knew I wanted more of it, and that meant not being killed by the gun lady. I now compulsively checked my e–mail after almost every session. She still hadn't followed up on her George Bush quote informing me that I could run but I couldn't hide. She would, of course. But how? And when? I couldn't just sit around and hope she wouldn't find me. I had to find her first.

And then what? Ask her to please go away? Talk to her? My business involved making persuasive arguments, but my score with her idled at zero. Lower than zero, since she still wanted to kill me and that counted as a minus score. I needed a plan and I didn't think I had much time left to devise one.

***

Joel Marks and his mother sat in my office. Halfway through the session he became animated for the first time.

"I read that investment book. The one you recommended. The Siegel."

"Did you enjoy it?"

"He wrote another one after that. He says buy big companies that pay a dividend and re–invest the dividends. But how do I know that's the best way? What if there's a better way?"

He leaned forward, resting his arms on his ripped jeans. The Einstein T–shirt had been usurped by one that said Whoever Has The Most Toys When He Dies Wins. I hoped this didn't mean Einstein no longer rocked. Some day I'd have to give some thought to the younger generation's need to send the world a message via their chests.

"You ever hear of Warren Buffet?" he asked.

"Sure."

"He's the most successful investor who ever lived, right? He's made the most money."

"True."

"So I've got three hundred dollars saved up now. Why don't I just follow his system?"

"He's never written a book. He hasn't laid out his system."

"But he's written all those annual reports," Joel said excitedly. "They're on the web."

"Yes he has."

"And people have read those and written books about how he thinks. Some of them even have websites with lists of stocks they think he'd pick. So, what I'm going to do, I'm going to pick some stocks from those lists. Maybe three stocks, a hundred dollars in each one."

He sat back and regarded me. "How does that sound? You see anything wrong with that?"

"Just one thing, Joel. No one knows what Warren Buffet would buy except Warren Buffet."

"Yeah, but don't you think these guys who've read all this stuff could come up with some pretty good guesses?"

"They might. They might not. Certainly none of them has come anywhere near his success."

"Well, I'm gonna try them out like I said. But there's one thing I don't get. I mean, here's this best investor the world has ever seen, and people can see what kind of stuff he buys, well, bought in the past, and they can analyze that, so why doesn't everyone just try and buy the kind of stocks he does?"

"A lot of people are trying."

"But?"

"But he's the best so far. No one has been able to duplicate his thinking."

"What about you? Do you try to figure out what he'd do?"

"I sometimes apply his methods as I understand them."

"Not always?"

"No."

"Why not?"

I shrugged. "There are other ways to make money in the stock market."

"But his is the best!"

"Possibly. Probably."

"So why don't you try to use his methods all the time? Why only sometimes?"

"Sometimes I see other opportunities that look like they'd give me a better short term return."

Joel shook his head. "Not me. I'll go with the best method, the one that made the most money. The one the best investor uses."

His eyes shone. He had a faint smile on his face, the first I'd ever seen on him. He sat straight, as if barely containing his energy and restraining himself from bounding out of the chair. I grinned.

"Sounds like a plan. Good luck."

As they started to leave, Dorothy paused at the door, smiled brightly and said, "Thanks."

It was the only word she had spoken the entire time.

21

Sally Carter, my last appointment for the day, had on another slacks and blouse outfit. She took a few moments to arrange herself comfortably. "I'm still thinking about what you said last time. About purpose and randomness."

Her blouse was plain white, with a single empty pocket over her left breast. I always wondered about that placement for women. Did any woman actually stuff objects, or even papers, into those pockets and ruin the beauty of their breast curve? Probably not, at least not in my experience. Then why did the manufacturers add the pockets? Another of life's mysteries that I would spend no time trying to solve.

"Did I tell you I was a very good student in school?"

I shook my head.

She nodded. "All A's. High school and college. I thought I had it made, you know? The question of what to do with your life never came up. They taught you things, then they tested you to see if you understood what they taught you, and that was it. You just gave them back what they already told you. That was your goal. It was set in advance for you by the school system, and if you could do it, you were a success. Success was defined for you in advance, you see? Then when you're twenty–two they hand you a degree and put you out on the street and say, 'go.'"

Sally's eyes were intent. She leaned toward me. "Go? Where? How? They never tell you that. You have to figure it out for yourself.

Suddenly there's no one to tell you what you have to do to get an A. No one pops up with a sign saying, 'Okay. Here's what success means from this point on.' You can look around and see what other people are going after. Money, power, sex, popularity. Whatever. But who says they know what they're doing? They're probably just as confused as you are."

She leaned back in her chair, looking exhausted now. Her eyes fixed on the coffee machine. I poured some and handed it to her. She took a few sips and reached over to rest the cup on my desk. The coffee seemed to both relax and energize her.

"I settled for a husband, kids, and a dog. And a couple of films." She drank some more coffee. "I think I sold out too cheap."

"You didn't find what I said last time convincing?"

"Which part?"

"All of it. Any of it. Bringing up your children in a creative way. Getting a message across in that film. Thinking of yourself as a work in progress that you're continually improving."

"It sounded good when you said it. Especially that last part. But when I got home, it kind of faded away."

She leaned her head back against the chair as if tired again. "I bet you get that a lot."

Actually I did, but people generally didn't have the self–awareness to know it, let alone express it explicitly the way Sally just had. Outside, a police siren shredded the air. A black and white spotted pigeon on someone else's ledge started cooing, hoping to persuade some fatally attractive lady pigeon to let him have his way with her. The cooing was increasing in volume, which either meant she was encouraging him or she wasn't. I figured that exhausted the possibilities. I wished him luck. Solidarity.

"It faded away because the old feelings and ideas you've held for so many years are more real to you. Bad ideas and feelings are like bad habits. In fact they are bad habits. They're physically encoded in your brain's neural pathways, which is one reason they're so hard to break. Replacing them with good ones can be a slow process. The way to do it is to go over the argument for the new idea every time a feeling that came from the old one crops up."

She nodded twice. "I can do that." But she glanced away, looking uncomfortable. "There's something else I want to talk about. This is going to sound strange."

"Go on."

"Well." She tucked her legs under her. "I don't know how to say this. It sounds so weird."

A full minute passed while she wrestled with it.

"I don't know who I am."

I started to reply, but she held up her hand.

"Wait. That sounds so stupid. Let me talk around it a little." She flicked her tongue over her lips.

"I mean, I knew who I was in the past. Know, I mean. Not knew. I can look back at my past, for instance when I was a teenager. I know who that girl was then. That Sally Carter college girl, I know who that was. The grown up wife and mother Sally, I know who she was. They all have a clear identity. But this Sally, the one sitting in front of you now, in a sense she's all of those, but in a sense she's none of them because all that's in the past, so the question is, who is Sally now?" She leaned forward, intent.

"Does that make any sense to you?"

"This is not a new topic, Sally."

She looked startled. "Sure it is. I haven't brought this up before."

"You have. Just in other words. When you first walked in here and asked me for a reason to get out of bed in the morning."

"I don't understand."

"We've been talking about why you have difficulty feeling, why you read so much, why your life feels empty, why you need a purpose. Now you say you don't know who you are, but you did know when you were in high school and college and when you were being a mother. When you had clear, specific goals. Which you don't have now." I smiled. "Yet."

Sally freed her legs, leaned toward my desk, closed both hands around her coffee cup, and took a succession of quick sips, like a bird with an eye out for a predator.

"Are you saying a person is their goals? That's all a person is?"

"People are of course more complex than that. A person is what she thinks about, what she reads, what she laughs at, what she cries at, how she treats other people, who she loves, and a lot more. But more than any other single thing, I'd say a person is defined by what she thinks worthwhile enough to spend her limited time on earth pursuing."

She clutched her empty cup between her breasts. A two–handed clutch. "Purpose again."

I nodded.

"You think that's the whole problem."

"For you. Right now, anyway."

She put the cup near a leg of the chair and sat for a while, considering. "I don't know if that's right, but it feels right." She became thoughtful again. I gave her whatever time she needed.

"I guess what you're talking about is something people seem to know automatically at some level," she said. "Isn't that why when people meet you the first question they usually ask after 'how are you' is 'what do you do?'"

I smiled. Sally smiled back.

Her smile was a lot prettier than mine.

✳✳✳

After Sally's session I walked up Columbus toward my apartment. The day was brisk and sunny, about sixty degrees. Not much wind. Perfect for an invigorating walk after too many sedentary hours sitting in my office exercising nothing bulkier than my vocal cords. People jammed the sidewalks, eager to get home to whatever they thought made them happy, their families, their TV, their dog or cat. Sadly, in my experience there weren't too many people who felt fulfilled by their work. Many people are clock–watchers who tolerate work only as a means to an end. Beyond staying alive, they're usually not too clear on what that end is. Happiness, sure. But what did that mean? Feeling good? How good did you have to feel? And all the time? Most of the time? What did most of the time mean? Was fifty one percent of the time good enough? Two thirds? Eighty percent? Most people just lived their lives the way everyone else did, going to school, getting married, acquiring two kids and half a dog, and expecting, if they thought about it at all, that whatever happiness was, they had done everything necessary to get it. Every now and then some of the more thoughtful among them shook themselves awake and asked themselves the age–old "Is this all there is?" My clientele, or at least some of them, came from that group.

I passed a new sandwich shop between Seventy–Third and Seventy–Fourth. They made a different kind of sandwich, a sandwich in name only, using a technique the owner had told me he had seen in Japan. Apparently it coined money in Japan, and he hoped Manhattanites would be as intrigued by it as the Japanese. It consisted of shaping a crepe into a cone and filling the cone with the sandwich ingredients – ham and cheese, beef, chicken, ratatouille, whatever. You ate it on the street as you walked.

The place was jammed so I walked on by. I hoped the owner continued to be right about Manhattan tastes once the novelty wore off, because I liked his food and the convenience and was rooting for him to stay in business. Another small entrepreneur risking his savings in the hope of pleasing the public and making a buck.

Cats have hearing far more sensitive than ours. Circe probably heard me and recognized my step before I even reached the staircase. When I finally finished plodding up the stairs and entered the apartment she was waiting at the door and started scolding me instantly. Where were you? How could you go away and leave me for so long? Don't you know how I worry? I didn't even know if you were coming back!

I cradled her in my arms the way she liked, belly up, and carried her into the kitchen. She started to subside a little and when I stroked and kneaded the underside of her neck her protests morphed into a steady purr. Cats not only see and hear better than we do, they also forgive and forget faster. A lot faster.

Only a little food remained in her bowl. I dumped in a can of chicken giblets and refreshed her water bowl. Then I settled myself on the couch and called Sheila's home number. She answered on the first ring.

"Hello?"

"That's what I like. Sitting by the phone waiting for my call."

She laughed. "Dream on. But I do miss you."

"Me too, babe."

"Oh good."

"Lot of stuff's been happening."

Without using their names I told her about the latest developments with Bernie, Jeremy, the Marks family, Valerie Marsh, and Sally Carter. Then I told her what I'd found out from Valerie about Clara Thompson. I left out the gun lady's YOU CAN'T HIDE e–mail. I saw no point in upsetting her over something she could do nothing about. I told her about my trip to Florida to visit my father, and I repeated his words to me before he went into the dining room. *I could have done more. Never be afraid.*

"The poor man. What do you think he meant?"

"Sounded like he was grieving for the risks he didn't take."

"Oh my. I hope not. Did he ever mention any ambitions to you when you were growing up?"

"No. He just went from one thing to the next. Never seemed satisfied. Now he's near the end and he's got some vague sense that he's missed something."

"But he had a family and he nurtured it and supported it. That's not nothing. I hope you told him that."

"Actually, no. It happened too fast."

"Well you tell him next time you see him. The poor man," she said again.

"I will."

"Good."

I got up and walked to the window. "Listen, there's something else I wanted to talk about."

"I hoped there was."

I cleared my throat of some obstruction that wasn't there. "You're way ahead of me. I was, ah, thinking about the last time we were together."

She was silent.

I looked out at a brick wall. "All this coast to coast stuff, seeing each other on the run. It's nice, but it sucks."

"It kind of does," she said softly.

"We need to be together for a while," I said. "A pretty long while. Maybe six months. Give it a try. See how it goes."

"Yes. And if it goes well?"

I felt my collar getting tight. Strange, because I was wearing an open–necked sport shirt. I had big reservations about whether our lifestyles could ever be compatible, and I didn't know how long it might take for those reservations to be put to rest. If they ever could.

"We might want to think about making it more permanent," I said in a voice I hoped sounded normal.

"Might?"

"Sheila, what do you want me to say?"

"I guess you've gone about as far as you can go. Have you thought about the practicalities?"

"Which ones?"

"Little things like my career is out here and your patients are out there."

"Clients," I said automatically.

"So there's no way you could come out here and live with me unless you were willing to abandon your practice, and I don't think you'd want to do that. Or could, financially. On the other hand for me to live there I'd have to sell or close up the house and take myself out of circulation here professionally. Not that I wouldn't get good roles any more of course, I'm too big a draw for that, but there'd be a lot of times when I wouldn't get first look at a project simply because I was no longer pressing the flesh."

"Well, but your agent would still be there."

"It's not the same thing. They like to see your face, walk over to your table, casually send up a trial balloon about their next project, sometimes one that they thought up on the spot and whose only hope of ever making it to the real world is if you indicate some interest."

"So what do you want to do?" I said after a brief silence.

"I could close up the house and make all the arrangements in about three weeks."

"But you just said — "

"Do you want me to come or not?"

"Yes. Or course."

"Then it's settled. We'll need a bigger place, of course."

"Why?"

"Please. Your closet space is pathetic."

"This place was hard to find. I don't want to give it up. If we live somewhere else for six months I'll be paying rent here and half the rent for our new place. I can't afford that."

"You don't have to pay half the rent."

"Sheila — "

"You said you weren't hung up on that man is supposed to have a higher income thing."

"It's not that."

"Then what?"

"I like to pay my own way."

"Even if it means we can't get together? What about if we decided to make it permanent, or as you put it, more permanent? Would you feel the same way? How would we get around that?"

I said nothing.

"I can afford a nice place and I want to have what I can afford. Do you think that's unreasonable?"

"No."

"Well, what's your solution? Mine would be that we rent a bigger place. If you want to chip in, which you don't have to do as far as I'm concerned, pay whatever you can afford or whatever you want to and I'll pay the rest."

I hesitated. She was right, but I was fighting a strong distaste for what still looked to me like being a kept man. Against that was the annoying fact that I couldn't fault her argument.

"Let me think about it."

"When will you get back to me?"

"How about tomorrow night."

"Until then," she said.

"Until then."

I replaced the receiver and sat down. Circe immediately staked out my lap. I chucked her under her chin so she was looking up at me.

"What do you think, Circe? Am I being a horse's ass here?"

But she just stared at me greenly. She never answered when the answer was obvious.

22

How people could be bright–eyed, not to mention bushy–tailed, early in the morning was an enduring mystery to me, but Diana Rogers was one of the lucky ones.

Before I'd left my apartment I'd checked my e–mail. The gun lady still maintained her silence, which made no sense to me. Why start a campaign of threats and intimidation and then just drop it? I had to assume a method to this particular variation of her madness. Maybe she thought the anticipation of what she might do next would unnerve me more than the actual fact. If so, she might have a point. I didn't know which upset me more, receiving her threats or not receiving them and wondering why. In the game of cat and mouse, being cast in the role of mouse was galling. And it hurt my pride as well as my equanimity.

Diana Rogers blew in uncharacteristically late and sat catching her breath for a few moments. She looked stunning in a light gray tweed suit and dark gray turtleneck. Her legs were bare. When her breathing returned to normal she flipped back her bangs. "I'm sorry."

I thought she was referring to her lateness. No.

"The way I walked out of here last time. I was hurt. When you asked me if I thought I was interesting, I thought you were saying that I wasn't. But then later I decided you weren't saying that. You were trying to find out if my opinion of myself was changed."

She stopped and looked at me. I nodded.

"Well, like I said. I'm sorry."

She glanced around the room. Without asking I poured her some coffee and slid it to the edge of the desk.

"Thanks. So I guess I should answer the question, otherwise what am I doing here, right? I guess the answer is no, I don't think my opinion of myself has changed all that much. Not really. I wasn't really being honest last time. Bruce thinks I'm an interesting person, and in the beginning I thought that was great. I mean, I still think it's great, but it scares me."

"In what way?"

"I'm afraid he'll change his mind. I'm afraid that when he gets to know me he'll be bored."

So we were back at the beginning.

"Why?"

Her face fell and her lower lip trembled. Her voice dropped to a whisper.

"Because I'm boring. What happens after he really gets to know me and he's heard all my opinions on things? I'll just be repeating myself and he'll be bored and leave me." She took a swig of her coffee, put the cup under her chair, then clasped her hands tightly in her lap.

"I don't want to feel this way."

I didn't blame her, but of course I couldn't change how she felt until I changed how she thought. Apparently I hadn't succeeded so far. I had to take a new tack.

"Diana, what makes a person interesting?"

"What?"

"To you. Let's say you meet someone at a party. It could be a man or a woman. How do you decide if they're interesting?"

"Well, what kind of question is that? They say something interesting. How else would you know?"

"So you know as soon as they say something interesting?"

"Of course."

"You don't have to hear any more? What if they've just memorized a lot of facts or are repeating something they've heard or read somewhere but can't come up with very much on their own?"

"I guess that's possible."

"Then they wouldn't really be interesting, would they? Your first impression would be wrong."

"I suppose so."

"So what makes a person interesting, and when do you decide?"

"When they say interesting things and you know them long enough."

"Interesting things, like what?"

"You know." She waved a hand. "Everyone knows an interesting thing when they hear it. You can't say in advance."

"Why not?"

"Because there are too many things. It could be almost anything. The list would be too long."

"Do you think different people would find different things on that list interesting?"

"Of course."

"So interesting depends on who you ask."

"I don't know what you're getting at."

"I'm getting at Bruce. He finds you interesting, and it's not just a first impression, which is all you need to know right now. Interesting is a word that has concrete meaning only in the minds of individual people. Bruce has known you a while and he thinks you're interesting. End of story."

She worried her lower lip between her teeth.

"Well, that's now. What about later?"

"There are no guarantees. There never are. Right now, we know Bruce is happy with you. Why look for trouble around the corner when there's no reason to think it's there?"

She could have said, 'because I'm a very insecure person and I can't help it,' which would have taken us along a different path, but she left it there for now.

***

As soon as the door closed behind Diana, I started obsessing about the gun lady. I knew she might find me any day. I also knew that if she found me and didn't immediately pull the trigger without any more talk, it could help me to know Clara Thompson's identity and her connection to the gun lady.

Besides, I was curious. Here was a book–reading woman who didn't want to waste her spare time but who worked as a prostitute and then suddenly disappeared. And she had some connection to a gun–toting lady whose threats I took seriously enough to carry a gun, although carrying it made me feel more foolish every day. What would I do if she found me, shoot her? I'd never shot anything in my life. Even the idea of hunting for sport made me nauseous.

So why did I have a gun strapped on like an old–time riverboat gambler or a cowboy? Did I have some kind of subconscious fantasy of outdrawing her in a confrontation like some tall rangy suntanned western hero?

Yes, I probably did, although I hadn't realized it until now. My subconscious embarrassed me. I felt my face flush and I started to take off the shoulder holster, but I stopped when it occurred to me that I could obviously drop the fantasy and still keep the gun.

One of my modes of relaxation, in addition to music, walking, chess, philosophy, and playing with Circe, is reading the occasional detective novel, and over the years I've read enough of them to have a general idea of how a detective works. Massive amounts of data exist out there, and now, especially since the advent of the internet, almost anyone can be located if you look hard enough. There are data bases on motor vehicle registrations, homes, apartments, mortgages, credit cards, landline phones, cell phones, local taxes, federal taxes, deaths, and who knew what else.

Well, detectives know, or should know. Finding people for one reason or another is their business, and knowing which databases to access and how to access them is part of their professional expertise. If I could find a competent detective who charged reasonable fees, which in my circumstances meant low, I would be able to tap into that expertise, which is to say, hire him. I pulled out my yellow pages. Were private detectives listed under D or under P?

As it turned out, under I, for investigators.

The first three detective agencies I tried had the most impressive looking boxed ads. Their prices all seemed high to me, although I really had no standard of comparison until I called one of the listees who, out of modesty, laziness, or impecuniousness, hadn't bothered to take out an ad of any sort. His agency was called Tracers, which certainly sounded promising. His name was Sam Kashinsky. His rates were low compared to the other three. I knew this could be good news or bad. Good if he was competent, bad if his competence matched his rates.

"So it's by the day, not by the hour?" I said.

"That's right."

"And there's no minimum after one day?"

"No minimum."

"If I give you the information I have about this person and what I want you to find out, can you give me an estimate of how long it will take you?"

"No."

This was not a man of many words.

"Why not?"

"Each case is different. Some people hide better than others. They take longer. Some people are smarter than others and they do more than just hide. They also leave fake trails."

"Fake trails?"

"Fake death certificates. Fake dental records. Fake addresses and deeds. You name it. If it can be used for ID purposes, someone has thought of a way to fake it."

"Oh."

"You want me to get started or not?"

So I told him everything Valerie Marsh had told me about Clara Thompson/Courtney Felton. When I finished he said, "That's it?"

"Yeah."

"Not much to go on," he grunted.

"I know. That's why I'm calling you."

"She a fugitive?"

"Not that I know of."

"This could take a while."

"Let's take it day by day," I said. "I'll check in with you to see what you've come up with."

"You don't want me to call you?"

"If you have something you think is particularly urgent. Otherwise I'll call you."

"How would I know what's urgent if I don't know why you want this info?"

He said info.

The man had a point.

"Just use your judgement."

He grunted. "Send me a check. You might want to make it for a full week. If I find her sooner, which I don't expect, I'll send you back a refund."

"I'll send it out today."

I got one last grunt before he hung up.

23

The rain had been sluicing down all afternoon in intermittent downpours that spent their energy in a few minutes and then subsided into wet fog. Ever the optimist, I decided to walk home anyway, betting that I'd make it before the next Niagra.

Bad bet. The rain got me at Columbus and Seventy–Fourth. It washed the street clean of everyone but me and a few intrepid souls who had come prepared with humongous umbrellas. Since I couldn't get any wetter because my clothes were completely saturated in the first four seconds, I decided what the hell and sloshed along until I made it home.

Circe never saw me sodden like this. Instead of her usual scolding for my being gone so long, she stopped after the first meow and stared at me. I plodded into the bathroom, stripped off my clothes and treated myself to a hot shower which left me feeling vaguely human again. Then I filled her food and water bowls and padded into the living room to call Sheila.

"Hi, I'm looking for the sex queen of the western world," I said when she came on the line.

"Speaking."

"Great. How about a little hanky–panky?"

"Not a problem. Oh by the way, who's speaking?"

"An admirer."

She gave a theatrical sigh. "I have so many of those."

"The one who wants to rent an apartment with you."

"Oh, that one."

"How about you come down for the weekend and we'll look at the real estate section and wander around town a little."

"I have a better idea. A friend of mine has a sister who owns a real estate agency. I can call her and tell her what we're looking for and she can take us around."

"What are we looking for?"

"Trust me," she said.

"With my heart? Again?"

"That too, but in this case to come up with some apartments you'll like."

"Not just what I'll like. Also what I can afford. Or I should say what I can afford half of."

"That'll be your decision, darling."

I was silent. Darling. I didn't feel like making any more wisecracks.

"This weekend?"

"Yes."

"Kennedy or La Guardia?"

"I'll call you when I've got my flight number."

The cat, as usual, was curled up on my lap. "Want to say hello to Circe?"

"I'll wait till I get there."

"See you soon."

Circe had looked up when I said her name. When I hung up she knew her lap gig was over, and she jumped down and sauntered back to her food bowl without a backward glance.

Well, I was used to that.

***

Life looked a little better. Back in the office waiting for Bernie Feld to appear I realized I felt calmer, comforted not only by Sheila's coming but also by the knowledge of Sam Kashinsky out there doing his Tracer bit and the reasonable chance that he would uncover some good information about Clara Thompson. I no longer felt I was just marking time awaiting the gun lady's pleasure.

Bernie arrived wearing a navy blue suit, a white shirt with French cuffs, and a pair of oxblood cordovan loafers. Before Bernie I didn't know bank officers were allowed to wear loafers. Or any color shoe but black. Apparently standards went downhill when I wasn't looking.

"You said I was on a perpetual motion machine," Bernie said. His tan was deeper today, which made his blue eyes seem even more electric. Since summer was gone I ruled out weekend sunning at the Hamptons, which left a tanning salon as the probable place of acquisition. Unless we were dealing with that modern mini–makeover, a tube of self–tanner. I glanced at Bernie's right hand. His knuckles stood out darker than the rest of his hand.

Self–tanner.

He crossed his legs with his left ankle over his right knee.

"Actually you said it," I said.

"You're way off. I'm doing exactly what everyone else does. I'm working for a living. If I'm on a treadmill, then so is everyone else. So is our whole society."

He spoke as if most of our conversation last time never took place. I continue to marvel at peoples' ability to believe what they want to believe and remember only what they want to remember. They think reality can be safely ignored whenever it suits them. In fact reality always finds a way to have the last word. That's why it's called reality.

"Sounds like the fifty million Frenchmen can't be wrong argument," I said. He didn't respond, so I went on. "Making a living is not what we're talking about here. Sure, everyone has to do it, but not everyone envies people who are making more than they are. That's the treadmill. We discussed this, Bernie."

Bernie's eyes blazed defiantly. "So some people are cows, they graze with their heads down all their lives. I'm in the same pasture, but I look up now and then to see what's going on around me. What other people are doing. How much grass they're getting. I don't think that's a bad thing."

"Not unless you can't handle what you see."

He recrossed his legs, right ankle on left knee. He shot his left cuff and glanced at his gold watch. He pressed his lips together. "What about ambition. What about getting ahead. You want to throw all that out? You got to be dissatisfied with your situation or else where's your motivation? You feel satisfied all the time, you're a cow, not a man."

He had latched onto this cow thing and was pushing it beyond its value and my tolerance limits. But I had no need to make an issue of it. Good things happen in this life. He might switch to horses or rhinos or sheep or brontosaurs. Anything but cows. I was tired of cows.

"There's more than one way to be dissatisfied," I said.

"What's that mean?"

"You can be perfectly convinced that whatever you're doing, you're trying your best, doing your best, and still be ambitious to learn more and become even better. That's a healthy motivation and a healthy kind of dissatisfaction. That kind of person is not necessarily unhappy with his present situation. And he doesn't feel any need to constantly compare himself with others."

"Sure he does. Why do you think he wants to become better? Because he sees that others are better than him."

I placed my elbows on the desk and interlaced my fingers.

"You don't think someone could want to be the best he could be, even if right now there's no one better than he is?"

Bernie gave an emphatic headshake. "Nah. What for? What would be the point? That's a lot of crap."

I stared at him. It's one thing to be dumb, but Bernie wasn't dumb, at least not IQ dumb. It's another thing entirely to be blind because you can't get past your own messed up psychology, although a person often could not control that, at least not in the short term. But ordinary politeness is almost always in one's control, and I had become increasingly tired of Bernie's undiminished stream of casually insulting language.

"Bernie, you don't get to say that in here."

He stared back at me. "Huh?"

"You get to tell me what you want to talk about. You get to disagree with me any time you want. But you don't get to be uncivil."

"What, because I said crap? What are you, some kind of hothouse flower? A sensitive poet?"

Abruptly he pushed back his chair and stood up. He took out his wallet and threw a check on my desk.

"Fuck this," he said, and stormed out.

I had probably lost a client I could ill afford to lose, over a matter small enough that most people in my profession or in the related profession of psychotherapy would have easily let pass. I asked myself whether it was worth it.

Yeah, it was.

I extracted a small sliced pizza from the mini fridge and took it to the window. Dark clouds had started to drift down among the buildings of Manhattan. The Jersey shore loomed barely visible, a jumble of indistinct shapes. I thought about my clients. Those who did best were the ones able and willing to think things out without letting their emotions cripple their thinking processes. Once on vacation from college I had my first experience of how wrong this crippling could go. My mother chain smoked. She wanted to quit but didn't know how. Knowing her to be a thrifty woman who would not spend money unless she felt it absolutely necessary, I proposed a solution. She'd owe me a dollar every time she smoked a cigarette. She thought it a great idea. On my next vacation a few months later I asked her how much she owed me. We'd come into the tiny kitchen. She looked away and fixated on the white top of the shoehorned washing machine.

"Nothing."

"Great! So it worked? You stopped smoking?"

My mother had a small, slight frame, a startling contrast to my father's hearty six feet plus. I spent my home years looking up at him and down at her.

"No." Her mouth trembled. She looked as if she might cry.

"Wait. I thought we agreed — "

She shook her head. "No. I can't do it."

"But we said...you said..."

"No. I can't stop. I don't want to."

I just stood there. I didn't know what to say. For every one of my eighteen years my mother always kept her promises. I could depend on her. My father erupted often, especially when work became particularly frustrating. But my mother was a rock.

She also loved poetry and felt deeply. I'm sure her awareness of my dismay at that moment in the kitchen cut her. She knew too that the money didn't enter into it at all and that my image of her had been shaken. She took out a cigarette and lit it with a single flick of her lighter. She took a few puffs, which seemed to settle her.

"It wasn't fair," she said around the cigarette.

Another first. She had never been given to non–sequiturs. But she was my mother, and she was hurting.

I didn't argue.

Could it be possible that she hadn't simply let her emotions overrule her reason? Maybe she had a physical dependency. Did that mean that when I, and her own reason, told her years in advance of the fact that she was killing herself, she could understand that and actually be unable to stop?

Science says it has no definitive answer, but free will is what makes us who we are. As the source of our power and whatever glory we may have, it can hurdle obstacles that seem insurmountable. The main thing is to never give up. Winston Churchill said it best, if not succinctly: "Never give in, never, never, never, never, in nothing great or small." He didn't. My lovely mother did, and so do some of my clients. But not all. Thankfully, not all.

I finished the pizza. To my delighted surprise, the last piece tasted as good as the first. According to the law of diminishing returns, that's not supposed to happen, and in my experience it never had until now.

Thank goodness for black swans.

24

I met Valerie Marsh at a coffee shop. She had telephoned shortly after Bernie Feld made his genteel exit, saying she didn't want to see me professionally but had a few things she wanted to ask me and something she wanted to tell me. She said I owed her for the time she spent answering my questions about Clara Thompson. I saw enough truth in this to agree to the meeting, so we sat in a booth with red leatherette banquettes, her with a latte, which apparently all coffee shops had on their menus post Starbucks, me with a huge iced coffee, black.

"Aren't you at all curious," Valerie said, "about why I decided not to see you professionally any more?"

While my curiosity fell far short of overwhelming, there was no need to be impolite and quantify my interest, so I nodded encouragingly.

"You probably think it's because you keep refusing my, ah, advances." She shook her head. "It has nothing to do with that, believe it or not. The real reason is that there's really nothing I need to talk about any more."

This seemed highly unlikely to the point of impossibility, but I felt locked into an ambiguous situation here. She and I no longer had a practitioner–client relationship, but neither were we friends.

"I see," I lied.

"My business is going great. I'm making more money than you would believe."

I, on the other hand, had probably just lost a client, and now she'd told me I'd lost another one. If I kept losing clients at this rate, maybe she'd give me a job as her bookkeeper.

I shifted to the end of the banquette so my back rested against the wood partition. "I believe it," I said, still waiting for her to get to the purpose of the meeting.

She ordered another latte. "Making a lot of money answers more questions than you might think."

"Uh huh." I threw back a jolt of strong black coffee. Nectar of the Gods compared to the stuff I made.

"Independence," she said. She put her cup on the green formica. "Freedom from not knowing where your next meal is coming from. Power, when you know you can buy whatever you want, well almost, and hire people to do things for you. Respect."

My eyebrows went up at this last, and she said, "Oh yes, respect. People don't know what I do for a living, but they can see I'm successful, and that's what respect is all about. Some people make it in life and some don't, and everyone respects the ones who make it and wants to be one of them."

"What do you say when people ask you what you do?"

"I make something up. Sometimes I say I'm a consultant. Sometimes a physical therapist. Sometimes an entrepreneur."

I couldn't resist. I guess I'm a compulsive p.p.

"It doesn't bother you that you feel you have to lie?"

"Why should it? Everyone lies. Besides, it gives me kind of a kick, because they're all true in a way, I'm all of those things, if you look at it right."

She took a delicate sip of her new latte while she eyed me over its top.

"What do you tell your friends? Your family?"

Her eyes clouded. She put her cup down carefully and pushed it a few inches away from her.

"I didn't come here to talk about me. I told you, that's all over."

I refrained from reminding her that that's all she'd been doing so far.

"I wanted to ask you something." Her words came out a little clipped. "It's kind of amusing, seeing what we've been talking about. But here it is. Why do you do what you do? All those hours you spend talking to people I'm sure you don't find very interesting. For what? I know it's not for the money. You'll never get rich doing what you do. So you don't work for the money, which I find kind of interesting, because I sure do, and so does everyone I know. But if you don't do it for the money and you don't do it because you meet interesting people, then why?"

"You're wrong about my clients. Of course some are more interesting than others, but their problems are always interesting. And helping them is satisfying." I paused. "And I like spending my time thinking about philosophy, and applying it."

"And psychology. You do a lot of that with your patients, right?"

I gave an inward sigh. I'd never break people of the habit of saying patient instead of client. Maybe the better part of valor was to stop trying.

"Yes. I like doing that too."

"But you don't have any training in it, right? Your degree is in philosophy."

"I took a few psych courses and I do some reading, but yes, my degree is in philosophy."

I took another swallow of coffee. This stuff was the strongest I'd ever tasted. It felt as if only seconds passed between swallowing and having my brain hit with a bolus of adrenaline. Who could ask for anything more?

"As I mentioned in my office, there's a lot of overlap. I use psychology and some psychologists use philosophy, even if they aren't aware of it and it's only implicit. Everyone, including therapists, has a philosophy, or a mish mash of philosophies, and it comes out in what they tell their clients."

Valerie seemed suddenly restless. She cradled her cup in her hands while she glanced around the shop. There wasn't much to see, just a couple of college kids on the couch at the far corner pounding away at their laptops and an old guy in a denim shirt and faded corduroys drinking alone and staring out the window. Valerie turned to me.

"The other reason I wanted to see you," she said, and stopped. She drained her cup in one long gulp.

"What I wanted to tell you, I mean, I thought you might want to know." She searched my face. "Clara Thompson. When she recommended I go to you, it was right before she disappeared. She said you were smart. But she seemed...I don't know. A little uncomfortable when she said it. Maybe that's not the right word."

"Uncomfortable in what way?"

"She had a funny kind of smile on her face like she liked talking about you, you know? Maybe uncomfortable was the wrong word. I don't know why I said that." She hesitated. "I thought you might want to know," she said again. "I stashed your address away somewhere, but when it turned up a while ago you weren't at that address so I went to the post office and asked them for your forwarding address, and that's when I came to see you."

I closed my eyes. As simple as that. I hoped the gun lady didn't think of it. Tomorrow I'd stop by the post office and rent a mailbox.

"Anything else you can remember? About Clara?"

"I'm sorry. Why is it so important?"

"Do you remember what you were talking about? Why did she think I could help you?"

She shrugged. "I was having a problem, and I guess I was a little blue. I'm always having problems. In my business, you can imagine." She grimaced. "No, maybe you can't. I don't remember which one I was having at the time."

"Why didn't you come to me then, when she gave you my name?"

"I don't know. I'm not even sure why I came when I finally did."

There didn't seem to be anywhere to go with that. I signaled for the check and when it came I left some money on the table.

Valerie opened her bag. "I'll pay. I invited you."

"No. You've helped me. And many thanks, by the way."

"I hope so," she said as we left. "Whatever your interest in Clara is."

I wondered if I would ever see her again.

***

The day before Sheila's arrival I spotted the gun lady. Or I should say we spotted each other, pretty much at the same time. After my last client session for the day I'd decided to treat myself to a meal at a small Chinese place just off Times Square, and afterward I walked a couple of blocks to the subway. I got there around ten minutes to six, so I knew I'd be caught in the rush, but I was only going a few stops and being a sardine for a few minutes isn't as bad as legend has it.

When the train ground to a halt at the Forty–Second street platform the doors spewed out a stream of humanity. A shoving crowd of commuters who wanted to be sure they wouldn't have to wait for the next train and waste maybe two and a half minutes of their lives bore me inside. After the third try the doors closed and we started moving.

I always try to stand near the door in crowded trains to minimize the chance of the doors closing at my stop before I can push my way out of the crowd, so I was looking out at the opposite track when I saw her, jammed into a car that was just starting to move out of the station in the other, downtown direction. I knew she saw me because our eyes met and hers got wide and in those few seconds before our steel cages whisked us off in opposite directions I watched her expression go from surprise to shock to glaring frustration. Then we flashed past each other and she disappeared.

25

Ipicked Sheila up at the airport, and in the taxi to my place I told her about yesterday's sighting.

"What was your reaction?" she said.

"I don't know. Shock, I guess. There wasn't time for anything else."

She nodded and placed her hand on my thigh. "What are you going to do?"

"How about we dump your luggage in the living room and jump into bed?"

"Good plan, but we have to get there first. What are you going to do about the gun lady?"

"Nothing. There's nothing I can do. I'm no closer to knowing anything about her than I was before. Although there are a couple of new developments."

I summed up my conversations with Sam Kashinsky and Valerie Marsh.

"So this Clara Thompson must have known you. Which means she must have met you. If she recommended you in your professional capacity, the obvious conclusion is that she was one of your clients."

"Except that I never had a client by that name. Or by the name of Courtney Felton, which is the name she gave to her customers."

"Her Johns."

"Yeah."

"So maybe she never met you and just recommended you because she heard about you from a friend."

I shrugged. From what Valerie had said, this didn't seem likely. But I supposed it was possible.

"A friend who was one of your patients," Sheila said.

"Clients."

"You could go over your old client files."

"And what? Call each one and ask them if they ever knew a Clara Thompson or a Courtney Felton? Call only the men and ask if they've been to a tall dark prostitute in the last few years?"

"Yeah, not too professional. And not something the men would appreciate being asked."

Sheila looked out her window for a little. She turned back to me.

"Tell me something. Did you ever fail? With a client?"

I looked at her, surprised.

"I don't always know." I reflected briefly. "There was a woman once, about eight years ago. I couldn't help her at all."

"I don't believe it."

I smiled. "Sorry to burst your bubble."

"What was wrong with her?"

"You mean what was her problem."

"I mean what was wrong with her. If she was a normal, functioning person she would have been helped."

"Nice to have a cheering section."

"So what's the answer."

"Well, she had a little trouble distinguishing the reality of the outside world from the reality she experienced in her mind." I paused. "She also had a few misconceptions about Einstein."

"So she was crazy."

"She thought time was unreal because two of her friends had just died and they were as clear in her mind as they were when they were alive. They didn't fade from her mind because they were dead. She said it was the same as if they'd moved to China. All that changed was that she couldn't see them face to face any more."

"She thought being dead was like moving to China?" Sheila shook her head pityingly. "What about the Einstein part?"

"She said Newton thought time was absolute, but he was wrong. Einstein proved it's relative. So, she said, that's all she was saying. If her friends were still young in her head, then they were young. Relative to her. If her dead friends were still alive in her head, then they were alive. Relative to her. And relative to her was all she knew."

"No wonder you couldn't help her."

"I tried to show her what was wrong with her concept of Einsteinian relativity."

"But you couldn't get through."

"A person has to be willing to reason with me."

Sheila nodded. She glanced at her watch.

"When do you start looking at apartments?" I asked.

"An hour and a half from now. The agent has two places she wants to show me today. I won't even bother to change. Just dump the bags and out the door."

"No hopping into bed first?"

She patted my leg. I took that as a no.

"You're welcome to come along."

I shook my head. "Let's leave it the way we discussed. I'll come when you've got it narrowed down."

She patted my leg again. This time I took it as a yes.

26

With Sheila out looking at apartments and Sam Kashinsky, I hoped, looking at databases, making phone calls, and tooling around the web, I relaxed a bit. I had my feet up on the desk, reading a new book by a philosopher whose thesis was that if we paid more attention to our feelings and less to what people called reality, we would find that reality would conform to our feelings.

The jangling of the phone gave me an excuse to stop reading. I tossed the book into the wastebasket and picked up the phone. Jeremy was calling to talk about coming to see me with his wife. I asked him again why he wanted to bring her.

"I still have feelings for her. When I ask you questions, I want her to hear the answers."

"What would be wrong with just coming yourself as usual and telling her about the session afterwards?"

"I can't remember everything. Besides it wouldn't be the same. I want her to hear it in real time."

"Why?"

"I want to see her reactions. Her spontaneous reactions."

"Jeremy, are you thinking of getting back together with her?"

A beat went by. "Yes. Maybe. I'm not sure, but I'm thinking about it."

"Does she know that?"

"I didn't tell her in so many words. But she probably knows. She's smart."

"Have you discussed this with her? Does she want to come along?"

"I was waiting to talk to you first. To make sure it was okay."

I mulled it over. As before, my first inclination was to say no, because I'm not a marriage counselor and have no desire to be one. Also Jeremy gave me no real reason for his wife to be there. Still, I couldn't see any harm. I always try to monitor myself to avoid being too rigid. Don't always succeed. I decided to go with it.

"All right. If she wants to come along, bring her next time."

"I'll find out when she's free and call you."

***

This was the second time Martin Marks had come along with his wife and son. They lined up before me in my three client chairs. Martin's chin now sported blue–black stubble. He either forgot to shave or felt he needed a new look in his middle age. Joel sat between his parents. Once again all three wore jeans and running shoes. These people had hit upon a wardrobe simplification program the whole family could share. Martin spoke first.

"So, I understand we have you to thank for my son turning into a gambler."

"Dad..." Joel began.

"What? You're not a gambler? You sit staring at that screen for hours at a time. What are you looking for? I'll tell you what you're looking for. A free lunch. Well, you can stop looking, boy. There are no free lunches, and the sooner you learn that, the better. There are no shortcuts in life."

He turned to me and opened his mouth to speak but turned back to his son again.

"You don't want to get addicted to this stuff, son. Believe me. Gambling is a disease. You'll make money when you're old enough to get a job. Until then just stick to your schoolwork. After you gradu-ate you'll go out and get a job like everyone else. You're only sixteen. Don't pick up any bad habits."

"I don't want to do what everyone else does," Joel said. "And I'm not gambling." He shifted his gaze to me, clearly wanting confirmation.

"There's a difference between gambling and investing," I said in a neutral tone.

Martin Marks' face darkened. "Wait a minute. Wait a minute. What kind of snake oil are you selling here? I bring the kid here for some guidance and you tell him to look for pie in the sky. Let me ask you, can you predict the stock market?"

"Not short term movements, no."

"And neither can anyone else, right?"

"I believe that's right."

"So when you buy stocks you can't know if you'll make money or lose money."

"Not for certain, no."

He leaned back and folded his arms. He looked at his son, then his wife, who looked away, then at me again.

"So it's a gamble, right? Fine. You want to gamble with your own money, go right ahead. But don't tell my son that gambling is an okay lifestyle."

Where to begin? Defining the difference between gambling and investing in terms of the criteria for picking one's stocks would be wasted here. Mindset was something he'd be more likely to relate to.

"If you look at the record, way back to the stock market's beginnings under the buttonwood tree in 1792, stocks have shown a strong upside bias over the long term. There can be some very sharp downward moves, but if you do your homework and buy stock in good businesses and hold on for the long term while the companies grow, chances are you'll do pretty well. That's not a gambler's psychology."

"Chances? You're talking about chances, and you're telling me it's not gambling?"

"I'd say taking a calculated risk when the odds are significantly in your favor is investing, not gambling."

Martin's mouth tightened. He sucked in his cheeks and folded his arms closer to his chest, almost hugging himself.

"If it's not certain, it's gambling."

I shook my head. "It's like everything else in life. Calculated risks are the best we've got."

Dorothy spoke for the first time. "That sounds right." Martin glared at her.

"He's right, dad," Joel said.

Martin got up abruptly.

"Let's go," he barked, and his family stood with him. At the door he turned back to me.

"I'm not paying for any more of this." And he slammed the door behind him.

27

J eremy Long's wife had long legs and red hair. She looked composed and attractive in a tan knee–length skirt and a green silk blouse open at the throat, displaying a necklace of three thin braided gold strands.

"This is Alice," Jeremy said. When he said nothing more I introduced myself. She inclined her head in acknowledgement.

"How do you do," she said in a rich contralto. She didn't seem nervous, which I found surprising, given her situation with her husband combined with the newness and awkwardness of discussing her private life with a stranger.

"Alice knows how I feel," Jeremy said. "There aren't any secrets. Everything I told you about the two of us I told her. She knows about my, um, ambivalence."

I looked at Alice, who simply nodded.

"So, how can I help?"

Alice said, "You're not a psychologist, right?"

"No, I'm not."

"Or a psychiatrist."

"No."

"So I don't suppose it would be helpful to ask you what you think is going on with my husband."

"At this point it might be more helpful to talk about what you're both feeling about each other," I suggested.

She fingered a bracelet on her wrist. "I don't mean to be rude, but as I understand it you're not a marriage counselor either."

Jeremy turned to her. "He's a smart guy, Alice. Otherwise I wouldn't have brought you here."

She seemed to consider this.

"Apparently we're going to pretend that you're both. With a few philosophical reflections thrown in whenever you think it appropriate."

I looked at Jeremy. He stared at his wife. Then he seemed to gather himself. "All cards are on the table. Alice and I have grown apart in the last few years. I was focused on business and she was busy with the kids, and we didn't have much time together and didn't have much to talk about. We sort of drifted apart and as you know a few weeks ago I moved out for a while — "

"Twelve days ago," she said.

He glanced at her, hunched his head forward in a gesture of acknowledgement, and soldiered on.

" — but I missed her and now I'm going to move back."

"It might be significant that you seem to know what you want after such a short a separation," I said.

Alice raised her chin. "It doesn't matter what he wants. Not unless I want it too."

Jeremy's features contracted into a deep frown. This was not going according to his expectations.

"What — "

His wife cut him off.

"Talk to me, Arthur, not to him. Tell me why you left. No, don't. Tell me why you want to come back."

Arthur's face turned red. Whether because his first name was now out in the open or because his wife had taken over I couldn't tell.

"He knew me as Jeremy," Arthur said thickly.

Now it was his wife's turn to look confused.

"What?"

"Never mind." He took a deep breath, then another.

"Okay. I want to come back because I miss you. I don't know what else to say. I was lonely."

She gave a minimal head shake. "Lonely is a kind of general term. You can be lonely without wanting to be with anyone in particular."

"I was lonely for you. I missed you."

She turned and faced him.

"Why? You just got finished saying how we drifted apart. How we didn't have much to say to each other. So what were you missing? And please don't say the sex."

Arthur's face reddened again, and he looked away toward the window. When he faced his wife again his voice had grown softer.

"I can't answer that. I just know I was lonely, and I missed you."

She continued shaking her head. "Not good enough. Fourteen years of marriage, you walk out on me and your two children and twelve days later you want to waltz back in again and expect me to welcome you with open arms as if nothing happened?"

A beat of silence hung in the air. Arthur opened his mouth and closed it, then tried again.

"What do you want me to say?"

She considered him. "Please think about this before you answer. Don't say anything off the top of your head." She turned her body so she was facing him squarely, her profile to me.

"Tell me why you think I'd want you back."

He gaped at her. Here he was, a powerful businessman with big bucks to calling all the shots. Now his world had tilted, like a ship that encountered rough seas beyond what the designers planned for. His desires controlled his world, not anyone else's. Others proposed, he disposed. Until now, when his wife suddenly revealed unplumbed depths of character and will.

He decided to play the role of the aggrieved party.

"This is preposterous. It's also embarrassing. You know what I've given you. The house, the cars, financial security. How many women can say they have that? How many men, for that matter? I've done my part and I've done it in spades. You're not involved with anyone else, I presume. So what's this all about?"

Alice looked at him sadly, then at me.

"You haven't said much."

"Arthur," I said, and he winced at my use of his real name, "I think Alice is focusing on your feelings for her, which she's implying have a lot to do with whatever feelings she has for you."

Alice clasped her hands in her lap. "Thank you."

Arthur turned to her. "I told you I missed you. Isn't that enough? That's why I came back. What do you want me to say? That I love you? Come on, Alice. That's kid stuff. It's what you say when you're just out of school and you're a walking hormone factory. But then you get married and have kids and you do the best you can and after fourteen years if you can say you miss your wife after being away from her for twelve days, that's as good as it gets. What else do you want from me?"

Alice regarded him for several moments.

"I want a divorce," she said quietly.

***

After Jeremy/Arthur left, trailing along behind his wife as if unsure how to approach her now, I made two quick calls. One was to Tracers. Sam Kashinsky told me he hadn't found any leads on Clara Thompson yet but was optimistic. This did not provide me with much comfort since no leads meant to me no reason for optimism, but I let it pass. No point in getting him defensive. Besides, a positive attitude is essential for getting things done. Especially difficult things such as finding someone who probably doesn't want to be found.

I next called my friend Burt Lidsky. I gave his secretary my name and he came on the phone instantly.

"Hey," he said. I knew he was probably staring at a computer screen watching flashing red and green numbers that told him whether to buy yen and short dollars or buy dollars and short yen, and the same for all the other currencies and stocks he played with. He wouldn't want to stay on the phone long, but what I had to tell him wouldn't take long.

"Hey. Just wanted you to know Sheila's in town."

"Sheila? What's she here for, a promo for one of her films? Wait, don't tell me, are you by any chance seeing her again?"

"We're going to live together. For a while."

"Jesus Christ. How did you manage that? After all these years. Well, Jesus, my hat's off to you, fella."

"I thought we might get together. The four of us."

"Absolutely. Listen, I can't talk now, but I'll check with Nancy and get back to you. We'll set it up."

I hung up and went to meet Sheila at an Indian restaurant I knew on Columbus. I found her waiting in a booth at the far end of the room in one of her disguises. She had on a kerchief that hid most of her hair, no lipstick and round tortoise shell glasses which she didn't need.

"I can't remember the last time I saw anyone in a kerchief," I said as I sat down.

She smiled. "Hello to you too. And how was your day?"

"It's unusual enough that it might attract attention, which I don't think was your plan."

"I'll chance it."

She rested her hand on my forearm. "Ask me if I found anything interesting."

"Did you find anything interesting?"

"As it happens, I did."

"Wow. That was fast."

"My agent has a pretty specific idea of what I'm looking for."

"Is it just interesting, or is it something you love?"

"I'll tell you after you've seen it."

"Okay. How about tomorrow lunchtime?"

"How about today after I have some tandoori chicken under my belt?"

"At night?"

I looked at my watch. Five twenty–four. The sun already sat low on the horizon over New Jersey. We probably wouldn't meet up with the agent for a couple of hours.

"Shouldn't I see it in daylight?"

"You will. In the meantime, the sooner I get my chicken, the sooner we can go."

***

The real estate agent, a bleached blonde of uncertain years, had flawless makeup and projected a perky cheerfulness that seemed real. She was polite and appeared competent, and if she treated us any differently because of Sheila's fame I didn't see it.

She showed us an apartment on the thirteenth floor of a building on West Fifty–Ninth, which isn't called West Fifty–Ninth but Central Park South in deference to the fact that it runs the whole southern length of the park and sounds a lot tonier than West Fifty–Ninth. Using the same logic, the western border is called Central Park West, but the logic breaks down on Fifth Avenue, which should be Central Park East upwards of Fifty–Ninth but instead clings stubbornly to its identity as Fifth Avenue, probably because the powers that be once decided that the worldwide fame of Fifth Avenue conveys even more prestige than Central Park. They were probably right, because the decision had never been revisited.

Apartment number 1300 had at least three times the space of mine. More space, I thought, than two people needed. I remarked on this to Sheila as we stood in the huge living room gazing out at the park while the agent remained discreetly in the background.

"Yes," she said, "but there's a difference between needing and wanting."

I nodded. Truth is hard to argue with. I decided to defer the question of cost until we were alone.

On the elevator down the agent said, "The view is so spectacular. You can see forever, the whole length of the park. You can watch the seasons change so it would never be boring. I'd love to live here myself."

"I don't know if I could live on the thirteenth floor," I deadpanned.

She looked startled. Her eyes widened and her mouth opened but she didn't know what to say. Sheila came to her rescue.

"He's kidding."

"Oh." She gave a little relief laugh. "You know, this is one of the few buildings that actually has a thirteenth floor. Most go from twelve to fourteen."

"That says something," I said.

"Yes it does," she replied.

I suspected we might not agree on exactly what it said but we had reached the lobby and I thanked her for showing us the apartment and Sheila said she'd get back to her and we both shook her hand and started walking west. Sheila took my arm at the elbow.

"Is there a place nearby we can have dessert and talk?"

Fifty–Sixth is lined with restaurants on both sides. I told her to pick one. She hugged my arm tighter. "So, what did you think?"

"I thought you wanted to wait till we got to the restaurant."

"Come on, spill it."

I wanted to choose my words carefully, but I didn't come up with much.

"We're kind of back at the beginning."

"Uh oh."

As we turned up Fifty–Sixth I said, "I probably can't afford half that rent."

"I thought you were going to think that issue through."

"Yeah, well, I didn't come up with any easy answers. Are you looking at the restaurants?"

"The one across the street. The Greek."

We crossed the street and went in. "Just dessert," I told the hostess. After we ordered, I said, "About that difference between needing and wanting. How about going for just what we need. We could probably find a place the right size in the building we just saw, or if not one very much like it, with the same view if that's something that's important to you."

Sheila gave my hand a little squeeze.

"I went through all that when I was just starting out. It was cramping and limiting and depressing. I had to limit the clothing I could buy and the food I ate and the space I could live in. I couldn't afford a car or travel or restaurants. I had to count every penny. It got old pretty fast. I don't have to live that way any more, Eric. And I don't want to, so help me out here."

We were silent for a while. Neither of us knew what to say next. Sheila tried first.

"Like you said, we're kind of back at the beginning."

"Yeah."

The waitress brought our desserts, baklava for both of us.

"Just let go of your double standard," Sheila said. "Look, I know it's hard."

Was she patronizing me? If so I deserved it. Some atavistic ancestor in me was fighting with teeth and claws. The rational part of me knew Sheila was right. It kept trying to put the atavistic part in its place and having a hard time of it. I speared a forkful of baklava and let a little honey drip off.

"Tell you what. Find the smallest place you could be happy with. I'll chip in whatever I can afford. But I won't be able to afford half, so I'll owe you the difference between half the rent and the amount I can afford."

"Fine. Great. Deal."

"Hang on. I want to be clear. That debt might be outstanding for a long time. Because I don't know where the money will come from to pay it off."

"I don't care if it never gets paid off. You know that."

"Yes, but I care."

"I know." She leaned over and kissed my cheek.

"I will pay you back. I can't tell you how long it will take, but I will do it."

"Okay. Let's not talk about it any more."

"How about we walk back home and fool around a little," I said.

"How about we take a taxi."

So we did.

*****

When your nights are fulfilling, the problems of the day seem to fade, maybe not to insignificance, but to pale versions of their former selves, like images in a mud puddle. Sheila and I had talked and made love far into the night. I was at peace. My problems with the gun lady seemed far away.

I was in my office reading my underlinings in Becker's *Denial Of Death* when Diana Rogers called. Becker got a Nobel prize for his work. He claimed we went about our business as if our lives would last forever, pushing away thoughts of our own death as if death might happen to others but never to us, because if we didn't, if we kept at the forefront of our minds the realization that one day we would cease to exist, we would not be able to function. We would lose the incentive to ever do anything. We might even go mad. I thought he was probably right about most people, though not about all.

"I won't be coming to see you any more," Diana said, her words rushing together. "I wanted to tell you why. It's because I'm happy now."

"I'm glad to hear that, Diana. Not that I won't be seeing you, but that you're happy."

"Don't you want to know why?"

"Sure."

"I'm getting married. Bruce asked me, and I said yes."

"Well, that's terrific. I wish you all the best. And if you ever decide you want to talk some more, you know where to find me."

"We're looking for a house. Out in Queens. We looked at Brooklyn Heights, but you get more for your money in Queens."

"Found anything you like yet?"

"Oh, lots. There are so many choices. It's hard to settle on just one and say this is it and let all the rest go."

"I'm sure you'll make a good choice."

"I hope you're not mad or anything."

"Diana, why would I be mad? I'm happy for you. Really."

"Well, all right, then. It's been nice knowing you. I mean it."

"Thanks for calling and letting me know. And again — best wishes and congratulations."

I hoped I'd helped her and that she'd be happy. She still had problems, sure, but she understood some things now that she hadn't before, and if each of us could keep saying that as our lives progressed, how much else was there?

I stood looking out at the clouds for a while, thinking about losing another client at just the time my expenses were about to go up. I might have to owe Sheila more than I thought for longer than I thought and I hated that idea. I could liquidate my stock portfolio but I hated that idea too. It had been hard putting aside the little money I managed to save over the years and my portfolio, though small, gave me a sense of security I didn't want to lose. Not that that made too much sense if I was going to go into debt over the rent. Well, no sense brooding about it. I'd either get some new clients soon enough to help out my straining finances or I wouldn't. And at least I was pretty sure I could sublet my apartment quickly.

A pigeon with iridescent purple and green neck feathers fluttered down on my window ledge and cocked a beady eye at me. It stood no more than a couple of feet away but showed no fear. Somehow it knew there was a barrier between us, although I didn't know how since so many birds killed themselves crashing into plate glass windows that they apparently mistook for air. Of course there were many more birds that didn't crash into windows. Maybe it had something to do with the angle of the light, which could change the reflections the bird saw. Or didn't see. Or maybe only sick ones crashed.

I left the pigeon to whatever urgent pigeon business brought him to my ledge and picked up the phone. I wanted to check in with my father. I had no way of knowing how lucid he would be, but if he was lucid I wanted him to know I was still there for him.

He answered on the second ring. The attendants had told me he spent a lot of time in his room watching television or reading. When I asked them what they meant by a lot, they said maybe it wasn't really a lot, he just sometimes liked to watch TV in his room rather than in the communal lounge.

"Hello." His voice sounded hollow, as if he were talking through a muffler.

"Hi, dad. How are you doing?"

Silence. This might not be a lucid day.

"Dad?"

Silence.

"Dad, are you still there?"

"He died."

"What?" My heart jumped. Was someone telling me my father was dead? No, impossible. Even though his voice sounded a little strange I knew that voice. I'd heard it all my life.

"Dad? Who died? A friend of yours?"

I heard him breathing. "Maury."

"Maury? One of your friends? Did you know him a long time?"

"Long time," he repeated. I waited for him to go on.

"Was he a childhood friend, dad? Someone you went to school with?"

"Always trying to impress him. Now he's dead."

"Was it someone you were close to?"

"Now he's dead."

"Dad, do you need me there? Should I get on a plane?"

"In the end it didn't matter."

He wasn't responding to me. Maybe he just wanted someone on the other end of the phone to listen to him. I waited. I listened to him breathe. I started to say something to prompt him when I heard a click. The line went dead. I dialed his number again and heard it ring ten times before I gave up.

I needed to go down to see him again. Soon.

28

Sometimes when I think about a problem and I'm not getting anywhere and I want to kick it back to my subconscious to work on for a while I take out the chess set in my office drawer and play against myself. I had another set in my apartment.

My father's words troubled me. When he was confused I had no idea what he experienced because he couldn't tell me, and in his more lucid moments his moods seemed darker and darker. I didn't know what to do about it. I suspected I could do nothing, but I thought I'd let my subconscious poke away at it while I moved the pieces around. After half an hour of getting myself in and out of chessic complications my subconscious hadn't yet come up with anything so I put the pieces away and called Sheila on her cell.

"Are you free?"

"I could give you the names of some movie producers who'd laugh in your face."

"Can you meet me at the park, the Central Park South and Fifth entrance?"

"I'm in Bloomingdale's. I can be there in fifteen minutes."

I found her perched daintily on a bench under a tree just inside the entrance, her face and sunglasses dappled by the light dancing down from the shifting canopy of leaves overhead. She had on a royal blue velour running outfit, light blue Nikes with a red swoosh, and a floppy blue denim hat. As I approached she rose and smiled and took my arm and we started walking.

"This is no walk in the park," I said, trying to lighten my own mood. It didn't work.

"Could have fooled me. Let's walk through the zoo. I love zoos."

I told her about my conversation with my father.

"Eric, he's how old now? Over eighty–five? He's lived his life and he's come to his own conclusions about it. His feelings have been hardening all those years. He's not going to change now."

She looked up at me. Her eyes were kind, her voice soft. "There's nothing you can do."

We entered the zoo gates and stopped at the railing surrounding the seal habitat. We'd come at feeding time, which seemed to be an event. Clusters of people grouped at the section of railing directly opposite where the attendant, in thigh high rubber waders, tossed fish from a bucket high in the air near the seals, which swam over and snatched them before they hit the water. They never missed. We watched until the bucket was empty. When the fish stopped coming one seal swam over to the attendant and started barking like a hoarse foghorn. The attendant upended the empty bucket to show the seal and the barking stopped. Smart animal.

"Where next?" I said.

"The polar bear."

I put my hand over hers on my arm. "He's with people his own age, his needs are taken care of, and the staff treats him well. And there's a doctor on the premises."

"Yes, and you call him and visit him."

"Yeah."

"You've done all you can do."

We walked for a while in silence. A light breeze played with the hair that stuck out under her hat. I reached over and pushed a tendril away from the corner of her mouth. Where the pavement ended at the sides of our path little dust devils whirled and died in the bare patches where no grass grew.

The polar bear lumbered out of his cave and began playing with a tire in his swimming hole. He threw it into the water, dove in after it, retrieved it, and repeated the process. After he did this a few times he tired of it and stretched out on the rocks outside the cave, face turned toward the sun, eyes closed against the glare. With the bear supine, people started moving off, hoping to find more energetic animals to entertain them. We went with them.

"I've found another place," Sheila said.

"Ah."

"Central Park South again, overlooking the park. You can see it from here." She pointed. "Look between those two trees. The white brick near the end of the block."

"It meets the requirements we discussed?"

She gave me an injured look.

"Yes. You'll love it."

I nodded. "What do you want to see next?"

"Don't you want to ask me anything? What floor, how many rooms, how much rent?"

"Tell me later."

She looked at me and made a moue with her mouth.

"In that case, take me to the tigers."

"I don't think they have tigers here."

"Lions, then. Panthers. I like big cats."

"I'll see what I can scare up."

***

The effects of my conversation with my father lingered into the next day so when Dorothy Marks came to see me in the afternoon I had to make an extra effort to concentrate.

Dorothy came alone. She had on a gold silk blouse which went well with her red hair and a tan skirt which ended modestly below her knees. The running shoes had been replaced by light brown pumps with a dark brown stripe along the sides.

"I wanted to thank you. Joel is a changed boy. So far he's read six investment books from the library. I think he's going to go through their whole collection." She gave a little laugh.

"Sounds like he's checking out whether he likes any system better than Warren Buffet's," I said.

"I wouldn't know about that. I'm just happy he's happy, and it's all due to you."

"What does Martin think?"

"Well, you probably know. You saw him when he was here."

"Is he giving Joel a hard time?"

She clasped her hands in her lap.

"You have to understand about Martin. He may seem hard, but he's really a good man. Joel is his only son, his only child, and he wants the best for him. You must understand that he's doing what he thinks is right. He has Joel's best interests at heart."

She hesitated, looked at the wall to her right, then back at me.

"Sometimes he makes mistakes. Sometimes he doesn't see things. He's not perfect. But he's under a lot of pressure. He tries his best. He works hard to support us, and he loves his son. Truly."

"Okay."

"I know it looks bad with him not letting Joel come see you any more. But actually, you've helped Joel so much, he's got so much direction now with this investment thing, he really doesn't need to come back here any more. He's a changed boy."

"Martin doesn't mind him reading those books?"

"He doesn't like it, but it isn't as if he can stop the boy from going to the library the way he can stop him from seeing you. The library is free."

I nodded. Dorothy Marks' face relaxed and her eyes softened.

"Martin even bought Joel a dog the other day. He thought maybe Joel needed some companionship."

"Joel never mentioned wanting a dog," I said.

"It was all Martin's idea."

I put my hands on the edge of the desk. "As long as Joel is okay with the responsibility. It's a lot of work. Training, exercising, feeding. Looking after the dog's health."

Dorothy smiled.

"No, see, that's where Martin was so smart. He knew Joel might not want to do all that, so he solved that whole problem."

"He did?"

"He bought Joel a dog that didn't need all that." She paused for effect.

"Martin bought Joel a robot dog." She looked proud.

"It even comes with a remote control."

29

We had dinner with Burt Lidsky and his wife Nancy at a place on West Fifty–Seventh called simply, Nine. We had a quiet booth away from the bar and the kitchen. Nancy seemed thrilled to be dining with Sheila, who kept getting covert glances from everyone in the room because I prevailed upon her to drop the cloak and dagger stuff for this occasion. I found it only mildly annoying because she'd warned me and I'd been expecting it.

Burt was oblivious to everyone but Sheila. They spent most of the meal reminiscing about college and catching up on each other's lives, although much of Sheila's was in the public domain due to all the news coverage and magazine articles about her. Nancy and I took it patiently and managed to get a little conversation in edgewise during the infrequent pauses. When the meal ended Sheila and I stopped off to visit the furnished sublet she found. We could move in the day after tomorrow. The place had tasteful modern furnishings and lots of wood paneling, a new kitchen of mainly brushed chrome, and an unobstructed view of the park, a Central Park South trademark. I complimented her on her choice, asked about the cost, and managed to keep a straight face when she told me. I had resolved not to tell her how my client list had wound down and what that did to my income. I'd made a deal and I'd stick to it. Bellyaching about it was not an option.

***

I had no appointments at all the next day but I went to my office anyway, partly out of habit, partly because walk–ins were always a possibility. As soon as I got in I called Sam Kashinsky and asked him if he learned anything.

"You know how many Clara Thompsons are in the New York City phone book?" he asked.

"No."

"Would you believe a hundred and sixty two?"

"She won't be in the phone book. I told you that."

"I know you did, but you might be wrong."

"I'm not wrong. I told you what she did for a living. Even I have an unlisted number, and I'm not nearly as secretive as she is."

"Yeah, well, I'm just jerking your chain a little. Actually, weird as it seems, there are none. Not a single one. But I checked other databases to see if I could find a Clara Thompson in any of them."

"And?"

"Had to go through a lot of databases. Thank God for the internet."

"Give me a break here, Sam."

"I found two who might fit. Looked at graduates of local high schools and colleges. One Clara Thompson is a college graduate, the other a high school graduate. Both about the right age and height, from what you told me, but only one might be a brunette. The other is listed in the DMV as a blonde. On the other hand with women you never know about hair color. She could have started out life as a brunette. So they could both be brunettes."

"No listing for the other?"

"Apparently doesn't own a vehicle."

"She the high school grad? The one without a car?"

"Yeah."

"You got addresses?"

"Sure. I'll give you the high school grad first. Keep in mind, though, this is old data. The address for the blonde is up to date, but the high school kid's listing in her yearbook is from ten years ago. I had to take a guess, the address is probably her parents'."

"Thanks, Sam."

I wrote down the addresses, started to replace the phone in its cradle, and brought it up to my mouth again.

"Nice work."

On the other end of the line there was a grunt, then a click.

***

The ten–year–old address for the high school grad who might or might not be a brunette was in Brooklyn, on East Forty–Ninth street between Clarkson Avenue and Lenox Road. It turned out to be a nar-row semi–attached brick building, half a block from Kings County Hospital. I walked past a small garden between the brick house and its identical neighbor and up a high red brick stoop. I had no guaran-tee that anyone would be home, but I didn't want to call ahead and risk being told by the parents not to bother coming by. That is, if the parents still lived there. Nevertheless this was my best lead, and I thought it worth a subway ride.

A locked aluminum screen door protected the wooden door and bell. I rang, then stepped back to appear less intimidating.

A gray haired woman with a sagging throat but fairly youthful face opened the inner door. She could have been anywhere between forty–five and sixty. She wore a pink dress with large red flowers which ended above her kneecap and might have been appropriate for a woman of twenty–five or thirty. In her left hand was a tumbler half filled with a colorless liquid. There was always the possibility that it was water.

Nah.

I smiled my most disarming smile.

"Mrs. Thompson?"

She gave me a blank stare, not making any move to open the screen door.

I tried again.

"Mrs. Thompson? I'm here about your daughter Clara. If I could have a moment of your time?"

A momentary spark in her eyes at the mention of her daughter's name, but then the dead stare returned.

"You knew Clara?"

"I'm not sure. I know this sounds strange, but someone I know claims I knew her, and, well, this person seems to think we had some kind of relationship. It's possible she might have been using a different name. I'd like to get in touch with her, see if I can get to the bottom of this, so I came here hoping you could help me out."

She blinked at me. "What?"

"Mrs. Thompson, I'm trying to find Clara. Can you tell me where she is?"

She looked at me for a few moments, then tilted her head back, drained the rest of the tumbler, and inspected it. Then she looked at me, licked her lips once and said, "You want a drink of water?"

"Yes. Thank you."

Progress. She was going to invite me in.

"Wait here."

She wasn't going to invite me in. Closing the door in my face, she disappeared inside, returning shortly with a glass of ice water in one hand and a book in the other. She cracked the screen door, handed me the glass, and retreated behind the screen.

"I haven't seen my daughter in five years."

"I'm sorry. Do you know where she is?"

"If I knew I'd have seen her in five years."

"Yes. Of course." I drank up to buy thinking time.

"I don't think you knew Clara."

I didn't know what to say beyond repeating myself, which didn't seem productive.

"It's complicated," I said lamely.

"Yeah, you told me." She snaked her hand out for my empty glass.

We stood there looking through the screen at each other. Finally she came to a decision. She put the glass on the floor and opened up the book to the last page. It was an album.

"This is the last picture I had of my Clara." She held the page up to the screen.

I recognized the picture immediately. I knew her several years ago. But not as Clara Thompson or Courtney Felton. The name she used was Cathy Stone, and yes, she had been a client of mine.

"You know her? Yes or no."

"Yes."

She pushed out her lips, fishlike, as if considering whether to believe me.

"You find her, you let me know," she said, and shut the door in my face again without waiting for an answer.

I had just had a peek at Cathy/Courtney/Clara's earliest role model.

***

My stubborn status as possibly the last man in Manhattan without a cell phone finally did me in. Maybe everyone else was right and I was wrong. I had to wait the length of a subway ride to our new home on the park before I could call Sam Kashinsky. I gave him Clara Thompson's original home address and told him the name she used when I had her as a client. I gave him a physical description. I told him her mother said she'd been missing for five years.

"That might help," he said.

"You think so?"

"I said might. It narrows things down a little. On the other hand it might not. Especially if she changed her name again."

"All you can do is try."

"Hey, that's my line," he said.

We hung up and I went to the kitchen where I found a note from Sheila propped up on the table. She had gone shopping. Circe, as usual, followed me into the kitchen. She wasn't happy. Moving to a new location is hard for a cat. Even the new furniture is threatening. The pieces she used to be familiar with were still in my apartment, which I hoped to sublet for the planned six–month duration of the trial arrangement. In an unfamiliar place cats never knew what cat-eating monsters could be lurking in a nook or cranny just around the corner. Every now and then, when the enormity of the danger hit her full force, she let out a low wail.

So I opened a can of her favorite food. She sniffed at it and dug right in. Distracting a cat for a while is easy because they have a lot of trouble resisting whatever stimulus is in front of their face. Lots of people are like that too. One of the defining marks of intelligence is how much a person is influenced by abstractions as opposed to the concrete of the moment. And of course the new connections he or she makes among those abstractions.

Except that some people have no idea how the abstractions they use are tied to the real world. In effect, they live in a dream world. Compared to them Circe's way might not be so bad after all.

I thought about my own reaction to the move. While unfamiliarity is a danger signal for animals, humans are able to view it as excitement and opportunity. The new apartment was right across the street from beautiful, lush Central Park and much closer to my office and almost everything else I liked walking to in New York. The public library. The IBM and SONY atriums. The shops lining Fifth, Fifty–Seventh, and Madison. The Plaza hotel. The Whole Foods on Columbus Circle. The Apple store a block away. Rents had shot to nosebleed heights in this neighborhood for a reason. Everyone wanted to live here.

Having decided I was going to like it here, I went back to the living room to wait for Sheila, who with perfect timing arrived as I settled on the couch. She carried a Bergdorf Goodman shopping bag which held a package big enough to hold any of a number of costly items, but knowing her penchant for shoes probably contained shoes.

I gave her a hello kiss.

"What's in the bag?"

"Shoes."

She once told me how many pairs of shoes she owned. It was a very large multiple of the number of feet she had. I had four pair. Three black, one brown. Five, if you included my running shoes, which you probably should since I used them for walking rather than running.

"You don't have enough?"

"Remember our conversation about needing and wanting?"

"Yep."

"So?"

"Why don't you stash the shoes. I have a few things to tell you."

When she came back to the living room I told her about my trip to Brooklyn, the picture I'd seen of my former client, and my call to Sam Kashinsky.

"What are you going to do?"

"Any suggestions?"

"Well, you wanted to find out who Clara Thompson was so you could figure out why the gun lady wanted to kill you, right?"

"Yes."

"So now you know Clara Thompson was a client. Did anything unusual happen during any of your sessions with her?"

"No, not that I recall."

"Which? No, or not that you recall?"

"What's the difference? I only know what I can recall."

The couch was on a raised platform to allow a better view of the park, and if we looked to our left we could see the sun starting to slide behind the buildings on Central Park West.

"You don't have notes?"

"Actually I do. I'll look them over tomorrow, but I really don't need to. I remember her very well. I remember why she came to me and what we talked about."

"And? Anything that would explain why some woman you never saw before threatens to kill you, which you take seriously enough to keep wearing that silly gun?"

"Silly gun?"

"Well, don't you feel a little silly wearing it every day?"

The sun had just about gone now and the streetlights had come on. Circe finished her meal and went into stealth mode, slinking through the living room to keep a low profile to the monsters. I reached down and petted her as she crept past me. She paid no attention.

"Maybe just a little."

"I'm not sure I'm with the program here. The gun is supposed to be for self defense, in case the gun lady finds you, right?"

"Yeah."

"But you're trying to find her before she finds you. Suppose you do. Then what? You take out your gun and shoot her?"

"I was thinking I'd try to talk to her."

"What if she doesn't want to talk? What if she opens her purse or wherever she keeps her gun and takes it out when she sees you?"

"If I'm pointing my gun at her she's not going to do that."

"A rational person wouldn't do that. But from what you've told me this isn't the most rational person in the world."

"True."

"So, what if she goes for her gun? What would you do?"

I looked at her. She could be like a bulldog sometimes, which would turn a lot of men off. I loved it.

"That thought has occurred to me. I don't have an answer yet."

"You bought a gun for self defense and you don't know if you'd pull the trigger?"

"If I thought it was me or her, I'd pull the trigger."

She nodded. "Sorry. I didn't mean to sound like a cross–examination. I just wanted to know."

"And you wanted me to be clear on it."

"Yes."

"Suppose we give it a rest now."

"Sure. What would you like to do?"

I smiled at her.

"Oh. That."

"Silly question."

"Apparently," she said as we moved off to the bedroom, getting in what would be the last word for quite a while.

30

Since I now knew Clara Thompson's identity, at least a possibility existed that in any future confrontation with the gun lady that knowledge could help me, even if I didn't know how. Small progress, but progress.

My new apartment's location, an easy walk to my office, made life a little easier. In the morning I arrived ten minutes before my appointment with Jeremy / Arthur.

"My real name is Arthur Kravitz," the man I once knew as Jeremy Long said. He had abandoned his usual dark suit and tie for unpressed chinos and a sport shirt done in blue–brown tattersall which had a couple of days worth of wrinkles. At least three days of stubble shadowed his face. The hairs on his chin had grown in gray.

"I'm on vacation. I took a week off."

"Why are you telling me your full name?"

He shrugged. "It doesn't matter any more."

"Why did it matter before, and not now?"

He draped his right arm across the back of the chair next to him. He spoke in a flat voice.

"I was trying to protect myself before. She left me, you know. She filed for divorce."

"I'm sorry."

He nodded. "You wonder what it was all for, you know? The years of school, the years of work, the years bringing up the kids, all of it."

"Any chance she'll change her mind?"

"No. I tried. Believe me, I tried. I reminded her of how we first met, all the years we had together, all the good times. I told her it would be bad for the kids, which I believe. Broken homes are hard on kids, and I know she cares about them. She loves them. She's a good mother."

"But she wasn't convinced."

"She just kept saying it was over. Nothing I could say made any difference. I'm still living in a hotel."

"A whole lot of people have been through divorces and come out the other side," I said.

"So? What are you saying, I shouldn't care? It hurts, dammit!"

"It's hard, but it's not the end of the world if you can't get her back. I know you're in pain now, but sometimes a longer term perspective helps."

"What do you mean, *if* I can't get her back? I just told you how it is."

"You also told me how you tried to change her mind. So I can kind of figure out what you didn't say."

"What, all that 'I love you' stuff? That's embarrassing, you know that? That's such an overused word, it doesn't mean anything any more. It means different things to different people. If ten different people tell a woman they love her, they mean ten different things by it. I'm not going to get into that nonsense. I already told her how I feel. I'm feeling lonely and I'm feeling I miss her and I'm feeling I want her back. What else does she want from me? That's me. That's all of me. That's all there is."

"But it wasn't enough."

He sagged. "No."

"Go through it again for me. Why you want her back. What you told her."

"I just told you."

"I know, but maybe you could tell me a little more."

He gave a deep sigh and spread his hands on his thighs. "What do you expect me to say? It's no different than a million other men.

We've been married fourteen years. We had three kids together. We had a lot of good times. We could have had a lot more."

"Arthur, I heard what you said about overuse of the word love, and I agree with most of it. But tell me this. If I ask you what the word means to you, just you, forget about what it may mean to other people, what would you say?"

He sat back and looked up at the ceiling, as if the answer were printed there.

"It's wanting to be with someone. Caring what happens to them. With a man and a woman, wanting to touch and have sex. Wanting to share when good things happen. Someone to listen and care when bad things happen. Laughing together. Liking the same music and books and movies and plays. Feeling good when the other person walks into a room."

He pulled his gaze from the ceiling and looked at me.

"You're going to tell me I should have told her this."

"Might be worth a try."

He fixed his gaze on the wall behind me for a long time. He ran his tongue along his lips. Then he nodded.

***

After Jeremy left I had some free time, so when Sally Carter called and asked if she could drop by for a few minutes I said yes. She arrived a little breathless and began talking as soon as she was seated.

"I decided you're right. I need a purpose again. I'm going back to making documentaries. Although I have to say I'm not at all sure I'll be able to make a difference."

"You don't know that. And besides, it doesn't really matter all that much, as we've said. What matters is doing what you love and doing it the best way you know how."

"But if I don't succeed?"

I shook my head.

"If it turns out well, great. It's an added bonus. But however it turns out, you did your best. That's all there is."

Sally didn't answer for a while. Then she spoke, measuring her words.

"Even though I know it's going to take a lot of work raising the money and hiring the right people, and even though I don't know if any of the films will be good or if I'll be able to get distribution deals, and even though I'm scared, one thing outweighs all that."

"I think I can guess."

She beamed me a luminous smile.

"I'll have a reason to get out of bed in the morning. I came to tell you that."

***

When Sally left I punched in the phone number for the management office of my father's retirement home. He'd been reasonably lucid last time we spoke, but he'd been depressed, and he didn't seem to be enjoying himself during his increasingly rare lucid episodes. If there was no enjoyment left, what was the point? I didn't want to think that way, but I had to talk to a person there who saw him every day. Maybe they could tell me something I didn't know that might help me to help him. Or that would make me see I had it wrong and he was all right after all.

A woman answered. I recognized her voice immediately. It belonged to Susan Harris, an oversized black lady who favored colorful neckerchiefs and radiated friendliness. She seemed to truly enjoy helping the residents when they came to her with problems and requests. If their room was too hot or too cold, if a machine in the exercise room stopped working, if a vegetarian got a meat meal by mistake, if the valve on a faucet stopped working, she took care of it with a smile. I never saw her patronize anyone. The residents seemed to love her.

"Oh, he's fine," she told me after I'd introduced myself. "No problems."

"He seemed a little depressed the last time I spoke to him,".

"Oh, no. At least not that I can see. I mean, he eats with his friends at the dinner table and takes walks with them sometimes, just like before. Sometimes he has a bad day and he'll be a little withdrawn, but you mustn't read too much into that. It's something that happens with all the residents, you know. It's their age. Nothing's wrong. It's just that their attention wanders and their moods are unpredictable. It doesn't mean anything, really. Your father is fine."

"When did you last see him?"

"Just now. About half an hour ago."

"Is he around? Can I speak to him?"

"I can get him if you want, but I'd suggest you call another time. He's in the common room watching his favorite TV show with some of his friends."

I thanked her, hung up, leaned back in my chair with my hands clasped behind my head and my eyes closed, and wondered whether she really knew more about my father's state of mind than I did. I wanted to think so, but I knew she couldn't spend any time with him one on one. She saw him only in a group setting. Not much comfort there. I'd need to fly down and see him again.

31

Circe started in on me as soon as I entered the apartment.

"She jumped right off my lap and went to the door a couple of minutes before you came," Sheila said from one of the sling–back chairs. She looked stunning in anything. Today she managed it in gray sweats and a burnt orange T–shirt. A black binder lay on her lap. "I don't know how she does it. How does she know?"

"Best guess is she heard me say hello to the doorman. Cats have really great hearing."

"We're fifteen floors up."

"Really, really great hearing."

I sat opposite her and put Circe on my lap, belly up. She lay there with all four paws in the air looking at me with that green stare and what would have been a smile if she could smile.

Sheila picked up the black binder. "Guess what I've got."

"Looks like a script."

"My agent sent it today. The producers want me to do a one–woman show."

"In New York?"

"Of course in New York. Broadway is the only place that counts in theater."

"You going to do it?"

"Well, I've only done movies, you know. But I love the script."

"What is it, a lot of different character parts or a straight monologue?"

"Monologue. It's a woman recounting a life of childhood abuse and neglect and poverty and all the people who told her she'd never amount to anything and what she did to lift herself out of it and where she is now and where she wants to be and how she feels about the whole thing."

"The whole thing being her life."

"Yes."

"Sounds like you're going to do it."

"I'm leaning that way."

"When will you decide?"

"There isn't that much to think about. I'll sleep on it. Want to read it?"

"You want me to?"

"Up to you."

"How about if I come to the show instead."

"That'll be fine."

"Can I come every night? How long a run?"

"Can't tell that in advance. Until I get tired of it or ticket sales drop off or the theater kicks us out, whichever comes first."

I put Circe on the floor and stood up.

"What's for dinner?"

"Lucky you. I stopped at a deli on Sixth Avenue. We've got corned beef, tongue, pastrami, coleslaw and potato latkes."

"What's latkes?"

"If you don't know you've got a treat in store. Oh, and there's applesauce. Goes with the latkes."

We went to the kitchen, took out the food and put it on the table.

"Orange juice or wine?" I said.

She sat down. "OJ will be fine."

"Healthy."

"So is wine."

"But not deli," I said.

"On the other hand you only live once."

"I've heard that."

"If you do it right, once can be enough."

"I never heard that."
"You've heard it now."
"I want to believe it."
"Eat your pastrami," she said.

✳✳✳

Sheila was a big theatergoer. The Los Angeles theater scene was nothing like New York, and now she reveled in Broadway's sumptuous productions. We went to a mystery, a new musical, and a play in which a woman dies, enters heaven, and finds her long lost high school love, only to find that there's no sex in heaven, so she petitions Saint Peter for a change in policy. He refuses, so she brings suit in Heaven's Court, and there's a trial in which arguments are given for and against heavenly sex. I won't give away the ending in case it comes to a theater near you.

At these theatrical events Sheila could not hide behind sunglasses and kerchiefs and floppy hats. Flashbulbs went off in our faces both before the show and afterward, when we stepped out of the stage door onto the sidewalk. I hadn't gotten used to it. I wasn't sure I ever could.

And what if the gun lady read the theatrical section of the newspaper or fan magazines? What if she found a photo of the two of us on one of the websites she frequented? The longer I continued squiring Sheila around town, the more likely these things became. The odds were good that she would find me. What then? True, I now knew who Clara Thompson was, but I didn't really know how or if the knowledge would help me. That last time in my office the gun lady had said simply we would talk about Clara Thompson before she killed me. My complacency of a few days ago had evaporated.

Sheila no longer seemed bothered by being recognized. She smiled and waved at the photographers and gave every indication of enjoying all the attention. I asked her about it.

"So, what's with all the incognito stuff all the time if you enjoy being recognized?"

"It's hard to explain."

"Probably not. Think about it."

"You think every problem can be solved if you just think about it?"

"Most of them. For sure the little ones."

"A lot of people think their problems aren't little."

"True."

"Maybe this one isn't little."

"Sheila, what are we arguing about here? I just wanted to know how you felt about the fans and the paparazzi."

"Going to the theater is different from everyday life. It's an event. It's glamorous. People don't act the same."

"Including you."

"I guess I don't mind attention in a, ah, festive atmosphere. In fact I kind of like it."

"Theater is festive?"

"You know what I mean. People are excited. They expect exciting things to happen."

"And you like being part of what excites them."

"I suppose I do."

"But not if they're excited to see you on the street in everyday life."

"Look, do you have to dissect everything down to the last detail?"

"Not if you don't want to."

"I'm happy with the way I am. I don't need to analyze it to death."

"Okay."

"Okay, drop the subject, or okay, that's fine?"

"Okay, we don't need to talk about it if you'd rather not."

It occurred to me that we might have just had our first fight.

32

At mid–morning, the time when office workers throughout the land took their first coffee break, Arthur Kravitz looked badly in need of sleep. Bags puffed out under his eyes. His face sprouted stubble again. His uncombed hair, jeans, black western style sport-shirt, and blue Adidas running shoes completed the picture. No one would mistake him for a high powered executive. I offered him some coffee, which he declined.

"I quit my job."

"I never knew where you worked."

He looked surprised.

"You never Googled me? After you found out my name?"

I shook my head.

"I was CFO of Balfour Industries."

"The conglomerate?"

"Yeah."

"Why did you quit?"

He shrugged. "Didn't see the point any more."

"Balfour is one of the Fortune 500," I said. "As you know. A lot of very bright people spend their entire lives trying to make it to CFO of a Fortune 500 company."

He shrugged again and said nothing.

"I take it things didn't go too well with Alice."

"I told her what we talked about. All those things about how I felt. She said it was too late. She said she wanted to move on."

"I'm sorry."

A few silent moments went by.

"What will you do?"

"I don't know. I'll have plenty of money, even after the divorce, so I can do whatever I want. The trouble is, I don't particularly feel like doing anything. Maybe I'll get a little place in the country and do some reading."

"Arthur, you've been a very active man with an exciting career. Do you think that will satisfy you?"

"You don't think reading is worthwhile?"

"Of course it is. But it's contemplative, and you're used to a lot of activity and being in the thick of things."

"Yeah, well, that was...how do the kids say it? So yesterday."

He rose to leave. It took him a long time to get to his feet.

"Remember what I said when I first came to see you? That maybe everything was an illusion? I know you don't believe that, but I'll tell you, you're wrong. Okay, maybe not everything, I'll give you that. But the big one, happiness, that's an illusion for sure. You think you've got it and it's solid, but then suddenly a crack opens under your feet and the center doesn't hold."

I started to answer but he shook his head, made a cutting gesture with his hand, and left.

I didn't think he'd be back. He was a sad, bewildered man, but he was not a bad man. I wished him luck.

***

Glitterati packed the opening night house for Sheila's one-woman show. A lot of her Hollywood friends flew in for the event. Some came because they were genuinely fond of her, others because they wanted to be in her good graces. As a bankable star she held a lot of power, even if inadvertently. If she attached her name to a project some studio would finance it. If she stated a preference for a particular co-star or character actor, that person would probably get the part. If she felt strongly enough to make it a condition of her being in the film it became close to a foregone conclusion. As long as she remained at the top of the heap the whole pecking order wanted to be on her good side. Producers, directors, actors, writers. Even studio heads, although they had so much power they didn't need to make trips to New York to prove anything to anybody, except in some cases their board of directors.

At the end of the show she got a standing ovation which lasted several minutes. When I went backstage to her dressing room I found the small space already crowded with famous faces who got there before me and who surrounded her, congratulating her after the obligatory air kisses with things like fabulous, fantastic, incredible, brilliant, edge of my seat, masterful, unbelievable, and a few others. The favorite according to my off the cuff count seemed to be fabulous.

When Sheila saw me she broke through the circle around her and gave me a quick kiss on the lips. This caused a few of the men, including two marquee faces I recognized, to stare at me, some with thinly disguised hostility and some with no disguise at all. The women stared with open curiosity. I could see one or two of their expressions morph from curiosity to calculation. I wasn't handsome, they could see that. I wasn't famous. Therefore I must be rich.

"Go," I whispered in her ear, indicating her admirers. "I'll wait until they leave."

"I'll have to go out for drinks with some of them," she said in a low voice. "Come with us."

Drinks turned out to be late dinner for most of the dozen or so people who tagged along to Sardi's, which Sheila liked for its place in theater history. The conversation was almost exclusively about which projects were in the works, which films had been given a go by some studio but had not yet cast some choice role, who led the pack in the running for the role, who wanted it but had no chance, which high profile directors had busted their budgets, and the latest rumors about which stars had crashed the gross club, which meant they could command part of gross receipts from dollar one instead of a piece of the net profits, which as defined by the studios were almost always zero, as everyone in the business knew.

During a break in the conversation, a lovely young thing on my left who, as an unknown, had been chosen by a budget–conscious director to play the female lead in a B film which had just grossed seventy–three million in its first week couldn't contain her curiosity any longer. She turned to me and said, "So what part of the business are you in?"

This caused all eyes to focus on me as everyone perked up at the delicious prospect of finding out what possible madness had possessed Sheila in getting involved with a total unknown. A few were probably hoping that maybe, somehow, I could be a stepping stone in their careers.

"I'm not in the business," I smiled.

She blinked. I was a civilian. On her mattering meter I had just dropped down to near zero, but she had to say something more out of politeness. A wide smile stretched the lower part of her face as if I had just said something very clever.

"Oh, and what do you do, if I may ask?"

"I'm a philosophical practitioner."

She stared at me.

"What?"

"I talk to people about problems that are bothering them."

"Is that, like, a psychiatrist?"

"No, a psychiatrist is an M.D. and does psychotherapy. I do more of a philosophy oriented counseling."

"Oh."

She seemed at a loss for words, having exhausted both her knowledge of counseling and her interest in me. After a few more moments of polite silence around the table the conversation turned again to the film business. Now everyone, even those who didn't read the gossip columns, knew a civilian dined in their midst. No one tried to speak to me again, and I didn't make any effort to join in a conversation about a topic I knew very little about. Sheila graced the head of the table. I sat a good distance away to give her friends easier access to her. A couple of times she quirked an eyebrow at me in a way I knew meant what can I do, this will be over soon, and I smiled an everything will be fine smile back at her.

Afterward, when we were on the living room sofa back home with Circe on my lap and a couple of drinks in front of us, Sheila said, "Was it really so bad?"

I pulled her over so her head was on my shoulder.

"What are you talking about? You were great. Your delivery was perfect. You were completely at ease and natural. You shone. You sparkled. They loved you."

"Thanks, but you know what I mean. The dinner. You hated it." She snapped her fingers. "We forgot to get the *Times* review."

"It doesn't matter. You were great."

"It matters. Very few shows can survive a bad review from them."

"If they have any sense at all, they loved it."

She smiled. "What about the dinner?"

"Oh, that."

"Some of them are pretty shallow, aren't they."

"Well, they're caught up in their work."

She snuggled closer. "You're very tactful."

"Is that why you love me?"

"Let's say it's a plus." She pulled back a little.

"You don't have to spend much time with them. In fact, you don't have to spend any at all if you don't want to."

I nodded. "Let's go to bed. It's nearly three in the morning."

"God, I just realized how tired I am," she said, and we called it a night.

33

I met Burt in a white tablecloth Thai restaurant in the financial district a couple of blocks from his office. The weight of my gun and my continual need to keep it concealed constrained the natural movements of my left arm and made me feel awkward. I didn't think Burt noticed. On the phone he sounded a little ragged, so when he asked if I could meet him for lunch the day after Sheila's Broadway debut I hopped on the subway and got off near Pine street, and now we feasted on skewered meats and fried rice with more ingredients than you find in your usual plethora.

"Nancy is a good woman," he said out of the blue. "I just want that to be clear."

"Understood."

"What it is, I'm getting older. Yeah, I know, I know, I'm only in my thirties. But I've been thinking about it a lot."

He slipped a piece of chicken off his skewer and chewed it for a while.

"I thought everything would fall in place. Does that make sense? You see what I'm saying?"

"I think so."

"That's good because I'm not sure I do. I feel like something's missing but I know that doesn't make sense. If I don't know what's missing how can I know it's missing?"

"You can know you have a feeling of, call it incompleteness. That's real knowledge."

"Yeah, but what if it's all smoke and mirrors. Half of me says it's based on nothing, because there's nothing my life is missing. But that doesn't make the feeling go away, the – what did you call it? The incompleteness."

His gaze fixed on some meat on a rotating spit behind a pane of glass. "Maybe this is just your average midlife crisis ten years ahead of time. Like early Alzheimer's but a lot less serious. Maybe I should just slap myself upside the head and get over it."

We finished the meal. Our waiter came over and we both ordered Thai coffee.

"This is your field," Burt said. "You've studied this stuff. Where do you think I'm going wrong here?"

"I didn't say you were wrong."

"Okay, so what's your diagnosis? You got any theories?"

"I've got a lot of clichés, but I don't have one answer that fits everyone. There is no one final answer. That's one of the clichés."

"Yeah, but some answers are better than others, right?"

"Always."

"So give me some of the good ones."

The coffee came. It sat on top of a layer of sweetened condensed milk in an espresso glass. I took a sip. Lush. Piquant. A few more sips and I realized it lived in a space beyond my store of adjectives.

"Burt, you see what kind of question you're asking here? Asking what's missing in your life isn't much different from asking what life is all about, which isn't much different from why life is worth living. It's the same category of thing, looked at in slightly different ways."

He gave me a rueful smile.

"Why bother with small talk? Anyway, none of that lets you off the hook. You owe me some clichés."

"How about, you'll never know if you've reached your destination unless you know where you're going."

Burt drummed his fingers on the table.

"Or," I said, "there are as many meaningful ways of living life as there are people."

"What does that mean? There are over six billion people. Six billion solutions, all equally good?"

"All potentially equally good."

He drained the last of his coffee.

"That doesn't tell me what's missing in my life."

"True."

"You're implying only I can answer that?"

"Yeah."

He laughed. "In one of six billion ways."

"In your unique way."

He glanced at his watch and frowned. He put some bills on top of the check and held up his hand when I reached for my wallet.

"Please. You came all the way down here. You don't know how much I appreciate this."

"I can't see that I've been much help."

He held out his hand.

"You'd be surprised. I think I've been looking for something that isn't there."

"That's not what I was trying to say."

"I think it was. Only you didn't know it."

34

Both the audience and the *New York Times* loved Sheila's show, *Celebration Of Life*. The entire planned run sold out, and Sheila became a star on Broadway as well as in filmdom.

She wanted to walk home tonight, so to leave the crowd and the paparazzi behind we ran out the stage door and popped into the limo the producer had on call for her. The fleeting thought occurred to me that if the gun lady was in that crowd there was no way for me to know it. I pushed the thought aside, since there was nowhere to go with it. A few blocks later we asked the driver to let us out on Seventh Avenue.

I told Sheila about my conversation with Burt but kept his name out of it as I thought he would prefer.

"So you think he misinterpreted what you were saying."

In the clear, crisp night air we walked north up Seventh Avenue and she held my arm again, which made me feel big and strong and protective. Even beyond the bright lights of Times Square couples of all ages thronged the street. Occasionally someone would recognize Sheila and whisper excitedly to their partner, but thankfully no one barged over to ask for her autograph and we were able to have an uninterrupted conversation like normal people.

"He misinterpreted what I meant. Maybe he didn't misinterpret what I said."

"You think you weren't clear?"

"Well, I thought I was."

"It sounds like at the end there he thought that if there were six billion solutions that was the same as saying there were no solutions."

I nodded.

"But that wasn't what you meant."

"No, and I don't think it's what I said either."

"Forget what you said for a minute. What did you mean?"

We passed a pizza parlor that had a counter open to the street. Steaming hot slices oozing with melted cheese strategically placed on a circular pizza tray near the street edge of the counter produced an aroma that took a stronger man than I am to resist. I stopped, pointed, held up two fingers to the counterman, paid, and handed a slice to Sheila.

"What makes you think I want pizza?" she said, and took a monstrous, unladylike bite as we continued walking.

"What I meant to say was every life story is necessarily different but they can all be meaningful as long as they include the right elements."

"Elements?"

"Actions. Principles. Principled actions."

She shook her head. "Sorry, I don't think that's very clear. No wonder the man was confused."

"Hard to explain with a mouthful of pizza," I said.

"Hell, I've waited all my life to hear this, I can wait until you swallow."

"Sorry to disappoint you. There's no magic formula."

"Cop out," she said, but she gave my arm a squeeze to take the sting out of it.

"Still," I said, "some life choices are more equal than others."

"How do you put that together with there being six billion solutions?"

"What you do with your life, there are lots of ways to go. How you do it, that's where the principles apply."

We reached our building.

"For me," she said in the elevator, "the way to go is acting. Of course if you look at it one way, all I do is say lines made up by clever people." As the doors opened on our floor she added, "Sometimes I worry about my lack of originality."

We entered the apartment and Circe fussed at me until I picked her up. We went to the kitchen.

"Plenty of originality in your interpretation. No one else could do it quite the same way." I refilled Circe's water bowl.

"How about the fame part. Not the fact that it happens, but that I want it. We never resolved that."

I took a chocolate muffin out of the fridge and sliced it in half. We ate it at the kitchen table.

"I thought we did. It's only a problem if you need it to feel good about yourself."

The muffin went fast. Sheila took out another one, sliced it, and gave me half, half of which I chomped off in one chomp. "Someone once said no one courts fame out of happiness. It's the difference between having an internal compass and letting every random wind push you around."

She stared at me. "You think people push me around?"

"You know I didn't say that."

"Are you thinking it?"

I got up and stood behind her chair with my hands on her shoulders. I massaged the back of her neck.

"You might have been that way once. In the beginning. I don't think you are now."

"But you aren't sure."

I massaged a little deeper. "I'm pretty sure, but the only one who knows for certain is you. That's just the way it is."

She was still for a while. Then she stopped my hand. "I'm tired."

Circe was sitting by her bowl watching us.

"Want to let the cat sleep with us tonight?" I said.

"Won't it confuse her? Set a precedent?"

"Nah. She's a smart cat."

"Then sure."

Circe ended up sleeping at the foot of the bed. We fell asleep to the strains of her purring. She was better than a white noise machine.

***

The call came on Saturday, just before Sheila had to leave for a matinee performance. My father had a heart attack, they said. He'd been rushed to a hospital. Miraculously, he seemed lucid, but they didn't think he had much time.

I gripped the phone. "How long?"

"Get here as soon as you can."

Sheila wanted to go with me.

"I want to meet him."

"You have two shows today."

"I'll cancel them."

I shook my head. "You don't want to see him like this."

"Yes I do. It may be the only chance I'll ever have."

"I don't want you to see him like this. It's not fair to him. Having you there, a new face, it might confuse him."

She cupped my face in her hands.

"Are you absolutely sure? I'm happy to come. The shows are not a problem."

I kissed her and stroked her cheek. As I crossed to the door she said, "Call me."

***

The hospital was an eight story affair a few blocks off I–95. The receptionist gave me the floor and room number. When I got there a middle–aged nurse with a pleasant face whose nametag said Shirley was just exiting the blue curtain surrounding his bed. She immediately took my arm and led me back into the hall.

"You're his son?"

I nodded. "Is he–"

"He's still with us, but I don't know for how long. The good news is he's awake and aware."

I made a move to go, but she tightened her hold.

"Just one thing. You have to tell me how aggressive you want us to be."

I looked at her. "Life is all there is. If you can give him life, do it. Unless he's in unbearable pain."

She locked eyes with me and slowly nodded.

"Got it," she said softly, and left.

I went over to the bed and parted the curtain. My father lay there, eyes closed. They had strapped his right arm to the side of the bed and taped an intravenous drip to the back of his hand. It caused a purple bruise that spread like an amoeba from the spot beneath the tape where the metal point of the tube pierced his papery flesh. Another tube emerged from his right nostril. Two wires snaked out from a machine behind him and disappeared beneath the olive green blanket that covered most of his chest.

His left hand lay flaccid at his side. Large brown liver spots covered the back of the hand. The skin looked like crumpled cellophane. I took his hand in both of mine.

"Pop, it's me."

His eyes fluttered open.

"Eric?"

"Right here, pop."

His chest moved up and down.

"Hurts."

"Where? Your chest? You want me to get the doctor?"

He moved his head slightly from side to side. He took two breaths.

"Not chest. Hand."

I looked at the angry amoeba on the back of his right hand. I reached over and pressed the call button. Shirley came in less than a minute. Had to be some kind of record. She looked at me inquiringly.

"His hand hurts where the intravenous is going in. Can you give him some aspirin?"

"Not a good idea. We already gave him all the salicylic acid and clot busters we think he can tolerate. Let's try a topical anesthetic. I'll be right back."

She spoke to my father.

"I'm sorry you're having pain. Is it bothering you a lot?"

She returned a few minutes later and applied a thin gel to his hand. She patted his forehead. "I'll leave you with your son. If it wears off, one of you press the call button and I'll be back."

I pulled over a chair and took my father's hand again. We stayed that way for maybe half an hour, him lying there with his hand cradled in the two of mine, his eyes closed, his breathing shallow, his sunken face relaxed and peaceful. Shirley came in once and looked at the readings on the machines behind him. Later a young doctor came in and did the same. I followed him into the hall.

"How long?"

He frowned. They were taught not to answer questions like that.

"I can't tell you that."

He shifted his weight to his other foot, the action of a man who either had back problems or a small store of patience. He looked too young for back problems.

"What's your best guess."

His frown deepened.

"He's very old. His heart has suffered major damage, and it wasn't very strong to start with. Does that answer your question?"

"Is there anything more you can do for him? Anything, even if it's risky, that you haven't tried yet?"

"We've done everything we can. It's up to him now. And the God who made him."

I wasn't going to pin my hopes on a God who was killing him. The doctor started to go but I caught his arm.

"How long?" I said again. "A week? A day?"

He was about my height. He looked at me and shifted his weight again. He pulled his arm back, pursed his lips, and shook his head.

"He could go any time. Not days. Hours maybe. Maybe not even that."

I went back to his bed. He hadn't moved, but I could see his chest rising and falling ever so gently. Shallow, birdlike breaths.

I remembered a time when I was nine years old. We lived in Brooklyn and had very little money. When I wanted to take a ride on a bicycle my father or my mother would take me to the bicycle store a few blocks away and rent a second–hand bicycle for me because we couldn't afford to buy one. One day on a weekend my father took me down to the store and as usual asked me to pick the bike I wanted to ride on. I picked a Columbia, which I liked better than Schwinn because I thought it pedaled easier. Its chipped red paint had long ago lost its shine but I had the same reaction to it that I have to a beautiful woman today.

"This one," I said excitedly.

"You're sure?"

"Yes," I said, my young eyes wide and bright.

My father went over to the shopkeeper and paid him some money. On the way home I walked the bike on the sidewalk with him walking next to me. Halfway home I looked up at him and said, "Daddy, how long do I have it for?"

His black eyes twinkled and he started to smile.

"How long do you want?"

"I mean, when do I have to take it back?"

"You don't have to take it back, Eric. It's yours."

"What?" I looked up at him to see if he was joking, which he did a lot when I was young.

"It's yours. I bought it for you. You never have to take it back."

I don't remember what I said next, but I remember that I grabbed his hand and kissed it, and I remember the look on his face when I kissed his hand. It was his left hand. The same one I was holding now.

His eyes opened and he seemed to squint, as if trying to focus on my face. I squeezed his hand.

"Pop?"

His mouth worked and he said something but it came out as a whisper. I leaned closer and he whispered again and this time I heard him.

"Save me."

A tear had formed at the corner of one eye. He blinked and it ran down his cheek. I racked my brain for something to say, but it was all I could do to hold my own tears back and before I could get anything out he squeezed my hand and said something else but the whisper was even lower this time and I had to lean very close and he said it again.

"You'll know it when you see it," he whispered, and stared into my eyes and died.

35

W e buried him in a cemetery in Queens next to my mother. None of his Florida friends showed up for the funeral, and none of the Brooklynites either. Only me, Sheila, and his sister, my aunt Ruth, a heavy, loud woman whom he never liked and who never liked him. To my knowledge she never visited him at his nursing home. She stayed for the minimum time she thought decorum demanded before jumping back into her chauffeured black limousine and driving back to the bakery she owned in Brooklyn Heights. She didn't want to lose any more business than she had to.

I no longer had a father. I felt overwhelming anguish at the depth of my loss. So much of him had already gradually slipped away in the years before his death. I thought I had adjusted, but it didn't work that way. It wasn't the dementia–ridden husk of him that stayed with me but the image of him in the fullness of his manhood, strong, laughing, Godlike.

I told all this to Sheila. I told her everything, including his enigmatic last words, which shook me even though I didn't know what they meant.

"He wanted you to save him, and of course you couldn't." She put her hand on my knee. "You want to talk about how that made you feel?"

"At the time, or now?"

"At the time."

"It ripped my heart out."

She squeezed my knee. "And now?"

"I don't know. The memory of him saying that, the look on his face and those words. I'll never forget that. Never."

Sheila twined her fingers in mine. "You loved him very much."

"He was my father. He gave me life."

She began caressing my hair. "You want to make love?"

I shook my head. She nodded. We sat a few moments saying nothing.

"He was scared," she said.

"He was terrified." I felt clammy. Something was closing my throat. I squeezed out some more words.

"At the end of his life, he asked me for help. For the first time. He never asked me for anything before. And he knew I failed him."

"What he was asking was impossible. You know that."

"But he didn't. He wasn't thinking. There was too much fear in him. He was just feeling, and what he felt at the end was that I failed him."

"Maybe not. There's no way to know. What do you think he meant by that last thing he said? What exactly was it again?"

"You'll know it when you see it."

"What does it mean?"

"I have no idea."

"Why don't you guess."

I stared into the unlit fireplace. He was my father. I'd known him all my life. Surely I could make some sense of his last words.

"I don't know. Maybe he didn't mean anything. His mind was going."

"But you said he was lucid at the end."

"Sort of."

"And the nurse said so too."

"Yeah."

"So if we assume he knew what he was saying, what would be your guess?"

I started talking before I knew how I would answer. "It's the last thing he'd ever say," I said slowly. "He was afraid and confused. I think he was groping for words. Maybe he felt his life slipping away. He was trying desperately to hold on to something."

"Like what?"

"Maybe like what it was all for. The point of it all."

"He was talking about the meaning of life on his deathbed?"

"His life. And maybe mine. I think he never found what he was looking for, and he knew it, and maybe he was trying to tell me to keep looking."

"And you'd know it when you saw it."

"Yeah."

We remained quiet a while. Sheila ran her fingers through my hair a few times. "Feel like making love now? I'll do all the work."

I managed a weak smile. "Sounds like an offer I can't refuse."

36

A few days after the funeral I left the apartment and turned the corner from Central Park South onto the Avenue of the Americas, heading downtown to catch Sheila's show again when I saw the gun lady. She had been looking into the window of a store that sold handbags and she turned to face me when I got within ten feet of her.

So, finally. Waiting for me around the corner from my building, timing it to my daily walk from the apartment to Sheila's show, she obviously knew where I lived now. She'd probably stumbled across some publicity shot of Sheila and me together and followed us home one night after a performance of *Celebration Of Life*.

Not that it mattered now. I almost felt relief for this whole cat and mouse thing to be finally over.

Almost, but not quite, because she'd buried her right hand in a pocket of her textured black raincoat and part of the pocket tented out at me in classic Bogart fashion. I had no doubt about the pocket's contents. Having seen her gun in my office made the likelihood of a bluff remote.

I had just passed the gate to an alley that ran behind several of the buildings that faced the park. We stood alone on our side of the street except for an elderly man on the corner of Fifty–Seventh facing south, away from me, waiting for the light to change. My gun was under my armpit covered by my corduroy jacket, but I had no way to get at it with a gun pointed straight at me.

She stopped a few feet from me and made a motion with the bulge in her pocket.

"The alley."

"What — " I began.

"Don't argue. Don't say anything. I'm not going to tell you again."

I didn't know if she would shoot me on the street in plain sight, but I wasn't in any hurry to find out. I had enough experience with this woman to know that my ability to predict what she would say or do was not something I would stake my life on.

The gate to the alley looked unlocked, which I supposed she had either known or arranged. The alley itself was narrow and dirty. Surprising, given the price of Central Park South real estate. In stark contrast to the gleaming facades of the buildings, grime covered the walls facing on the alley. Most of the residents probably never set foot there. They had no need to. Service people used it almost exclusively.

Maybe thirty–five feet past the gate she said, "Right turn." We'd come to a little cul–de–sac no more than ten or twelve feet long. We could no longer be seen from the street.

"Back against the wall."

I had to find a way to reach my gun. I rubbed the ball of my index finger against the wall. It came away black. I held it up for her to see.

"Can I take off my jacket?" I had some vague plan of pulling the gun while the jacket was obscuring her vision.

She took her hand out of the raincoat and pointed the gun at me.

"Don't be ridiculous. I'm going to ask you a question. Do you remember who Clara Thompson was?"

"I do now."

"But you didn't when I asked you before."

"No."

"So how come now."

"She was a client of mine a few years ago. I didn't remember her before because she used a different name when I knew her."

"You're lying."

"No."

"Why would she use a different name? She had no reason to do that. She was proud of her name, of who she was."

"Proud?"

"Of course. All those families she helped. She did God's work, and she knew it."

"God's work."

"Those families all loved her. Everyone loved her. She wasn't just an ordinary social worker. She told me how much time she spent with those mothers. Real quality time. She didn't just get them government money. She cared about them. As people. She told me how the kids would see her in the street and yell, 'Clara's coming, Clara's coming,' all excited, and then the mothers would come outside before she even got to the door, they were so glad to see her. They all knew her name. So why are you lying and telling me she changed it?"

"You're saying she was a social worker."

"She was my aunt and she was a force for good in this rotten world. But all that was before she met you."

"The woman I knew wasn't a social worker."

"That's not just a lie, it's a pitiful lie."

I hoped her anger wasn't causing her finger to tighten on that trigger.

Time was running out. No choice now.

I had to go for the gun.

I darted my hand inside my jacket, pulled out the gun and leveled it at her. "Standoff."

"She killed herself," she said as if nothing had happened. "Jumped from her apartment. Twelve stories. Do you want to see the note she left?"

She reached into her right coat pocket, pulled out a white envelope, and tossed it at my feet. I let it lay there. No way I'd take my eyes off her.

She nodded. "Then I'll tell you what it says."

She began to recite.

"Nothing matters. It's all for nothing." Her eyes blazed at me.

"I put that together with some entries in her diary about some conversations she had with you."

We still faced each other, maybe fifteen feet apart.

"We can talk about this," I said. "Why don't we put the guns away and — "

And she shot me. It wasn't like you see in the movies. Burning lava spurted through my body. I couldn't see. I dropped to my hands and knees, my gun gone, my head hanging, blind, jaw muscles clamped against the pain. The lava melted the wires of my veins. My lungs squeezed shut. I couldn't think. I couldn't breathe. I could barely support myself on all fours, but some inner voice begged me to stand up. Inch by inch, I pushed myself up against the wall until I stood nearly upright. It took a long time. I raised my head. It fell back down on my chest. I raised it again and it fell again. I raised it one last time and blinked hard. Finally I made out her blurry image in front of me, but I couldn't make it stand still. Her left hand stretched out toward me as if to help me up. She was crying.

Then she shot me again.

37

I was an astronaut. I floated in space outside the ship. They had sent me out to repair a loose tile, but something went wrong with my air. My lungs were heaving but they weren't pulling anything in. I started back toward the ship but it seemed so far away, a silver toy outlined against the dense blackness and the pinpoint stars that watched me and didn't care. I opened my eyes wide looking for the hatch and saw Sheila's face. I saw her eyes get big and her mouth open and I saw her shoot to her feet and heard her yell, "Doctor!", and my air ran out and I had no way to reach the ship, no way to breathe, and I gave up.

✱✱✱

Someone kept punching me in the chest. I couldn't stop him. I felt a sharp stabbing pain and I opened my eyes to see who was doing this to me. A man stood over me with a long needle in his hand and I said, "Don't do that again," and went to sleep.

✱✱✱

Sheila was the first thing I saw the next time I opened my eyes. She sprawled in a chair at the foot of my bed, her eyes closed, her head tilted to one side. My room didn't look much different from the

room my father died in. From this, plus the IV dripping into my arm
and the monitors attached to me, I recklessly concluded that I was in
a hospital. I opened my mouth to call to Sheila but only managed a
loud groan. This caused her eyes to snap open. She looked around
wildly, then jumped up and came to my bedside. She leaned over me
and put her hand on my forehead.

"Hey," she said in a voice just above a whisper. "You made it."
She left her hand on my forehead.

I coughed. In a voice that made me sound ten years old I said,
"Did you ever doubt it?"

She smiled. "Not for a minute."

I squeezed her hand. I had so little strength I'm not sure she even
felt it. The room started to spin. Spin and tilt. Spin and tilt. I blinked
and looked up at her.

"Why are you crying?" I croaked.

She bit her lip and shook her head and her face started to screw
up and I went away again.

***

The next time Sheila came into the room I'd been awake a few
minutes. A young nurse checked my IV and my monitors. When she
saw Sheila her eyes went wide.

"Oh, you're..."

"Hi," Sheila said, extending her hand.

"My boyfriend isn't going to believe this. He loves you."

Sheila came over and kissed me. She mussed my hair. To the
nurse she said, "How's he doing?"

"My boyfriend? Oh." She reddened. "BP's back up, heart rate's
back down. The infection is gone. Everything's in the normal range."

I tried to sit up. "Infection?"

The nurse pointed to my upper chest.

"I can't move my arm," I said.

"You will soon. You took two bullets right below the shoulder.
Tore things up pretty good. The second one clipped the top of your
lung. All in all I'd say you're pretty lucky."

"Lucky to have someone pump two bullets into me."

"That's not what I meant." She turned to Sheila. "Can I have your autograph?"

"Of course."

Sheila signed and the nurse left. I let my head fall back. "I never understood that."

"What?"

"The autograph thing. What's the point?"

She shrugged. "Who knows. It makes some people happy."

"How long have I been here?"

"This is day nine."

I nodded. I would have nodded if she said two days or twenty.

"Maybe they think people will be impressed that you were standing next to them," I said.

She sat next to me on the bed. "Maybe they want to sell them to autograph collectors."

"Yes, but why would the collectors want to collect autographs?"

"Because they could sell them to other collectors?"

"But..."

She placed a finger on my lips. "Shh. Get some rest."

I wanted to pursue it and solve the autograph puzzle, but thinking hurt so I stopped trying and drifted away.

***

The next time I awoke I still felt tired and knew I needed to sleep some more, but that seemed like a waste of time so I compromised and lay still in the narrow hospital bed with my eyes closed. I tried once to move my right arm but a bolt of pain changed my mind. Hearing a noise, I opened my eyes and saw Sheila sitting across from me in her chair.

Only it wasn't Sheila and it was no hallucination.

My mouth felt sandy, my tongue thick. "You tried to kill me."

Alone in the small room with her, I lay weak and helpless, anchored to the bed by tubes and sensors. It seemed obvious that she'd come to finish the job. With my left hand I fumbled for the call button, but she had moved it to the far side of the bedside table out of reach.

"You could yell for a nurse, but it would be pointless. The nurse's station is way at the end of the hall. Besides, I'm not going to do anything."

This assurance fell a little short of filling me with confidence, as did her funereal appearance. Black slacks, black turtleneck. Her limp uncombed black hair had lost its shine.

"Which is no doubt why you took away my call button," I managed.

She gave a curt shake of her head.

"I just want to talk."

"Right. What happened to bang bang, you're dead?"

She shook her head again. Her eyes looked puffy, her lips blood-less without lipstick. She looked drained. Grasping at straws, I took that as a hopeful sign.

"I vomited afterwards," she said.

"Am I supposed to be impressed?"

"All over my shoes."

"I get it. You're here because you want me to buy you a new pair."

"You're a very sarcastic person. There was nothing like that in Clara's diary. She thought you hung the moon."

"Try to forgive me." I felt faint. I fought it. "I'm not really up on the etiquette of how to have a conversation with your killer."

"I'm not your killer. You didn't die."

I stared at her. "I'll try to be more precise."

Sheila could walk in any moment. So could a nurse. Or a doctor. All of which I knew was not lost on this woman. So why had she come here?

She poked at her hair in a pointless and vain attempt to control its messiness. "You know you killed her."

I shook my head. It hurt.

"I didn't kill anyone."

"I just want you to know what you did. When you told her there was no God, and heaven knows how you got her to believe that, her whole world fell apart. She stopped singing in the choir. She stopped going to church. One day I found a CD I thought she'd like and I went to her apartment house on my lunch hour to leave it with the doorman and he said she was in so I went up and she was still in bed and I asked her why she wasn't at work and she looked confused and said she quit her job. A few days later she killed herself. We covered it up because it would break my grandmother's heart. She's a God fearing woman." She stared at me. "But it was really you who killed her."

"I never told her that."

"You never told her there was no God?"

"We talked about a lot of things. She asked a lot of questions about right and wrong. She wanted to know how right and wrong are handled in different philosophies and in different religions."

I took a few quick breaths. I didn't know how long I could keep talking.

"Different religions? She was a Christian."

"As I said, she wanted to know about various philosophies and religions."

"Why? She knew she was doing God's work. She knew what she was doing was good and right."

I thought of telling this woman what her aunt's job had been, which she'd hidden from both her and me. She'd told me she had a job as a legal secretary. After all, this woman had tried to kill me, and it would feel good to hurt her a little. Or a lot. But that would mean letting someone else's actions determine the kind of person I was. I remained silent.

She nodded. "No answer. Why am I not surprised."

"She asked me to give her the arguments for and against the existence of God and I did. That's all. If she changed her beliefs, she came to her own conclusions."

"Well, obviously she did change her beliefs because of what you told her, and now she's dead. So who would you say is responsible for her death?"

I closed my eyes. My head still hurt. My shoulder hurt. This was going nowhere, and I remained awake by sheer willpower, which could give out at any moment.

"All right, you've told me what you think. Is that it? You're done? You've said your piece and you're going home now?"

She stood up. Her eyes blazed down at me.

"You know, I hate your guts."

I held her gaze. I hated being helpless.

"Given the circumstances, I'm not too crazy about you either."

"You really do deserve to die. But I was wrong. Killing you is not the answer. It's too easy. The best punishment for you is having to live with yourself."

She turned and walked to the door.

"Have a nice life."

✳✳✳

A couple of minutes later Sheila walked in. I perked up.

"Getting out of the elevator I thought I saw a woman coming out of your room. Dressed in black?"

"Too bad you didn't come a few minutes sooner. Would have been interesting."

"Who is she?"

"She's the shooter."

Her eyes got wild. "What? What are you talking about?" Then, "We've got to stop her before she gets out of the building." She grabbed the call button, then thought better of it and went for the phone on the table.

"No," I said.

She stared, the phone still at her ear.

"What? But she..."

"I know. Put the phone down."

She did. She went to the chair and sat down.

"What's going on. Why are you letting that woman get away?"

I told her about our conversation.

"So what am I missing here? She tried to kill you. Why are you letting her go?"

"It's hard to explain."

"I have a lot of confidence in you. Try."

"She loved her aunt. Clara Thompson. She thinks I was responsible for her aunt's suicide."

"She also tried to kill you."

"She's not a killer."

"What, because she missed the first time? Because she didn't try this time out? Because she said she changed her mind? What's to say she won't change it back again?"

"Sheila, let it go."

She fought for control. She won. "The police were here. They want to talk to you. Are you going to press charges?"

My energy started slipping again. "Against whom?"

"Will you talk to them? Describe her?"

I shook my head.

She went silent, her disapproval palpable.

So now I had two women mad at me, and one of them I cared about a lot.

38

I was sitting up in bed in our apartment. Burt had just left after a long visit during which he'd shown me some problems on his pocket chess set. His way of reestablishing normalcy. Sheila had made chicken soup, which rested on a tray across my lap, along with a plate of braised beef, carrots and peas. Sheila sat near the foot of the bed watching me eat, although not as intently as Circe, who perched between us and whose eyes never left the beef. Sheila's hand served the dual function of petting the cat and restraining her, although Circe was much too well behaved to need much restraining. I hoped she didn't feel insulted.

"I still don't get it," Sheila said.

I kept eating soup.

"You let that woman just walk away."

"This soup is great. What's for dessert?"

She shook her head. "It's crazy. She tried to kill you. She might try again."

"I don't think so."

"But you don't know. You can't predict the actions of a crazy person."

"She's not crazy."

"Of course she's crazy."

I started on the beef. It was delicious.

"Beef's good too."

"All right, you don't want to talk about it. But I still think you made a big mistake."

"I don't think so," I said again. "But you might be right."

"I am right. Although I hope I'm wrong. I hope nothing happens. I don't want anything else to happen to you. Even if nothing happens, it was a crazy chance to take."

I let her have the last word.

"What about that dessert?"

"I made jello." She stood up. I passed her my plate. "When you get to the kitchen, why don't you give this last piece to Circe."

"You're spoiling her. The cat food we give her is perfectly nutritious."

"Let her live a little."

"At least you didn't feed her on the bed."

"That would be a big mistake," I said. She gave me a look and headed out to the kitchen with Circe padding along behind her.

***

Another three weeks went by before I felt strong enough to go to my office. Although I no longer had any clients, hope springs eternal. I took out my revised Oxford translation of Aristotle and settled down to wait for the phone to ring. I never minded the waiting before, but I had very little overhead then and could afford a few dry spells. Now the demanding nut of my share of the new apartment's upkeep changed things. The stock market had snagged on an interest rate spike, so my small portfolio was going nowhere. I couldn't afford to be out of work too long. Besides which I liked feeling useful. Well, at least I could enjoy the luxury of reading without the annoying weight and bulk of a gun under my arm.

Since I wasn't expecting anyone, the sound of the doorknob turning surprised me. I hadn't bothered to lock the door since there no longer appeared to be any threat. And so the gun lady waltzed in again and sat down in a client chair as if our confrontation in the alley and our talk in the hospital when she'd wished me a nice life had never happened.

She was all in black again, the same outfit she'd worn in the hospital, except for her handbag, shoes and lipstick, which were all a single glaring shade of red. This lady didn't do things by halves. Today her hair was combed, her eyebrows freshly blackened. She looked relaxed.

When I got past my initial shock I said the first thing that occurred to me. "What are you doing here? I thought we were done. What happened to 'have a nice life'?"

"I want to talk."

I looked at her in disbelief.

"In the hospital I had no choice. Now you come to me again and want to talk? First you shoot me, then you want to talk to me? The time for talking was before you pulled the trigger."

"How come you didn't try to stop me." She could have been talking about the weather.

"In the hospital. You could have called the front desk. They could've stopped me before I got out."

"I'd like you to leave now. Just go."

I knew I was taking a chance. She might have her gun in her purse, and in my present condition I couldn't reach her fast enough if she wanted to use it. But I thought it unlikely since she had all the opportunity she needed in the hospital. Or in the alley, for that matter.

On the other hand, she might be crazy. Sheila might be right. In which case all reasoning about her motives was an exercise in futility.

She did something between a pout and a grimace but settled her features back to normal an instant later. "What if I want to become a patient."

"Client," I said automatically.

"Whatever."

This is how Alice must have felt when she first hit Wonderland, I thought.

Out of curiosity I said, "What happened to 'I hate your guts'?"

She reached down for her bag and started to open it. My breathing got a little shallower.

"Mind if I smoke?"

Apparently she thought her special dispensation might be in jeopardy. She had it right.

"Yes."

She put the bag down with exaggerated slowness. She looked at me a long moment.

"Do all your clients have to like you?"

"No, but I've found it helpful if they don't dislike me enough to try to kill me."

"You keep harping on that."

"Forgive me. An overreaction."

"Can't we just move on. I mean, I'm not going to try that again."

"Good to know."

"So now that you know, what about my being a client."

On second thought, Alice never experienced anything like this. Wonderland didn't compare with the real world. After what she had done, this woman's request was not only off the wall. It was off the planet. Make that the solar system.

So why did I give it even an instant's consideration? I hadn't noticed any masochistic tendencies in myself before. Calling this woman unpredictable was like calling Everest a hill.

Well, Achilles had his heel. Superman had his Kryptonite. I had my curiosity.

"What possible reason could you have for wanting that?"

"I loved my aunt. I want to get to know her better. I want to really understand what happened to her. Also, I want to know what she saw in you."

"I can't help you understand what happened to her."

"Maybe you can and you just don't know it."

"What clients tell me is confidential. I can't help you."

She eyed me in silence.

"Maybe I want to ask you the same kind of questions she did. What you said in the hospital. About right and wrong. And God. How about that?"

"Let me get this straight. You shot me, and now you want to talk about right and wrong?"

"I thought we got past that." Her face never changed expression.

"You're past it. That makes one of us."

She moved a hand in an impatient gesture. "I've said what I came to say. Yes or no."

One thing she had going for her, she had plenty of gall. Guts. Nerve. Chutzpah. Whatever you wanted to call it, she had it. It's something I admire. Under normal circumstances.

But this situation bordered on the ridiculous. No, wrong. It crossed the border long ago. I should do the only sensible thing. Refuse and be done with it. No good could come of this. I threw one last sop to my better judgement, which kept screaming that I was an idiot.

"Three hundred an hour."

She shot to her feet.

"I won't need a lot of hours."

"What's your name?" I said as she started to go. "I've been thinking of you as the gun lady."

She turned around then and gave me the barest flicker of a smile.

"I'll call you."

***

"You did what?"

"I told her I'd take her on as a client. Well, I implied it."

Sheila shook her head. "You're as crazy as she is."

I had to admit she had a point, but I decided to quibble.

"You may have a point."

"What were you thinking? There's no way for you to predict what this woman will do."

"I know."

"Not to mention that she tried to kill you. And almost succeeded."

I nodded.

"So why are you doing this?"

"It's hard to explain."

"You say that a lot."

"I'm not really sure. It's probably curiosity more than anything else."

"For that you'd risk your life? To satisfy your curiosity?"

"I'm not risking my life. At least I don't think I am."

She stared at me. "Are you listening to yourself?"

I nodded. "Okay, so I might be taking a small risk."

"And you're good with that?"

"I could go into the one about how we all take a risk every time we cross the street."

"Please don't."

"Or not."

"This isn't funny."

I nodded somberly.

"But you're not going to change your mind, are you."

"No."

After a silence she let out a long sigh and shook her head.

"Then I'll have to live with it."

39

"So tell me about right and wrong," the gun lady said. "Tell me something I don't know."

"It would help things along if you told me your name."

She looked at me for a few seconds. She lifted her chin.

"Trixie."

"Trixie," I repeated.

She nodded, watching me.

"Call me Ishmael," I said.

"What?"

"Nothing. Look, it's not going to work if I give you lectures. It works best if you have specific questions."

"Fine."

Lipstick, bright red. Hair, scraped back and tied with a red bow patterned with green herringbone. Almost made her look like a schoolgirl. She looked nothing like someone who had attempted a murder.

She looked up at the ceiling, where she evidently found inspiration because she smiled and then locked eyes with mine.

"Tell me why killing a person is wrong. The Bible says thou shalt not kill. What do you say?"

"In this case I mainly agree with the Bible."

"Why? Because God said so?"

"No."

She leaned back. "I'm waiting."

"Respect for life is the basis of civilization. Without that we have nothing. We're no better than jungle animals."

"That's it? Civilization would collapse if I killed someone? Lots of people have killed lots of people. Civilization is still here."

"Think about what the world would be like if by some magic killing disappeared from the face of the earth. Would the world be more or less civilized?" I said.

The inanity of addressing this question to someone who had tried to kill me was not lost on me. Her lips formed into a brief pucker which resembled nothing so much as a schoolgirl's first approach to a kiss.

"Good luck with the magic. In the real world what one person does makes no difference one way or the other."

"What would give you the right?"

Her head snapped up. "What?"

"People have rights. Everyone is equal under the law. Are those new ideas for you?"

"What's your point?"

"There's only one fundamental right. The rest all come from that."

"And you're about to tell me what it is."

I let that pass.

"Every one of us has the absolute right to his or her own life. So I ask again, what would give you the right to take someone's life?"

She glared at me for several seconds. She wasn't going to answer my question, which was not surprising, since there was no answer. "That's it?" she said again. "That's why you know better than God?"

I was getting tired. My shoulder scar felt tight and itched.

"You asked me a question. I gave you an answer."

Which I thought should suffice. I didn't see any need to get into metaethics with this woman. What a standard is, and how one validates it.

Abruptly, she got up and walked over to the window. A single horn blasted. Not the cacophony you sometimes heard this time of day. Traffic must be slow. Without turning around, she said, "Let's get this over with. You keep dancing around it. Do you believe in God, or don't you?"

"Is it important that you know that?"

"Yes," she said, still with her back to me.

"Then no, I don't."

She turned to face me. She walked to her chair and stood behind it with her hands resting on the back.

"Did you ever tell Clara that?"

I thought back. There was no way I could remember all those sessions, but I really didn't need to, because no client ever asked me that question and I knew I would not have spontaneously volunteered it.

"I told you before, no, I didn't."

She leaned forward over the chair back.

"Are you sure?"

"Yes."

"But you never hid it, did you. She could have picked it up from the kind of things you said, the way you approached things, like I just did when I asked you about killing. You weren't subtle or anything, were you. You said God was not your reason for thinking killing was wrong. Not too hard to figure out where you stood, right?"

"Where is all this going."

"Right where I always thought it was going. You killed her. She looked up to you, heaven knows why, and you broke her faith. Remember I told you she left the choir? Stopped coming to church? Stopped showing up at her job? And then she killed herself. They found her body in the courtyard. They said she probably jumped in the early morning. From the twelfth floor. That was all you and your atheistic philosophy."

"That's ridiculous. There were other reasons why she might have been depressed."

"Like what?"

I said nothing. Telling this woman that her beloved aunt was a high class call girl would shatter her.

"Yeah, right." She gathered up her bag, took out some bills and flung them on the desk.

"Maybe I should have killed you. But maybe you didn't realize what you were doing." She stopped and looked at me hard.

"You have a lot of power. You should learn how to use it."

She crossed to the door, heels clacking, and without looking back said for the second time, "Have a nice life."

I realized I still didn't know her name. Maybe never would.

40

Sheila had cancelled her Broadway run after I got shot, which left her with not a lot to do. Right now, the afternoon following the gun lady's melodramatic exit, we were having brunch at a hole in the wall off Columbus. To get to it you had to descend five brick steps below street level. The place had a hand–lettered sign in the window that said American Food. We both wanted to find out what that meant, and we had just picked out our individual appetizer assortment and settled down to sample our samples.

"I'm glad you're finally rid of that woman. She's a loose cannon."

"She sure is."

"You think she's finally gone for good?"

"She sounded pretty definite."

"Except that she's unstable, so who knows what she'll do in the future."

"There's always that."

"You don't have to take that risk. You could still have her put away for what she did to you."

"Seems to me we had this conversation. Aside from the fact that I don't know who she is or where to find her."

She cut herself a piece of something flat and speckled with green.

"What's that?" I asked.

"I think it's an avocado fritter."

"Is it good?"

She bit into it and gave it a few chews. "Mmm," she said, and reached over to put a piece on my plate.

"Mmm," I said.

"We agree."

"Makes for a strong relationship."

"Speaking of which, there's something we need to talk about," she said.

"Fire away," I said as I finished off some unknown pickled vegetable. Possibly not the best response, but I was oblivious. Normally it's a good idea to stop whatever else you're doing and listen very carefully when a woman says you need to talk.

"My agent phoned yesterday. He said a project has come together that's perfect for me."

"Film?"

"Yes."

"Have you seen the script?"

"No, but he described it to me, and he's been very right so far. The script will be here tomorrow. I'm almost sure I'm going to want to do it."

"Great. So what's the problem?"

She pushed a sardine close to a shrimp and then separated them on opposite sides of her plate.

"We're filming in L.A."

She looked up at me. "The thing is, I want to stay there."

Before I could answer she added quickly, "I want you to come too. Of course." She reached across the table and squeezed my arm. "Say something."

I tried, but my mouth was dry. I took a deep breath, which made it drier. I gulped down half a glass of water and set the glass back on the table with great care so it made no noise. Noise was out of place. I was out of place. The world had tilted.

"Give me a minute."

A large cloud had scudded across the sky and obscured the sun. I saw myself reflected in the darkened window. Only I wasn't seeing myself as I was today. I saw a boy just out of grad school sitting in a cramped office day after day, waiting for the phone to ring while his savings drained away. I saw him one month away from eviction. I saw him the day he got his first client, an elderly gentleman who wanted to explore whether there could be objective standards in art. Then came an editorial writer for a local newspaper who wanted validation for his political position and a writer of romance novels who wanted to know if love is really just the squirting of chemicals from our glands.

After that the referrals began. One man had a college degree but only took jobs where he could work with his hands because he thought society had alienated us from our work. The sixtyish woman with seventeen cats who wanted to understand rights because she wanted to work out an argument for why animals should have them.

I didn't want to lose my client base and start over. I was established here. True, this was a dry spell, but I had a growing network of happy clients who referred their friends and acquaintances. Not to mention New York's unmatched energy, sophistication, pace and excitement. Living in this city was like living an extra lifetime. But the main thing was my client network. My livelihood.

I told all this to Sheila, although she already knew most of it because she brought up the livelihood question back when we first discussed her coming to New York.

We lapsed into silence. We forgot about the delicacies spread out on the long tables behind us. The other diners gobbled their food with healthy gusto. I became abnormally aware of the hubbub of normal people in normal conversation. To my ears it sounded like a tsunami.

"My life is back there," Sheila said at last. "My work. My friends."

I felt as if I'd swallowed sand.

"You knew that before you came here."

"I didn't know how much I'd miss being there."

"But you know now."

She nodded.

"You're sure."

"Yes."

We sat a while more. "What about being one of those bi–coastal couples," Sheila said.

"Are you okay with that?"

"No, but it's better than not having you at all. A lot better."

The tsunami in my ears worsened. "Let's get out of here. Unless you still want the main course."

"I'm not hungry."

"There are always planes and telephones," Sheila said as we reached the street. She looked up at me, waiting for a reply. I put my arm around her and drew her close. I kissed her forehead and her cheek. "You think this will work?"

"Lots of people do it."

"Not lots."

We walked some more. Across from our apartment building the trees lining the park side of the street had begun their transition to red and gold. We passed a horse and carriage standing at the curb waiting for customers. The horse ate from a feed bag. Sheila stopped to run her hand along its side. The horse didn't seem to notice. She came back and took my arm. I freed it and put it around her shoulders.

"You know," I said, "they say love is not enough. So are we proving them right, or are we proving them wrong?"

41

I knew when her plane was scheduled to land. I gave her time to collect her luggage and reached her as her taxi, or probably limo, left the airport. We spoke awhile as if nothing had changed between us. I called her the next evening too. The night after that she called me. We told each other the events of the day and reaffirmed our feelings for each other. We made plans for her to visit me in New York and me to visit her in Los Angeles. We both wanted this long distance thing to work and would work to make it happen. I felt more and more confident that we would find a way. Life was looking up.

Nevertheless, I felt lonely with Sheila so far away. Entirely apart from the sex, there is a primeval reassurance in physicality – just being able to see, hear and touch someone you love. No matter how advanced we become, our senses remain our most direct and satisfying contact with reality.

Sitting in my office three days after she left, I mused on this, the Aristotle unopened on my desk. I finished two cups of coffee and was working on a third when I heard a knock on the door and a tall blonde in a miniskirt walked in. She had a heart shaped face and wore light pink lipstick that exactly matched her blouse, the top three buttons of which were undone. Her skirt, hose, and shoes were black. She gave me a crooked smile as she sashayed to my middle client chair, sat down, turned her body at a slight angle to me, carefully crossed her long legs, and made a token effort at arranging her skirt before fixing me with a heavy–lidded stare.

"I'm looking for someone who can tell me about the meaning of life. Is that you, or do I have to keep looking?"

The End

About The Author

Larry Abrams received an A.B. from the University of Chicago and an A.M. from the University of Pennsylvania. After working in the 9 to 5 world for four years, he left it forever at age 24 to reclaim his time and do a lot of reading, supporting himself by entrepreneurial efforts which were not time intensive.

In his misspent youth he became chess champion of New York Mensa and the state of Connecticut, neither of which feats he could remotely hope to duplicate today. He enjoys writing, reading fiction and philosophy, listening to music and to recorded lectures on various topics, fast cars, cats, movies, plays, and speed chess. He is currently catless and living in Houston, where he is working on his next book.

13421052R00147

Made in the USA
Lexington, KY
30 January 2012